I0610461

Evernight Publishing

www.evernightpublishing.com

Copyright© 2015

Cait Jarrod

Editor: JS Cook

Cover Artist: Jay Aheer

ISBN: 978-1-77233-298-8

ALL RIGHTS RESERVED

WARNING: The unauthorized reproduction or distribution of this copyrighted work is illegal. No part of this book may be used or reproduced electronically or in print without written permission, except in the case of brief quotations embodied in reviews.

This is a work of fiction. All names, characters, and places are fictitious. Any resemblance to actual events, locales, organizations, or persons, living or dead, is entirely coincidental.

MYSTIC HEARTS

DEDICATION

To my dad, thank you for always being there.

ACKNOWLEDGEMENTS

Special thanks to the awesome critique duo: Norma Redfern and Neva Brown. Their support has been invaluable. To my beta readers—Patricia Smart, Susannah Hutchison, and Julie Fowler—you're awesome!

Cheers to my friends and confidantes, DC Stone and Lea Bronsen, for your endless encouragement.

To my editor JS Cook and the rest of the Evernight Publishing team, thank you. A special thank you to Jay Aheer for a fantastic cover.

MYSTIC HEARTS

MYSTIC HEARTS

Band of Friends, 2

Cait Jarrod

Copyright © 2014

Chapter One

Charlene Smith gaped at the two-hundred year-old plantation house as she sat parked in the driveway. Reports of flying ghosts, peculiar noises, and floating hands surfaced, making her decision to stay at the eerie, menacing Greenwood Manor not only questionable, but her actions desperate.

When a member of the Band of Friends, Paul England, asked if someone could watch over the place on Halloween to ward off any vandalism, she'd volunteered. She believed if she could stay in a spooky place, the terrifying sensation she'd held onto since she was kidnapped and rescued would disappear.

She gazed at the back porch, her grip tightening on the steering wheel from the apprehension creeping up her spine. Her knuckles whitened as her stomach churned.

Two lights installed on the corner of the porch illuminated the outside. One angled toward the driveway, highlighting two outbuildings, while the other spotlighted a one-room schoolhouse in the opposite direction, closest to the field.

During the day, the white house with green trim had been welcoming and magnificent. At night, a totally different description came to mind...*ominous.*

What had she gotten into?

"Confront your issues." Her grandmother's words replayed like an old record. Her wisdom had helped lead her through troubled times on more than one occasion.

If she could stay the night in the haunted house, she trusted her edginess would subside. No more looking over her shoulder whenever a car drove past her home. No more flinching when a friend touched her shoulder. She'd be cured of the trepidation the abduction had caused.

The jury was still out if her idea to come here was brilliant or plain stupid. For her sake and her son's, she hoped the former. For that reason, she would follow through with her plan. She had to. Henry couldn't have a mother scared of her own shadow.

She sucked in a deep breath, shoved open the driver's door, and stepped onto the gravel driveway. A gentle wind brushed her skin and tumbled her hair over her shoulders. Crickets chirped. A cow bellowed in the distance.

Comforting sounds she recognized.

No heavy footsteps, no angry voices like in the mountains.

From the driveway, the sidewalk led to the back steps, and farther, past large bushes and the corner of the house. She had to walk by a tree and twenty yards of grass before reaching safety. *Not hard to do.*

She bent inside her compact car and snatched an overnight bag and purse.

A coyote howled.

Dark, black panic shot through her system. She jolted. Hit her head the car's roof and her hand landed on the door.

She straightened, rubbed the top of her head and scanned the area, wide eyed. Coyotes rated up there with ghosts. She didn't like them. None were in sight, but she hoped they didn't lurk behind the buildings, watching her.

After slipping her overnight bag's strap over one shoulder, she closed the car door and dug into her purse for the house key.

Oh, no!

She eyed the car's lock pushed down to her keys dangling from the ignition.

When Paul gave her the house key before he left town, she'd put the key on the ring so she wouldn't lose it.

She went to the passenger's side and jerked on the handle…*locked.* Her next breath slid through gritted teeth with a hiss and a throaty growl. She had to get her act together.

A hide-a-key had to be stashed nearby. Most people had them nowadays. *Right?* Hers was under the rock near her back door. Haunted houses shouldn't be any different. An odd awareness someone watched her wriggled down her spine. Each stride brought on more goosebumps.

She managed to reach the back steps without flinching, and smiled.

One step closer to attaining my goal.

Each rock and brick she looked under had worms, dirt, or cement. No hidden key. Disgusted, her vivid imagination making her flinch and causing a troublesome situation, she slumped onto the porch. Her bag and purse dropped to the boarded floor with a thump and echoed.

The situation gave her limited options. Leaving the farm, for one, wouldn't happen. She'd given Paul her word. That, and…well, she couldn't very well drive home with the keys locked in the car. Another, one of the Band of Friends, BOFs as they liked to be called, would come.

Then she remembered volunteering, how she'd begged actually, after Paul exhausted his options with the other members. Since they hadn't volunteered to help Paul when he asked, then they'd be unavailable to help her.

Not having one of them to call on left her feeling out of sorts. She had grown close and trusted each one of the members in the last few months. Their generosity, amazing and impressive, caused her to grow fonder of them than she believed possible.

With an elbow braced on her knee, she plopped her chin on her palm, and thought about another person who hadn't joined the BOFs despite his close ties with the male members: the man who had saved her son on that horrendous day.

The auburn-haired man stayed in her dreams, day and night. Her emotions toward him were so intense she didn't trust them, for fear they'd developed out of gratitude. Knowing she'd have a hard time letting her guard down in his presence, she'd avoided contact as much as possible.

That day, before they left the mountain, he'd given her his business card and said to call whenever she needed something or wanted to talk. She never called.

After months without communication, would contacting him be right? He would have the tools to unlock her car. It'd be silly not to call. She fished his card and cell out of her purse, and spun the thin rectangle of paper between her fingers. Once again, she pondered her choices. His driving out to the manor and unlocking her car would force her to make a decision. Did she take control of her trust issues and ask him to stay with her, or did she smile, say thank you, and insist he leave?

Or the alternative: she'd stay on the porch for the rest of the night…with the animals …insects…and whatever apparitions might decide to appear.

The desire to call Larry grew strong. Still, she slid her phone back in her purse. Her attraction to him stopped her. Feelings for someone equaled giving someone power over your life. "Been there, done that, have the scars to prove it."

She shook her head and searched the objects lying on the porch. Anything to keep her mind off Larry's honey-colored eyes that had gazed at her with such compassion she wanted to melt.

A picnic basket was positioned near the door, half of the top raised a few inches over the other side. She placed Larry's card atop her purse and lifted the lid. A bottle of Moscato, a plastic glass, and a cork opener, all the items needed for a romantic moonlight picnic.

Yet, no one was around. Even the wildlife and insects had quieted. So, who had left the basket? Paul said no one lived in the house and that he let the foreman, who worked during the day, know she'd be staying at the house tonight. Maybe he left the basket.

The promising taste of fruit teased her.

This time, the decision, should she or shouldn't she, was a no-brainer. Tomorrow, she'd replace the wine. She uncorked the bottle and poured some into a glass. She savored the flavor of pears, apples, and a hint of a fruit she couldn't name while the liquid warmed her veins and eased the stress. She drained the glass and refilled it.

"Whew!" The alcohol went straight to her head. The buildings and bushes wavered. She looked at the ground. "Hello!" The ground spun. She slid her gaze upward and fixed her sights on a small structure.

Time literally stopped. The buildings stopped spinning. The ground stilled. Her hand, holding the wine glass, halted near her mouth.

A white patch…with no shape…no defined lines…glided through the air.

Anxiety, so heavy, constricted her throat. Barely daring to breathe, she shifted to peek over her shoulder.

The whiteness glided past pine trees, and the hue grew more vivid. Still, she couldn't make out the shape.

A ghost?

The patch flew behind the one-room schoolhouse, disappearing.

"Oh, jeez." She jumped to her feet, lost her balance, and smacked a hand against the porch's interior wall. The wine glass tumbled to the floor. The adrenaline rush mixed with the little bit of alcohol turned her legs and head to mush. She wiped a hand down her face and reached for the doorknob, hoping the knob would turn.

It did.

Odd. Then why did I need a key?

She stepped into the screened-in porch, and a woodsy smell swamped her. Underneath the row of windows, a pile of wood was stacked hip high, the source of the overwhelming scent. An antique gumball machine rested on the corner of a yellow cabinet. A glow of light shined out of the double doors leading into the kitchen. She returned to the small exterior porch. Careful not to lose her balance again, she stepped through the spilled wine and slowly lowered to grab her purse and overnight bag. With the straps over her shoulder, she snatched the wine bottle and glass and moved into the kitchen. She locked the door behind her.

She rested against the door and caught her breath. The scent of flour and spices filled the air. The kitchen was double the size of hers. There was a table in the center, and cabinets lined three walls. A flour mill cabinet and appliances filled the empty wall spaces. The room looked at peace, yet everything about the extravagant home possessed an air of mystery, encouraging her to explore.

Adrenaline cleared her fuzzy head. She shoved off the door, set her belongings on the kitchen table, and filled her glass with wine.

An opened salon style door revealed the formal dining room. Flipping the light switch up, she gazed at the crystal chandelier over the brim of her glass. The light sparkled off the crystal and reflected onto the cherry table's dark surface, giving the furniture a hint of elegance.

Double doors in the room's exterior wall opened to a moonlit room with wicker furniture. Books and magazines covered a small table, a means to pass time.

The light from the chandelier dimmed then brightened. She emptied the glass of wine and scanned the room. Looking for what, she had no clue. The peculiar occurrences gave the impression someone was indeed there: the wine basket, the unlocked doors, and now the lights dimming when only a gentle breeze stirred.

She remembered the reason Paul asked someone to stay. On Halloween, he'd been worried about trespassers wanting to have fun with the old house. With the manager out of town, Paul had said no one was available to check on the place. Was he misinformed? Was someone here…now…aiming to play a trick on an unsuspected victim…on her?

Another step, the lights flashed.

Backtracking, her heart pounded against her ribcage as if a drummer beat against it, readying for battle.

Emptying her glass and setting it on the table, she opened a cabinet drawer, frantically searching for a flashlight, candles, anything for a light source. What a fix she was in. No car, no one around to call for help. Holding a knob, she paused. Why not call Larry? He'd come, but if she did she would be back into the same predicament, not facing her fears on her own. People couldn't keep babysitting her. It was time for her to confront her phobias and reservations head on and get a grasp on her overactive imagination.

The next drawer she flung open with more force than she meant. Silverware flew out, stabbing and hitting her hand and arm before falling to the floor. She knelt, picked them up, and after a few minutes of consideration whether to wash them first or not, she tossed them in the sink.

The electricity gave another warning as to what would happen shortly. Three times, the lights had blinked. At her home, the electricity would flick off any second and not return for hours. She yanked open the drawer closest to the refrigerator. Matches and a couple of candlesticks rested inside. Images of horror stories entered her mind, her walking through the old house, carrying a candle to guide her way. She shivered. *Spooky*.

Shoving the images away, she set the sticks on the kitchen counter and gazed out the window. The moon glowed and stars twinkled over the stirring trees and bushes. The schoolhouse looked cute, quaint, and harmless. Not the same thoughts she had earlier, when the ghosts hid behind it.

She covered her mouth with a hand, blocking the sound of a hiccup, and braced her elbows on the counter.

In the distance, an unusual glow of diamond-shaped sparkles dotted the hillside. Three…no, four dots glittered, similar to the way a lightning bug's nervous system turns on and off in short, rhythmic flashes.

But that couldn't be. The bugs didn't come out this time of year—the cool weather made sure of it. She pressed a thumb against a closed eyelid, fingers on the other lid, to clear her vision before looking again.

The lights vanished.

A loud noise vibrated through the house.

The coldness of fear spread through her body, threatening to tear her apart and sucking the air out of her lungs. She forced in a deep breath and gazed at the ceiling, waiting with nervous energy for what would happen next.

A loud thump, and she jumped.

Damn it!

At this rate, she'd be looking over her shoulder, beneath mattresses, in closets everywhere she went. The plan to move beyond scared was backfiring.

An eerie scrape came from outside. The noise sounded like nails dragging across a chalkboard. Charlene rubbed her fingernails against her palms, cringing, and lifted on her tiptoes to peek out the window. Uncertain of what she might find unnerved her, yet didn't sway her determination to see what caused the disturbing sound.

The breeze had picked up. Tree branches moved like disjointed arms. One of the branches hit the aluminum siding. Nothing serious. She dropped back to her heels and gazed across the field.

The fake lighting bugs blinked. This time the rhythm of the flashing lights was familiar: Morse code. Having been fascinated by the communication system, she studied it and learned the alphabet. Now, when her learning it would be beneficial, her vision was skewed from the wine. She couldn't decipher the dashes and dots.

The house lights flicked off. The moonlight produced dancing shadows on the cabinets.

"Come on!" The hair lifted on the nape of her neck. Her mouth grew dry. She ran a hand over the countertop, found the candles and matches, and lit a wick. On high alert, she glanced around the room, darting her eyes from one side to the other.

Overhead, scratching noises scampered upstairs followed by creaking.

Enough!

Weak or not, smart or not, she was phoning Larry. Either she called, or went berserk. She grabbed her purse and searched the contents for his business card.

It wasn't there.

She recalled picking up her bag and not paying attention to the card on top. She snatched her phone and slipped it into her pocket, grabbed the glass and bottle and headed outside, away from the creaks and thuds.

Since she'd gone inside, the autumn air cooled, sending goosebumps over her body and making her wish she'd dressed warmer than a cotton tee and a pair of jeans. The wind tossed her hair, blocking her view. She tucked the long locks behind her ears and made a quick survey of the outer porch.

Like she'd thought, Larry's card lay face up near the basket. She sat down on the top step, poured a glass of wine, and sipped. The fruity flavor soothed her dry throat and relaxed her tense muscles. Again, she contemplated the wisdom of contacting Larry.

She flashed back to that horrible day, high on a mountain, nothing but trees and a couple cabins nearby. Members of the Black Scorpions, a terrorist group, had kidnapped her son to force her to do their bidding. She'd had to persuade her boss and friend, Pamela Young, to go to the mountains so the Black Scorpions could enact their revenge on her boyfriend, Special Agent Jake Gibson, and Charlene would get her son. Things didn't work out the way they'd said. At gunpoint, they'd thrown her and Pamela in a cabin.

The worse part of the whole horrible situation had been the day she learned her son was taken. She ached just as much today as she had then. Tears filled her eyes. She sipped some more wine. No amount of alcohol would ever take the pain away, but she'd given it a try a few times since then. Either her mother or one of the BOFs stopped her from having too much. Thankfully, she had enough sense not to drink when Henry was near.

A cow hollered from a neighboring farm, distracting her briefly from the downward spiral she was sure to go through if she kept up this line of thinking. She couldn't help it. The image of her son taken from their home stayed fresh in her mind every second of every day, even kept her awake at night. The nightmares lessened, but a few still haunted her. Between dreams of Larry and the nightmares, she hadn't slept much in the last six months.

Charlene finished the wine. Her ex-husband was to blame for their dire situation. He sent their restaurant into foreclosure, a business she'd dreamed of since a young child. Second to her son, The Café had been her heart and soul. Andrew took their money and skipped town without a word, not caring what would become of their family.

She tilted the bottle over her glass and drained it.

That's when her already troublesome situation went belly-up. A man who presented himself as trustworthy and wanting to help loaned her money.

Charlene gulped the wine. That asshole was dead now. She shook her head. This was not the type of person she was. She wasn't hateful or vindictive. One horrific event in life can change a person, as it had her. She hoped she could find her way back to seeing the good in people, to trust. Outside of her family and the BOFs, she didn't.

Tears streamed down her face. The terrorist's group end game: to use Pamela Young as a pawn to trap an FBI agent. She helped it happen, to save her son.

Charlene set the empty glass in the basket, braced her elbows on her knees, and grasped the sides of her head.

The explosion that day boomed in her ears. More tears fell, wetting her jean-clad knees. She believed Henry had died.

She swiped a hand across her cheeks, gazed at the field toward the weird lights, and recalled the most heart-wrenching time of her life. Special Agent Larry Newman had walked toward her, holding her excited, yet frightened son's hand.

Relief had washed over her, lessening her nerve-racking anxiety.

She shifted her gaze to the person responsible for saving her son and locked gazes with the agent. A connection passed between them. Like a treasure at the end of a torturous journey, she discovered a sensation she couldn't have possibly fathomed. A draw so intense, she hadn't believed it existed with another human outside of her mother and son until that moment...a future.

The feeling had scared her then. Still did. Her ex had ruined any chance for her to have a healthy relationship with another man. And now, here, she considered calling Larry, bringing him into her life. A man she wanted to spend time with despite fear that if she did, she'd scare him away with her inability to trust. Time hadn't healed her heart or soul.

Voices carried on the night air, the anger in their tones bolstered through the evening breeze..

She froze.

****

Not twenty yards from the driveway on Greenwood Manor, Special Agent Larry Newman had his hands full.

"On your knees. Hands on your head," he ordered, his gun pointed at the peeping Tom. "Why are you spying?"

"Why you? You're the mother-fucker who'd been watching my crib and my girl."

Larry's jaw clenched. He wanted to punch dipshits who spoke as if they hadn't had a chance at an education. Judging by his shorts that covered half his butt and the rancid stink coming off him, he had no respect for himself either. "Your name?"

"You don't answer my question. I don't talk to you."

This line of questioning went nowhere fast. A feeling churned in his gut. This guy was a pawn, not the leader. "Who sent you?"

"I ain't telling you shit."

"Have it your way." Larry holstered his pistol and unclipped his handcuffs from his belt. With the right wrist secure, he informed, "You have the right to remain silent…"

"Yadda, yadda, yadda. I know the drill."

Larry twisted the man's left arm behind his back, clicked the cuff, then the other and spotted a worn wallet sticking out of the guy's left pocket.

"Glad you do," Larry shined his penlight on the license. "Mr. Mathews."

Larry tugged on the cuffs until Mathews stood. The scruffy redhead would realize soon enough that he didn't have the evidence to hold him. No matter how much Larry questioned Mathews, a man who he could tell went to great lengths by changing his appearance from the botched hair dye and shaggy beard, wouldn't care. He wouldn't give up anyone he was involved with, as Mathews called it, his crib. Still he had to try. "Nice costume. Did your mommy put it together?"

"Man, that's just wrong. Why yous treat me this way? I'm just walking by."

No way did he happen by. Larry gazed through Greenwood Manor's kitchen window. Charlene had disappeared. This guy watched her, but why?

"I know my rights. Your arresting me is wrong," the man sputtered. Spit flew out the sides of his mouth.

"Watching someone without his or her knowledge is a misdemeanor."

"You're no better. You watched her, too. I seen ya."

Guilty.

Charlene, showing up at Greenwood Manor on Halloween, surprised him. Since the kidnapping, her son and at least one of the BOFs accompanied her everywhere she went. So what gave tonight?

More shocking than her arriving alone carrying an overnight bag was his inability to tear his eyes off her. From the time she arrived until Mathews approached, he had lost sight of the reason he came to the manor. He watched as she sat on the porch drinking wine, then through the kitchen window when she moved inside, trying to figure out a way to approach her.

"No comparison," Larry said offhandedly. His brain wouldn't engage in an authoritative comeback. Having to explain his actions as to why he watched

Charlene floored him. Not that he needed to go into details with a trespasser. Still, the comment stirred an emotion inside he didn't want to address.

"Yeah, there is. We're both red-blooded males. A good-looking woman, we're gonna look." Mathews cracked his knuckles. "She's off limits."

Red flashed before Larry's eyes. The guy had balls. "Wrong thing to say."

"Bullshit. She's mine. You stay the fuck away."

Larry fisted his hands. He wanted to cold-cock him. If he'd checked on the mysterious lights in the field and not perched on the step of the one-room schoolhouse watching Charlene, he would have avoided the protectiveness burning a hole in his stomach.

"Nope." His noggin still hadn't connected. For a trained agent who thought fast and acted quickly on a daily basis, he turned to putty around Charlene, another reason to stay away. At least, he didn't act on his primal instinct. He hadn't beaten the shit out of this guy.

"I work here. You don't."

Mathews' comment snapped him back to the here and now. Larry had hoped his off-handed comment about Mathews' mother and costume would fire up the peeping tom so he'd spill the actual reason he roamed the yard. Larry had a hunch Mathews was up to more than snooping on a beautiful woman. At least his perception stayed intact.

"I should call the real cops," Mathews said. "You're worthless."

Mathews' comment tumbled around in Larry's mind. Rage pounded through him, racing past annoyance and damn near stealing his control. Bile rose in his throat and his hands fisted. He gulped in a fortifying breath and shoved away the stabbing remark—you're worthless—

that showed its ugly head when his passion interfered with a case...words his father had used often.

"Go ahead," Mathews retorted. "Make my day. I'll have you on assault charges."

Larry raked a hand through his hair and stepped back, letting his mind clear and his anger subside until numbness filled his consciousness, the only recourse he had to ward off the emotion invoked by his father's vile memory.

"Man, you feel me?"

Feel him? "Hell, no!" Larry flexed and clenched his hands, his mind not as dulled as he'd hoped. "Shut your trap before we both regret it."

Mathews looked as if he wanted to retort, but Larry's glare stopped him.

Larry stared across the field to remove the anger rushing through him. Emotions were getting involved, not what an agent wants to happen.

The moon glowed on the empty field. Cows didn't graze in this pasture. He wondered why. Before he could deliberate any more on the manager's management style, lights flickered in the distance. The illumination didn't display long. A few twinkles, maybe four or five, then darkness. He'd needed his night goggles to see the distance.

Several questions came to mind. What was the origin of the mysterious lights that landed him at the manor? Were they a signal of some sort? Who was behind them? Larry gazed at the kitchen window. If Mathews worked on the manor, did he stay at the house? Why would he creep around instead of going inside? Was he seeing Charlene? The last question brought the sting of jealousy. Damn, he had it bad for this divorced mother.

He focused on the matter at hand...figuring out
Mathews. "Are you staying here?" Larry nodded toward
the house.

The anger on Mathews's face turned
compassionate as he stared at the empty window.

Damn it. "What affiliation do you have with the
woman?" Larry's voice was stern, fortified by anger, not
leaving any room to recoil and try another angle, one that
didn't have jealousy in the tone.

"None of your business."

Unlike moments ago, Mathews spoke clear. The
gangster slang and inflection had disappeared.

Larry uncuffed one of Mathews's wrists, dragged
him to the column supporting the schoolhouse porch, and
cuffed him to the column. As if Mathews had a choice,
Larry said, "Stay here." He walked several feet behind
the ten-foot tall boxwood bushes and called the FBI
office.

Missy Richards, the administrative assistant
who'd recently passed the requirements to be promoted to
agent, answered. Missy working this late at the office
didn't surprise him. She often worked well into the
evening, like him. "Hi, Missy... would you run a history
on Allen Mathews?"

"Will do, Special Agent Newman."

Ever since she left her previous position, she'd
been calling him by his title, a habit he wished she'd
break. A few moments later, she returned to the line. "No
priors."

"Employment?"

"Greenwood Manor."

So, the guy didn't lie. "Anything else useful?"

"No. There's no history past a few months ago."

A spook? Certain military agencies cleared their men's past, but this guy? "Thanks. Are you heading home?"

"Not for a while."

He and Missy were similar creatures. Neither had a reason to rush home and neither wanted a reason. "Have a good evening."

"You, too." She disconnected.

Larry stuck his phone on his belt clip. With no reason to hold Mathews, he had to release him. The guy worked on the farm and had a right to roam. Arresting a person on gut instinct didn't fly. The Director would take issue.

With his gaze glued to the window, Mathews slid his cuff wrists down the column and settled on the porch step.

His focus on Charlene dug under Larry's skin. "You're gonna stay away from the house?"

"You don't live here anyways."

The gangster slang returned. *Interesting.* "As far as you're concerned I do. Tell your crib, FBI is watching.

"You big fuzz?"

Larry hadn't heard anyone call the Bureau big fuzz. Other choice words, yes. "You bet."

"If I stay away, you gonna take these off?"

Larry thought about his good friend Paul England's worried phone call, insisting odd lights in the manor's front field had to be the work of criminals, and tried to figure out if Mathews fit into the equation. His gut said Mathews was up to no good, yet he believed the feeling was directed more toward Mathews watching Charlene than the mysterious lights flashing on the hillside. "Yes," Larry barked, sick the decision felt wrong and pissed to have no reason to hold him.

****

Rage boiled in Mathews's blood. How dare the big fuzz order him to leave? He stormed down the field toward the barn where he'd parked the four-wheeler.

I'll show that agent.

Low man on the totem pole within the gang, Mathews still had a card to play to make the FBI quake, and make the other members of the Impalers give him the respect he deserved.

His back seared from the agent watching him. He wanted to flip him off, but why bother? The chicken-shit would just arrest him. Not that the law would be able to hold him, his alias was clean. Still, he couldn't afford any attention, not if he wanted to earn Charlene's trust.

The picnic basket had been a beautifully laid out idea. The laced wine would aid her into seeing strange apparitions. The banging and knocking he made upstairs set everything into motion, scaring her. He waited for the wine to reach its full effect so he could make his move. She would be so scared she'd need someone to protect her. Who knew what that protection would entail? Naked between sheets, he hoped.

The plan executed perfectly until the damn son-of-a-bitch showed up. The desire in the agent's gaze when he watched Charlene through the window formed a knot in Mathews' stomach.

The agent was an obstacle he hadn't counted on and couldn't afford. Mathews never shot anyone. Maybe it was time. He'd find the agent alone, away from the only person who could identify him, and take him out.

Mathews climbed onto the seat of the four-wheeler, started the engine, and stared at the one-room schoolhouse. Charlene walked toward it and toward big fuzz. Her unsteady gait, a sign the drug took effect. Any minute, the agent would hear her. He'd be her rescuer.

His gut burned.

Fuck!

Chapter Two

The surprise of the raised voices propelled adrenaline through Charlene's veins. Two people, near the schoolhouse, stood and argued.

The voice that melted her insides on the mountain that awful day drifted toward her.

Larry?

Heart racing, she stumbled by the boxwood bushes, and fell to the ground beneath them. The limbs encased her as if they were prickly tentacles, scratching her arms and scraping her cheeks.

"Whoa!" She braced a hand on the dirt and lifted herself on unsteady legs. Her surroundings passed by her as if she rode a merry-go-round. Waiting for the ride to slow, she held onto the bush's skinny branches, swayed, and focused on the porch.

When it did, her vision changed. She gazed at the fragmented porch and distorted steps as if she looked through a kaleidoscope. The wine's effects played havoc with her senses. Playful as if a young child, she lifted her arms to her sides, shoulder level.

"You're gonna stay away from the house?" Larry's commanding voice boomed. She looked in the direction of the sultry tone that heated her blood.

Someone else spoke, but she couldn't hear what was said.

The desire to see Larry grew stronger. As if walking a tightrope and not a wide sidewalk, she placed a foot in front of the other.

The voices ceased. She paused, looked down at her shoes. The toe of a sneaker touched a crack in the sidewalk. "Step on a crack, break your mother's back," she sang, scooting her foot backwards parallel to the other, and lowered her arms.

The concrete beneath her vibrated, and she jumped, straddling the sidewalk. The cement popped...snapped...cracked.

She stared down in disbelief. Lines formed, stretched in every direction, like roots spreading at rapid speed, until reaching the end of the walkway.

Larry's voice boomed.

"Larry," she said, her voice not much above a whisper and shaky.

He didn't reply.

She stepped to the right side of the walk and moved closer to call him again. At the corner of the house, the concrete ended and a brick path began. Lines crisscrossed, making the feat of not stepping on one impossible, worse than the sidewalk.

"Hmm." She stayed on the grass and followed the bricks toward the schoolhouse.

The hair on the back of her neck rose. Her skin prickled. The wind picked up, blowing her hair across her face. She stopped, smoothed down her hair and turned, facing the side of the house. The moon and outside light cast a glow on the far end, highlighting two windows.

Not long ago at The Memory Café, during BOFs weekly get-togethers, she overheard a few of the members discussing an old wives' tale. At the time, she dismissed it as a joke children devised to terrorize one another. Now, standing outside the old house, she wondered if some verity backed the story.

A hand without a body would appear in a second floor window.

Maybe, if she called out...

"Madison Hand! Come out! Come out, from wherever you are." She giggled. Somewhere in her subconscious, she knew not to mess with the spirits. Again, she had no control.

"What was in that wine?"

The air stilled. She braced her feet a shoulder width apart and stared.

The windows grew wider and longer. She smacked and pinched each cheek, trying to snap out of the haunted haze the alcohol had produced.

She should have stayed home, gone 'trick or treating' with Henry and her mother.

Well beyond his years, her son had understood her reasons for coming to the manor tonight. Guilt had seeped in when she dropped him off at her mother's house until he excitedly said, "I get to stay up past bedtime." At that moment, she knew she had to go. Henry needed his mother whole again.

Clear as day, a hand emerged in the corner window, ripping her thoughts from her mind.

She froze everything except her eyes. They stayed glued to the phantom object. Fingers wiggled behind the glass pane before jumping to the next window in a game of peek-a-boo.

An owl hooted. The hand vanished. She darted her gaze between the two windows, waiting. "I've gone mad. I've turned into Alice in *Alice in Wonderland.* Where's the rabbit?" She twisted, scanned the ground for a white furry creature, and caught sight of the one-room schoolhouse. A light twinkled inside.

Is Larry there? Did he leave?

Mindful of not losing her balance, she moved at a snail's pace toward a concrete slab in front of the building, side-stepping a tree and its wayward branches. A rosebush with petite, deep red blooms grazed her arm.

The merry-go-round ride started again.

She wobbled. Her legs felt like wet noodles. Colors and lights pirouetted. "Oh, jeez."

A cat screeched.

The ride she didn't ask to be on intensified. She stumbled and fell to the ground.

Flat on her back, she stared at the sky. A witch rode a broomstick in front of the moon.

This can't be happening.

A light weight with numerous paws scurried over her stomach. She turned her head. Every inch she moved, the act freeze-framed in time. A disjointed cat ran toward two enormous monsters. She closed her lids on the tears welling. "Someone help me."

"Are you okay?" A masculine, sexy voice asked.

No. She wasn't. She was tripping, a sensation she'd never experienced. "Make it stop." Squinting, she looked toward the person belonging to the voice. The edges of her sight darkened. At the end of the tunnel, fireworks exploded. "I can't see you."

A breeze caressed her face. The outline of a man materialized.

She drew in air, the frostiness of it stinging her lungs. "Where did you come from?"

"I've been here."

She opened her mouth...closed it.

Casper the Friendly Ghost.

Nothing she did or saw made sense. "Are you a ghost?"

He chuckled. "In the flesh."

Darkness stole her vision.

****

A puff of air caressed Charlene's cheek and earlobe, emitting pleasant tingles across her skin. She opened her lids in hopes to see a man and not a ghost, to see Larry.

No one was there.

Alarm shot through her, tensing her muscles. The enjoyable thrill that woke her vanished. No longer outside watching witches on broomsticks, she lay on a soft surface with an ice pack against her head in an unfamiliar room. Her vision warped. The same effect she had looking out fatal-vision goggles, like the ones her mother forced her to wear at a sheriff's carnival to scare her from ever drinking and driving.

If her eyes didn't lie, a built-in bookshelf lined the front wall, boxes filling its shelves. Windows on either side of the room let the moonlight in.

The closed area brought forth the similarities from the kidnapping. Locked in a cabin, the unknown frightening her, she'd prayed to be rescued. The thought sizzled through her mind like a stick of dynamite, bringing an explosive feeling of doom.

Unlike last time, FBI agents wouldn't search for someone they didn't know was missing. This time, despair fell short when the scent of chicken soup filled her nostrils. She rose, scooted her legs around until her feet touched the floor, and searched the room.

In the corner, a pot sat on a woodstove. Her throat tightened. A wooden spoon moved in a circular motion...on its own.

Recalling Larry's voice, she pressed her palms into her eyes and latched onto the strength he'd imparted that day on the mountain. She'd heard him outside, arguing with someone, then inquiring if she was okay. He had to be here. Or had she wished and hoped for him so much that she dreamed it?

Anticipating and wishing the world righted and Larry stood before her, she dropped her hands and opened her eyes.

The spoon continued to stir the contents in the pot. "I'm hallucinating," she mumbled.

"You might be."

She jerked. Her hand smacked her chest. *A voice without a body.* If she ever got out of this mess, she'd have to check into a mental institution.

As if the universe knew she couldn't take another setback, a man materialized. "No-o," she whispered. Her vision once again turned fuzzy. She focused on a man's back as he stirred the soup.

He twisted. A flannel shirt covered his shoulders. With the patches of skin alternating with the flannel, she believed it was unbuttoned. His hair hung over his forehead into his eyes.

"Hi, Charlene." Her name escaped his lips as if he knew her.

She jumped to her feet and lost her balance, falling backwards.

Strong hands touched her back and lifted her until she steadied. The simple contact soothed her nervous body and his lightning-quick-speed delighted her delicate core. "Ben?" The name slipped out without thought. *Where had she heard it?*

His body went rigid.

The fatal-vision hadn't left. She couldn't make out his features. From the angle of his head, she could tell he was studying her.

"You okay?" he asked.

Easing away, her legs shook. She wanted to know who he was. With her eyes playing tricks, seeing things that weren't there, she had to go on instinct. "You're not real."

The air shimmered. The man stroked a finger down her cheek. "I assure you, I'm very much alive."

She stepped backwards and hit the wall. "W-why couldn't I see you moments ago?"

"I don't know." He chuckled.

His breath drifted across her face, stirring a desire she'd only felt once before. Impossible, as Larry had been the only man who'd stimulated outrageous cravings. *A hallucination can't do that. Can it?*

He slid another finger down her cheek. She quivered. The electricity produced a throbbing in her body and prevented her from grasping onto any one emotion. One second, she was delusional, the next, she melted. "How can I feel you?"

"You're not asking the right question." His voice filled with mischief.

The one she asked seemed important. "What is the right one?"

His hands slapped the wall on each side of her head, trapping her. Anticipating an imprisoned impression, she tensed.

It didn't occur. "What is the right—" Her whisper broke off when he moved closer, aligning his over six-foot stature perfectly to her five-foot-five frame.

"Why do I allow you?" he asked, his voice teasing.

Good question, yet why did he joke? Was this a game to him? "Why?"

A mere fraction stood between their bodies, and she wanted to taste him, have his lips move across hers.

"I've wanted you since the day I saw you," he whispered.

Her vision cleared. She bit her lip and gazed into his eyes, watching as the gold flecks sparkled. "Larry?" she asked, her voice a little louder than a whisper.

His dark, intense brows that made guys look extremely sexy, lifted. "Were you expecting someone else?"

She shook her head and let her eyes drift down the open shirt. Broad shoulders, flat abs framed by a narrowed waist. He had that sleek, muscled look that said he had kicked ass.

He lifted her chin with his finger, bringing her gaze back to his. "A woman's wet lips captivate a man." His eyes shifted to her mouth.

She fought the urge to squirm. The man was potent.

"When moisture forms on them," his voice dropped an octave, "it lets him know if he's worthy to touch her."

The seduction warmed her already overheated body. "Are you…worthy?"

"Your lips say so."

The air crackled between them.

Her pulse raced, throwing her back onto the merry-go-round ride. This time, her vision wasn't distorted, her heart was.

"I've dreamed of doing this."

If she was hallucinating, she didn't want the delirium to end.

He leaned toward her, his mouth coming in for the capture. She couldn't wait. Her lips parted.

His soft lips glided over hers. The kiss so delicate, so gentle, she felt like the treasure at the end of a rainbow. A gem someone looked long and hard to find. The hallucinations had played tricks on her all night.

Is this another trick?

She had to touch him to find out if she lived a dream or not. She placed her hands on his hardened pecs. Every nerve ending in her palms shot a jolt of awareness between her legs. If this was an illusion, she wanted more. Lots more.

A low growl escaped him, vibrating through her body. He nipped her bottom lip before taking the kiss deeper. His tongue tangled with hers, urging a response and threatening to pull well-hidden passion out of the secure hiding place she'd created two years ago.

She eased back, breaking the spell, and shook her head.

Chapter Three

Ice-cold water to Larry's crotch couldn't have felt worse than Charlene shaking her head, saying a silent '*no more*'.

Her movements might say no, but her heavy eyes and fast breathing told him she'd enjoyed their strong connection as much as he had, giving him hope they might continue.

Mind-blowing was the only way to describe the way Charlene kissed him. The power of the touch shocked him. Larry wanted to take the electricity between them even further, so damn much. His response alarmed him.

The same reaction must have caused her to stop their embrace. He should take this time to ask questions. After witnessing the questionable lights Paul spoke of, he had to agree that unexplained activity, possibly criminal, occurred on the property.

Charlene looked at him from under her lashes, her eyes longing for more. He couldn't concentrate on the case with her looking so un-believe-ably adorable.

When she showed up at the manor, he felt what he imagined a child would at Christmastime. Receiving the present on Christmas morning they'd wanted so much they'd begged their parents for it every day, a thrill he never had the pleasure of experiencing...until now.

The taste of her was beyond his expectations...delicious...incredible. Her heated body beckoned his closer. He inched forward.

"Larry." She touched a hand to his chest, keeping him at a distance.

He gazed at her wet lips, the result of their connection. "Yes."

"This is fast."

Again, the water drenched his overactive erection. "Agreed."

He mulled over his growing list of questions to keep his mind off wanting to touch her. Why was she at the manor alone? Did she know Allen Mathews? Why'd she call him Ben, a name he hated, when she first saw him?

He pulled his lips inward, tasting her sweetness and the wine she'd consumed on the steps of Greenwood Manor.

Engrossed in dealing with Mathews, he hadn't heard her approach until he heard the *thump* followed by a grunt when she hit the ground on the other side of the schoolhouse.

At first, he thought someone working with Mathews showed up and harmed Charlene. He stayed on high alert while he checked her vitals, and did a quick examination to see if any bones had broken. Other than a knot on the back of her head, she'd weathered the fall unscathed.

Charlene's breath on his skin brought him back to the present. She leaned closer, staring at his neck, and running a finger over the little bit of chest hair. With each stroke, her caressing fingers came dangerously close to urging him to pull her against him so they could pick up where they'd left off.

He tipped her head up with a finger until she met his gaze. "Charlene, are you okay?"

"No," she sighed. "I can't believe anything I see. I don't know if you're real or not. I've seen things tonight that I can't explain. I think my vision is getting better one minute, and in the next, I'm hallucinating. I don't know if you're really here. You told me who you are, but how do I know you're actually saying this and I'm not dreaming

it up in my head... How do I know who I'm kissing?"
She stared at him. Tears welled in her eyes. "Does any of
this make sense?"

The size of her pupils and her off-kilter behavior
alluded to drugs. Was she tripping?

Had the kidnapping messed with her so much, she
started using?

Pamela Gibson, Charlene's boss, and Pamela's
husband Jake, Larry's best friend, knew his fondness for
this single mom and her child. Since the ordeal in the
mountains, they'd kept a close eye on her. If she showed
any outlandish behavior, Jake would have mentioned it.
He hadn't, which made her current spiel alarming. Had
someone slipped her something?

The only thing he could say was, "Charlene, do
you want to kiss me?"

"Oh my God! You don't have any other
questions? I just ranted like a lunatic. Where's your
investigative mind?"

"I have plenty of questions, but not right now.
You're charming when you rant. And to answer the last
question, my investigative mind has left the building. I
have other matters I can't ignore."

Her eyes shifted between his and she pulled her
lips inward.

The stress Charlene endured, mixed with the
longing in her eyes, suggested he should click off the lust
running through him, and snap back into agent mode.
After another taste of her sweet lips, he would propose
they move to opposite corners of the room so they'd be
able to talk. Sitting next to one another wouldn't work.
He'd never keep his hands off her.

He lowered his head, stopping a fraction from her
lips, and waited to see how she'd respond. If she moved

away, he wouldn't try to kiss her again…at least not tonight.

She rose on her toes and slid her tongue over his chin. A low, soft moan escaped her precious lips.

He went rock hard from want, not lust, for the third time within minutes. The reason he'd kept his distance from Charlene: he couldn't allow emotions to mix with the idea of sex.

But now, he tumbled into a dilemma he couldn't reverse. As much as he didn't want to admit it, he knew he was damaged goods and wouldn't be able to give Charlene what she wanted or needed.

Still, not able to stop from kissing the woman he'd dreamed of, he shifted. Their lips touched. Just like minutes ago, the earth stood still.

She kissed with such intensity he wished he could stay there forever.

He wrapped his hands around the curve of her waist, the spot he'd wanted to touch since she parked in the Manor's driveway earlier, and pulled her closer. Her breasts flattened against him.

Since his father's death, he kept his carnal thoughts concealed on the do-not-think list, the place where he buried his grief.

Tonight, he'd break the self-imposed rules and risk destroying the wall he erected. In the past, changing his ways hadn't been a concern. No woman had tempted him, not until Charlene.

She eased away. Her brown eyes searched his face. "How can you be tangible?"

He rested his forehead against hers, debating if he should commence the questioning.

"The strobe light is on," Charlene said, her voice raising decibels, as she lifted her head away from his.

Her comments and actions reflected someone taking illegal substances. He could no longer put off asking. "Besides wine." Stroking her arms, he watched her face, monitoring her reaction to his next words. "Charlene, have you taken something?"

"What? I'd never." She braced her hands on his chest and pushed. "How could you ask?"

The world shifted. Their powerful, delicious moment had been squelched by his investigative brain, kicking in. "I have to ask."

"Why?" She folded her arms across her chest, the sign no matter what he said, it wouldn't compute in her raging mind.

"There's no strobe light," he said as delicately as he could.

"Yes, there is." She turned toward the darkened wall and grimaced. "I saw it."

He grasped her elbows, tugged her to him, but she stood firm. Either she drank too much, which he didn't believe, or his earlier thought resurfaced. She'd ingested a narcotic, somehow. His mind churned with possibilities. Had Mathews laced the wine? Is that why he watched her?

"Please talk to me." Her voice shook. Her sweet face, glowing moments ago from their kisses, turned white. "The look on your face is scaring me."

He touched her back and nudged her toward him. She tightened her grip around his waist.

"I don't mean to." Inhaling her peach scent, he rested his chin on top of her of head and inched closer. No doubt she was aware of how much he wanted her.

"Ben!" Charlene shouted, pointing at the window behind him. "They're coming."

Larry crossed the room and gazed out. The neighbor's outside lights glowed, casting a light on their yard and part of Charlene's. No one was there. He faced her.

Slowly, she shook her head. "No one is there…?"

He pressed his lips together. How could he tell her someone drugged her, that everything she saw tonight wasn't real, except for him?

Her face turned whiter. Her eyes rolled back in her head moments before her body went slack. Larry rushed over, caught her by the waist before her head hit the coffee table, and laid her on the couch in the same spot he'd placed her earlier.

On the edge of the couch, he studied her angelic features. A slight smile covered her face as short breaths escaped on a soft snore. Whatever she dreamed, it was good.

He slipped a blanket over her, and kissed her head before heading to the kitchen to search for noodles to finish the soup.

****

Charlene gazed at Larry, not believing he stood before her.

"You have to know. I assume the human form once a year on this night," he said.

She searched his eyes. The honey color she'd glimpsed earlier had changed, and they'd darkened. "I don't understand."

"Tonight, I'll break my tradition and risk losing the next five years for the brief mortality I have on All-Hallow's Eve by being with you." He kissed her below the ear. "No woman has ever tempted me to cave in and give up the one night that keeps my hope alive."

She tingled, yet she didn't fully comprehend what he was saying. She blinked, saw fireworks, and blinked again. The colorful sparkles remained.

He leaned his forehead against hers. "I'm not in the mortal form, at least not all the time."

The strobe twirled, light bounced off the walls.

He stepped away and raked his hand through his hair.

"It's an alarm, isn't it?"

"Yes. They've arrived. I'd hope they'd abandon the idea and let me have one mortal night of peace."

What was he talking about?

"You need to leave before the battle commences."

Her mouth dropped open. "What? No. I'm not leaving."

"They'll kill you."

Her stomach tightened.

The rate at which the light spun grew wild. From the corner of her eye, she glimpsed long, furry ears curled down, as if to wave. She faced it. The rabbit from Alice in Wonderland smiled from beside the woodstove. "You're late, you're late, you're late for a very important date," it said and jumped out the closed window.

Shaking her head, she turned toward him. "Nothing is as it seems." She met his serious eyes and bit her lip.

"During this time," he said, "I'm mortal, which happens once a year. A group wants me not to exist between the two worlds. If they kill me during All-Hallow's Eve, I'll disappear forever."

Her heart dropped, fell flat to her feet. She should pick it up, but his gaze bored into hers, fixing her in the spot. She'd get it later. "Wh-what?"

The light spun like an angry tiger. She closed her eyes before one chased her and she peed her pants.

"The light signals the intruders' arrival. I cooked chicken soup to cover up my scent. In years past, I hid in *the hay, around cows...goats. I hoped they wouldn't find me."*

Cows? Goats? She twisted to look out the window to find one. Maybe they could go cow-tipping.

On the horizon, lights came forth, indicating the imminent battle he referred to. Fear rushed through her. "Look!"

"They're on their way. We have some time before they reach us."

The light spun faster, flew off the pedestal.

She ducked.

The ball shattered against the wall, killing the lamp's glow. The moon's beam seeped in, giving her enough light to see his face.

Someone wanting to fight him terrified her. She didn't want to lose him to some stupid Hallow's Eve nonsense. "Let's hide." She tore through a few boxes and found two paint cans and tossed him one. "Spray paint the window. They won't be able to see us."

"That works."

With each pass of the can, the hissing expelled a pungent odor. The spray passed over the window. The light flittering inside disappeared.

"Now what?" she asked.

He turned on a small lamp. "The last moment of immortality lends me strength to make it another year. I'm savoring each second. I refuse to let this time end without touching the woman of my dreams."

A hand fisted her heart and squeezed. The fireworks at the end of her vision vanished. His face grew clearer: the sweet smile, the gentleness of his eyes. Her insides stirred.

In the corner, flowers from the rose bush filled a vase. He chose one and approached. "I have an idea."

She eyed it, wondering what he had planned. The sexual glint in his eyes stimulated her nether regions.

He guided her to lie down on the chaise. The scent of the flower flowed through the air much like the white patch had. The pedals glided down her forehead, down her nose. When he reached her mouth, she kissed the petals.

"I want to feel the silkiness...on my skin," she breathed.

"Your wish is my command."

Their clothes disappeared.

Standing beside her, the deliciousness of his glorious toned body urged her to run her fingers along the ridges of his pectoral muscles and lower. She shivered at his sensuality.

"Not yet." He grasped her hand and placed it back on the chaise. "Let me spoil you."

The flower, floating on its own, slid along her neck.

He trailed the flower, nibbling on the delicate area beneath her ear before pulling it into his mouth. The sensation felt so good, she craved more and arched her back.

He rose and observed the petals sweep the area where she longed to feel him, her breasts. She moaned. The intensity in his gaze, pleasing and wanting, made her wiggle. "I like you watching."

"You're gorgeous."

The flower caressed her stomach, inched toward the spot she ached to be touched.

"I want you." He covered her body with his, his warmth stroking her from chest to legs.

"I have to keep reminding myself you're not real, you're a ghost."

"Hmm." He kissed the tip of her nose. *"Nothing is as it seems."*

The door crashed in.

Chapter Four

Charlene bolted upright, panting. Sweat covered her body and her head ached. A white dresser lined the wall on the left, her favorite piece of furniture, an upholstered bench, on the right.

Her bedroom.

She pulled her legs inward, keeping the sheet over her waist and legs, and rested her arms on her knees. Last night's memories came in bits and pieces: locking her keys in the car, a white patch…a rose…a man.

Larry.

Memories rushed forward. The way he caressed her body with the flower's soft petals, sending sexual tingles to the areas that hadn't reacted to a man's touch in a long time.

Charlene froze.

The silky, coral nightgown she bought, but never wore, covered her.

Her mind reeled with 'oh, no she didn't.' The erotic encounter of soft petals stroking her skin slammed into her memory, which meant…she and Larry…"No-o-o-o!" They couldn't have slept together. She would have remembered.

Sex on the first date? Who does that?

Technically, it wasn't even a date…

Charlene scoffed, dropped her head on her knees and closed her eyes. "What have I done?" Many nights flew by on fantasies of sleeping with Larry. Not once had she dreamt she'd act the slut, nor be intoxicated.

A wooden spoon oddly moving in circles seeped into her mind. No hand grasped the handle to force the movements. She shook her head as a hand waving in the window flashed in her mind's eye. Nothing that happened last night was factual.

She lifted her head and set her chin on her knee. If that was true, then the petals that brought her body to life didn't exist.

Was Larry real?

She touched her lips, reliving their electrifying kiss. No illusion tasted or felt that good, nor could it bring her home, put her nightgown on, and help her to bed.

The delusions she experienced last night, ones she'd hoped would dissipate by this morning, came back two-fold. For certain, her mother would take her for a psych evaluation.

Not only did she have to contend with wondering if she lost her mind, now she fretted with whether or not she slept with a man.

Gorgeous, compassionate Larry…what would she say the next time she saw him? "Um, thanks for the memories? Catch ya on my next drunken stupor? Ugh." She flopped back against the headboard and hit her head. "Ouch."

"Careful!" a low masculine voice warned.

The surprise of his voice pounded anxiety through her system. Her day went from out of balance to humiliating. "Not possible," she muttered under her breath.

The bedroom door creaked open. "What's not?"

The care in Larry's voice sent tingles down her body. To rub her arms and legs to warm them before the goose bumps covered her skin meant she'd have to raise her head and open her eyes. If she did, she'd see him. Right now, with humiliation ruling her life, she couldn't. She covered her face with her hands and prayed he didn't hear her say, "She'd catch him on her next drunken stupor."

"You're up," he said when she remained silent.

Not looking at him wouldn't make the problem go away. If he heard what she'd said, then he did. She slid her fingers aside and peeked at him. "Hi!"

Larry chuckled.

The husky tenor that sent warmth through her body last night shot straight to her core.

"No need to be embarrassed." He moved to the side of the bed, touched her arm, and nudged it down.

She dropped her hands to her lap. Unlike last night, she could see every nuance of his face, the shadow of whiskers on his cheeks and jaw, the laugh lines at the corners of his eyes. His auburn hair shined and his honey colored eyes zoomed in on her. He had one hell of a sexy grin. But they weren't his only features holding her attention. His shirt was off and the hard plains and muscle ridges of his chest and abdomen begged her to touch.

"I'm not."

A smile stretched across his face, displaying straight, white teeth.

The passion she fought back into its hiding place last night clawed at her soul to escape.

"Are you hungry?" He pointed to the nightstand. "I worked hard, making toast and brewing coffee."

She hadn't noticed the tray or the aroma of coffee. A scent she usually savored in the mornings fell short in comparison to the man.

He settled on the mattress, and his knee brushed against her thigh. His nearness made her skin tingle. She studied his chest and lowered her gaze, following his happy trail.

He rubbed the sprinkle of hair between his muscular pecs, his face flushed pink. "I should put my shirt back on. I took it off before I went to sleep."

"No need." She smiled. "Do you usually sleep in jeans?"

His masculine groan declared he battled over that decision and made her insides clench. "I usually don't, but thought, best not."

She grinned, enjoying his reaction. "Why are you here?" She hated to sound ungrateful with the caffeine and food he put on the nightstand. "I mean, how'd you get in my house…my bedroom?"

Moments passed as he studied her. A flutter of excitement flipped her stomach. She wanted to touch him, taste him.

His eyes narrowed, a puzzled expression crossed his features. "Do you remember any details from last night?"

"Not really. No."

"At Paul's request, you went to Greenwood Manor to distract vandals."

Did she tell Larry?

"When you didn't answer your cell this morning, Paul called the other BOFs, and then called me."

As far as she knew he hadn't joined the BOFs. Now that he had, she'd see him every week at Cocktail Hour. Keeping a handle on her growing feelings toward him would be next to impossible. "I hadn't realized you joined the group."

He shook his head. "I haven't. I'm an honorary member."

"Oh."

"So you don't remember anything?"

"I recalled the reason I went to the manor. The areas between drinking a glass of wine on the porch until now are somewhat fuzzy."

"The rest will come back to you in time."

"You sound so confident. I feel like I've been hit in the head."

He lifted her hand and drew circles on the back of her hand with his thumb.

Each soothing caress ratcheted up her desire.

"In the past, I've experienced memory loss. It'll come back in fragments, eventually, the whole picture falls into place."

Accepting his explanation, she nodded.

Questions whirled around in her mind. Before she could ask one, he said, "I heard you fall."

"Heard me? Where?" She raised her eyebrows and searched her memory banks: the walk to the small building, a rose bush. "I fell outside the building that looks like an old one-room schoolhouse."

"You did, and it is a schoolhouse. I found lots of old textbooks inside, though I don't believe anyone's taught in there for years."

"I heard you and saw the light. I was coming to find you."

Larry stopped watching his thumb rubbing her skin and locked gazes with her. "You heard me?"

"Yes, and some other guy."

A serious expression crossed his face, one that made her nervous. "I need to ask you a few questions."

To get the monkey off her back, so to speak, and allow her time to get her bearings before she answered a battery of questions, she said, "Okay, but me first."

He arched a brow and hesitated briefly before saying, "Shoot."

"Why were you at Greenwood Manor?"

"Checking on mysterious lights Paul told me about."

The lights that looked like lightening bugs. "I saw them, fireflies." She paused. "If Paul asked you to check on the lights, then why did he need someone else to ward off vandals?"

Larry lifted their join hands. "I think we were victims to a matchmaking scheme."

"Paul? A matchmaker?" She had never known any of the BOFs to meddle in each other's lives; then again, she hadn't been around them long.

"Surprises me, too. It's the only explanation." He studied her. "Remember anything else?"

She released his hand, braced her hands on either side of her, and straightened, rising higher against the headboard. The next question she dreaded, but she needed an answer. "Did you put my nightgown on me?"

He glanced behind him at the door, then turned back around, and cocked his head. "That explains what you muttered earlier."

She scooted back down and pulled the sheet over her head. "You heard me."

He gripped the edge of the sheet and lowered it. "Yep, 'fraid so. So you're clear, I would never take advantage of someone inebriated." His gaze turned intense. "No matter how much I want her."

Despite her reservations on pursuing a relationship, relief washed over her and little feet danced happily over her heart.

"Here's the deal. I came to check out the mysterious lights, ran into someone, and had words. Then he. A few minutes later, I heard you fall. I immediately scooped you up and drove you home. Since no one else was here, I put ice on your head, gave you some aspirin, and stayed." He pointed to the chair in the corner of her room. "I slept there."

She had hoped he spooned her during the night, but his caring for her was wonderful. "Thank you."

He slanted his head to the other side, reminding her of a cuddly puppy, and reached for something on the tray. "Do you remember this?"

A variety of reactions flitted over her: shock, excitement, apprehension, passion. None of them was she willing to latch onto and claim.

The rose.

"I thought you said—" Her words broke off. She touched a hand to her chest. With the other hand, she grasped the stem. "It looks so fresh."

"Ah-h, you do remember." He slightly raised and kissed her forehead. "You had me worried." He placed a hand on her knee when he settled back on the bed.

The ease at which he touched her, the flower…she knew more *had* happened, which brought her back to the confusion she had earlier. "What about my nightgown?"

He made a throaty noise. "I can't explain it. We stayed downstairs for a while until you drifted to sleep on the couch. You thrashed around, so I brought you up here to bed. Here's the part that might bother you."

She tensed.

"I laid you on the bed while you were still sleeping. I turned to figure out where I might snooze. When I turned around," he ran a hand down his face, "your clothes were gone."

Her eyes narrowed. "Huh?"

"A-ah, I don-n…I don't know," he mumbled and shook his head. "Charlene, I can't explain why you stripped." He pressed his lips together, the corners of his mouth twitched. "I will say I managed to find the willpower of a lion. I looked through your dresser, grabbed the first thing I found, and helped you put it on."

She eyed him. "That's it?"

His lower teeth slid across his lower lip and he gave a slight nod. "Yeah."

Emotions pinged back and forth through her mind between gratitude that he remained a gentleman in such a circumstance and being insulted that he hadn't wanted her enough. She decided on the high road…grateful. "You're a gentleman."

He gathered her hands. "Please, don't ever test me like that again."

She liked the sound of that. "Okay."

He looked like he wanted to say something more. Instead he watched her, the pulse in his neck ticking.

She smelled the rose. On the chaise…the flower. "If we didn't sleep together, then what I'm remembering with the flower, did it happen?"

"I don't know what you recall, but the rose did play a part in what we did last night." He leaned forward. Very gently, he touched the back of her head.

The area smarted.

"The knot is a lot smaller. Does it hurt?"

She must have hit something when she fell. "Not much." Her mind had played lots of tricks on her, leaving her unable to determine what was real or fiction. "Did we go inside the schoolhouse?"

He glided the back of his finger from her temple down to her jawline. "No."

If they didn't, then the romantic scene between them didn't happen? An ache of emptiness swelled in her chest. An occurrence she couldn't explain or understand.

The fear that jolted her awake in a sweat rushed forward. Men on horseback raced through the field toward them while they hid in the schoolhouse.

She eyed Larry.

He smiled. He didn't look like someone who had anyone chasing him.

Curiosity over what they actually did with the rose nagged her. Were they naked? Charlene's stomach flip-flopped, telling her to leave that question unasked. Another thing that bothered her was when she first saw Larry, she'd called him Ben. The name had slipped out without thought. Had she dreamed him up? "Who's Ben?"

He chuckled.

The sexy, masculine sound tightened her stomach like endorphins.

"Your mind is playing tricks on you?"

She nodded.

For several seconds, he watched her as if trying to gather his thoughts.

Any minute, he would realize she was crazy and leave. Not able to recall kissing someone or anything that might have passed between them was unforgiveable in her book. She hoped it wasn't in his.

His pupils grew darker. The gold flecks in his irises shined brighter. Shockingly, he cupped her face. Testosterone oozed from him. Her intelligible thoughts fled.

"Let me remind you." His heated eyes closed with the tilt of his head. Tender lips connected with hers.

Desire, hot, intense, and needy, throbbed through her body. The scrape of his teeth over her bottom lip renewed her memory of the sizzling, passionate kisses they shared.

Location and time were overrated. The details might come back to her later. If not, who cares? She parted her lips, inviting him in.

He deepened the kiss. A low, guttural moan vibrated. One hand slid to the nape of her neck. The other traveled down her spine, massaging and sending sparks of pleasure through the silk. His adventurous palm rested on the small of her back and pressed her closer. The kiss lasted until she grew so hot and damp, she didn't think she could speak, and eased back.

"Whoa," he panted. Confusion and longing settled in his enlarged pupils.

The sensual haze he generated anchored deep in her stomach, creating a sense they'd found each other. Logically, she believed souls didn't find one another and people played a part in their own fate, but this connection, meeting of bodies and minds, blew her theory.

She gulped down the giant ball of emotion. Needing something else to think about, she asked again, "Who's this Ben guy?"

"Last night, you called me Ben."

That part she remembered. "Why would I?"

"I wondered the same." He paused, studying her. "Have you spied on me?"

"No," she said on a half-laugh, lying a tad. Whenever FBI agents, or retired agents in Jake's case, dropped by The Memory Café, she'd looked for Larry. If he showed up, she watched him through a window in one of the saloon doors. "Why would you think I spied?"

"Benjamin Larry Newman at your service." He grinned.

Her chin dropped. She hadn't dreamed up the name. But how did she know to call him Ben?

"Are you all right?"

If he only knew the workings of her mind, he'd run. She twirled the stem between her fingers and flicked her gaze to his chest, appreciating the sight again…bare…muscular…wide shoulders. Before she drooled, she wiped the edges of her lips and focused on his eyes.

He didn't turn red this time and leaned in for another kiss. His chest rubbed against hers, silk sliding across her sensitive nipples.

What he did with the soft petals she couldn't forget. Still, the nagging memory they were at the schoolhouse stayed with her. She eased back. "The rose, did it come from the bush at the manor?"

"It did. You held the stem when I found you on the ground."

"I did?" her voice quaked. Lines muddled between what she hoped he did with her and what actually happened.

He tugged her close. "In time, you'll remember everything."

The intimate touch of his warm chest pressing against her responsive breasts increased her already elevated pulse. She sank more into his comfort, enjoying the touch of him, and received a whiff of burning wood. "Why do you reek of smoke?"

"I should take a shower." He shifted to rise.

She clutched onto his hand. "No, it's fine. Did you build a fire?"

The mattress dipped from his body weight as he relaxed on the mattress. He held her hand. "I did."

She remembered a woodstove in the schoolhouse. "At the manor?"

He did the cuddly puppy thing again and tilted his head. "No. I cooked it downstairs on your woodstove in the family room. I put the rest in the refrigerator. Do you want some more?"

"More?"

"You had a bowl last night. You told me your grandmother made chicken-noodle soup the same way when you were a kid."

"If you say so." She had no clue what she did or didn't say. "I wasn't quite myself."

"You were lovely. You are lovely."

She stroked his five o'clock shadow. "Have you always been so sweet?"

A robust laugh erupted. He kissed the palm of her hand. "I know some felons who believe not."

Larry's sincerity and considerate qualities put him on a whole other level than her ex-husband. "I can't imagine why you're not married."

The compliment backfired. Larry's expression turned impassive and his body went rigid, cat-like, ready to flee.

She read the signs…subject closed.

Since the kidnapping, she'd seen him a few times, daydreamed about him. This gorgeous FBI agent saved her and her son. How could she not fantasize? He never asked her out, yet here she sat in her bed wearing a nightgown she hadn't put on—with him shirtless as if they hung out comfortably together every morning.

He snuggled her into his embrace, pressing her face against his chest.

Memories flooded her from the day he rescued her and her son. Her watery gaze had met Larry's across the battlefield, a magical moment passed between them. An awareness she didn't understand, yet knew it existed.

Last night, his lips caressed hers. The intimacy, comforting, and soothing had driven away the ghostly apparitions and animate objects.

Now, the embrace sparked a fire so deep inside her she had to act.

"We need to have a replay. The experience is worth remembering, or in this case, repeating." His whiskers brushed her cheek along with his breath.

The tender words and touch made other body parts beg to be stroked. She sighed, pulling back until her gaze met his. "Now?"

His lips curled, his eyes brightened.

She dove into the kiss and sought out what she'd wanted since the day she met him.

Kissing him, the tightness in her chest, and wanting to press her naked breasts against his skin, she got it. A magical attraction ran rampant between them, explaining her perception she had moments ago, feeling like she'd come home to a place she didn't know existed.

Possessing such a strong chemistry so easily with someone she didn't really know frightened her.

He eased back, placed his hands on each side of her face, kissed her softly, and gazed into her eyes. "I'd rather keep kissing you, but I have a few questions I have to ask."

She'd forgotten about their deal. "Okay."

He grasped both of her hands. "This is delicate. Know that I have to ask."

The expression on his face bothered her. "Ask."

"Did you take any narcotics?"

She had to admit her behavior last night was totally out of character, but Larry asking her questions about her character after they had just had such an intimate kiss bothered her. She pulled her hands free, pressed her back into the headboard to put distance between them, and narrowed her eyes. "No."

"My questions won't hurt." He braced his hands on the mattress on either side of her hips, trapping her in.

She squirmed under his scrutiny.

"Do you know anyone who works at Greenwood Manor?"

"No."

"What about the overseer, Jed Bradley," he edged his upper body closer, "ever met him?"

"No."

"The wine you drank on the back porch, did you bring it?"

"Who was spying on whom?"

He rubbed the tip of his nose against hers. "My turn to ask the questions." His breath drifted across her face.

"No."

"Here's the scoop. Last night your pupils were large and your behavior was erratic. They're signs of someone taking hallucinogens."

She studied him. Did he think she popped pills? "I drank wine, nothing more."

"Okay. If you didn't bring the bottle, where'd it come from?"

"From a basket on the porch."

"Do you make it a habit to take other people's wine?"

Disappointment snaked down her spine from his insensitive tone. "Are you irritating on purpose or is it habit?"

He laughed. "Touché."

"And no, I don't. I thought I was locked out of the house. The bottle was there, ready for the taking."

"Didn't Paul give you a key?"

Larry already thought she was nuts, she didn't want to go into the ordeal of how the house key was locked in her car. "Long story."

"What was in the basket?"

"A bottle of wine and a glass."

He arched a brow. "Only one glass?"

"Yes."

One corner of his mouth rose. "Glad to know you can say the word."

The tension in her face lessened. "When warranted."

"I hope I'm worthy of a *yes* one day."

She let out her anxiousness by blowing out a puff of air, the hair on her forehead lifted. "You do know how to heat up a room."

"My charms are more than rusty. I'm glad they work."

"Me, too."

"Charlene," the intensity of his voice grew, "I-I—" He groaned. "I want to take what we have between us further."

She'd love to see what they might have between them. With her twisted history, not being able to trust men, she didn't know if it was wise or fair to Larry.

"But, I don't know if I can."

Her mouth fell open. She didn't know what to say. Thinking the words and knowing she'd only have to contend with her own wayward behavior was one thing, but for him to express the same…it stung. She closed her eyes and shook her head, figuratively shaking the cobwebs out of her mind. What a mess.

His warmth surrounded her. She kept her eyes shut and let him pull her into his embrace. She relaxed her head into the crook of his neck, inhaling the smoky, woodsy smell.

"Let's take this slow, okay?"

Slow was good. She needed time to wrap her mind around everything, too. To see if she could bury the hatchet of not trusting to be able to lower the walls she'd built up around her heart.

"So you know, when we are together, I don't want any confusion if it's a dream or not or if I'm real or not."

She slid her arms around his back and held on. *Is this man for real?*

"As for the wine, I think someone laced it with some sort of drug. I don't know why or if you were the intended target. Trust me, I will find out."

"Mommy!" The front door banged open.

She pulled back and whispered, "It's Henry. He can't see you in here. He won't understand."

"Mommy, where are you?"

"Sweetie, in my room," she shouted and turned toward Larry.

He moved off the bed and grabbed his shirt from the rocking chair.

Footfalls banged on the steps, then the hall's wood floors. Henry bounced into the room, wearing a Spiderman costume, no mask, his blond hair dangling on his forehead. He halted. His keen eyes skimmed over her in bed, the blankets pulled to her neck, to Larry, now clothed, standing a few feet away.

The only time Henry had seen Larry since the kidnapping was on occasion at The Memory Café, a party situation. Here in her room, she didn't know what he'd think.

"Mommy, are you okay?" By the sullen words and the concerned expression, her son had assumed the worst.

"Yes…no…Last night," she stuttered, not knowing how to describe what happened. "I was sick. Agent Newman helped me."

Her son nodded. He held up an orange pumpkin and dumped the contents onto the bed. "Look at the candy."

She curled over and moved the pieces of candy and mini games from a bubble gum machine around.

Larry joined them. "You made a killing, little man."

Henry glanced up, smiled, and giggled. "I'm only seven."

"Really?" Larry rocked back on his heels. "I thought you were at least ten."

The grin on Henry's face stretched. Charlene loved seeing him this happy. He hadn't really smiled much since the divorce. To be honest, he wasn't happy prior to the divorce either.

"You weren't well?" her mother asked from the doorway. The sunlight streamed through the window onto Doris's brown hair, sprinkled with gray. Her dark eyes twinkled. "How are you now, honey?"

Charlene uncurled, sitting up straight and keeping the sheet up to her neck. Telling Henry a little white lie about the reason Larry was in her room so as not to confuse him was different than lying to her mother, yet how could she explain someone drugged the wine she drank? She couldn't, and supported the lie. "Hi, Mom. I'm better. This is Larry Newman. Larry, my mom, Doris Weber."

"Nice to meet you, ma'am." Larry stretched out a hand.

"Forget the handshake. I've wanted to meet you for some time. You helped save my daughter and grandson." Doris hugged him. "You rescued my babies."

Larry winked at Charlene over her mother's shoulder.

Henry left the candy discarded on the bed and walked to Larry as his grandmother stepped away, his brown eyes questioning.

Larry knelt in front of him. "Hey."

Henry's chin wobbled and eyes watered, but he stood still. Charlene ached for her son, who'd already been through so much in his young life. The expression on his face suggested he wanted a hug. From her and Henry's many conversations, she knew how much her son thought of Larry.

Larry touched the Spiderman cape. "This is a great costume. You're my favorite action hero. I wanted to be him for years."

Henry tilted his head. "He's not real, like you."

A muffled sniffle escaped Doris.

Larry raised an eyebrow to Charlene. She knew what he wanted. He wanted to comfort her son in a way Henry's father never did. Once she nodded, Larry opened his arms. Henry studied him for a moment before walking into his embrace.

The sincerity of her son hugging the man who saved him along with Larry clutching him was more than she could bear. Tears slid down her face. She tried to suck in some air, but it hitched on a sob.

"Can I call you Larry?" Henry asked and shifted away. "That's what Mom calls you."

One side of Larry's mouth lifted. "She does, huh?"

"She talks about you a lot."

"I do not," she said on a nervous giggle and wiped her cheeks. She might think about Larry once or twice…a day, but she didn't talk about him all the time.

Her mother caught her gaze and lifted an eyebrow.

Maybe she did…once in a while.

Laugh lines outlined Larry's eyes and mouth. "You don't say?" His cell beeped. "Excuse me," he said before walking into the hall.

Her mother grinned.

Henry smirked.

"What's up with you two?" Charlene asked.

"Nothing. Are you hungry?" her mom asked as she put the candy back in the pumpkin.

"I have toast and coffee." Charlene nodded toward the tray.

Henry grasped the pumpkin's handle and darted out of the room.

"I found homemade chicken soup in the refrigerator, like my mother made when you were sick." The knowing eyes of her mom flickered with delight. "He cooked for you. He's a keeper."

"Mom, I don't know. We haven't been on a date."

Her mother kissed her forehead. "Maybe not, but what you two have done is much more intimate."

"Mom!"

"Not that." Doris waved a hand and made a disgusted face. "He cared for you while you were sick. Any man who sticks around to do whatever is necessary is a good one in my book. Not many are around. You and I didn't choose well the first time, yet we have beautiful children. I believe you will find a man who will treat you like a princess, the way you deserve."

"You deserve a good guy, too."

Her mother squeezed Charlene's hand. "Henry wasn't hungry when he got up. Too much candy, I think. I'll go fix him some pancakes."

Her mother exited, passing Larry reentering the room. "Jake called. I gotta go. Can I see you this evening?"

She needed a ride to Greenwood Manor to pick up her car. While there, she wanted to look around to settle some of the troublesome images that kept flashing through her mind. With Larry meeting Jake, maybe one of the BOFs would go with her. She'd rather not bring

Henry to the manor, yet, not until she knew for certain what she had seen was a figment of her imagination.

"Sure."

He closed the distance between them and brushed his lips across hers. Again, last night drifted into her mind, like the green chaise. Was it inside the building? The place Larry pressed his body on top of hers in her dreams… She had to find out. "I'm going out to Greenwood Manor," she blurted.

His body went rigid. "Why?"

The question caught her off guard. "To pick up my car."

"If you don't mind waiting, I'll take you over later this afternoon."

She could wait, but didn't want to. "Thanks, but I'll catch a ride."

"I wouldn't advise it."

For not knowing her well, he gave his opinion freely. "Are you telling me not to?" She hoped not. It'd be a deal breaker.

A vein in his forehead showed. His jaw tightened. *What is he not saying?*

"It's your decision. For the record, I don't think it's wise," he said in a restrained, yet irritated tone she hadn't heard before.

"So you've said."

"Let's talk later." He kissed her cheek and left.

A moment later, the front door shut.

The wonderful moment they shared ended with his abrupt departure and his silent order for her not to go.

Her ex-husband had manipulated and tried to control her. No matter how much Larry's honey-colored eyes made her melt, no man would ever have power over her again.

She tossed back the covers and headed for the shower.

Chapter Five

In the small hideaway at Greenwood Manor, Mathews fumed.

Once 'big fuzz' drove Charlene off in a black Suburban, he'd parked the four-wheeler in a building along the road leading toward the backfields and walked the quarter of a mile in case trespassers happened by. He didn't want any evidence pointing to him staying at the house.

Sitting on the floor in the musty room barely large enough to sleep in, he stretched out his legs, hitting the opposite wall, and leaned back. A pistol in one hand, he stroked it with the other, waiting to hear Charlene's sweet voice over the receiver from the bug he'd planted in the kitchen and bedroom of her house, and contemplated murder.

The taste to kill a man hadn't hit him until big fuzz got in the way of what he wanted.

His mind flashed back to Washington, D.C. One evening at a bar, he met a guy named Razor, wearing a brown leather jacket, a couple tear drops tattooed on his face. The man intrigued him. They talked for hours. Razor told him, "Once you get the taste of taking a life, you'll crave more."

Mathews looked forward to the day he could proudly wear the symbol on his cheek, letting the world know he was one bad motherfucker.

He aimed his gun at a picture thumbtacked to the wall of the person whose actions aided in defining the new him, and pulled the trigger. The gun clicked. He bent his arm at the elbow and blew across the top of the barrel as if smoke drifted out.

Soon, he'd earn two teardrops.

Not only would two less assholes clutter the world, but the peons, who dumbly called themselves the Impalers, who thought they could manufacture marijuana on Greenwood Manor without giving him his fair cut, were in for a surprise.

A single phone call a moment earlier now put his plans into motion, cementing his initiation into the Black Scorpions and giving him the respect he deserved on the manor. Ever since Sanjar, the Black Scorpions' leader, was murdered, word had spread. If anyone could find the whereabouts of his killer they'd be inducted into the gang.

As lucrative as belonging to the gang would be, he needed something in return for him to give up such valuable information. His deal: the whereabouts of Jake Gibson in exchange for the 'top dawg' position at Greenwood Manor's manufacturing circuit. Once the Black Scorpions arrived, they'd take over the operation and give him the position. No one argued with the ruthless gang

Mathews lowered the gun to his lap and tossed the godforsaken hat he had to wear as a symbol that he worked with the Impalers onto the floor and ruffled his oily hair. Soon, he'd wear the brown leather jacket with the Scorpion insignia on the back, and his gang name stitched on the front. He'd have to think of a moniker, like Bruno or Rockon.

He stared at Agent Gibson's wedding picture he'd cut out from the local newspaper. Why hadn't the agent left the area? Staying, Gibson was a sitting duck. Damn, how'd a nitwit take down a Monarch? If Mathews had done such a thing, he'd run like hell. No way would he parade around the city as if he owned it.

Rage flowed through his veins. "Gibson and that Band of Fuckers turned Charlene against me." He petted his gun as if a beloved pet. "That's okay. Payback was coming." For several months, he'd prepared by target practicing in the back fields every day.

Jed Bradley hiring him to oversee the restoring of the six-hundred acre farm fit perfectly into his plans.

All he had to do was falsify his work history, have his good friend vouch for him, and the old fart hired him at their first meeting. He hadn't seen Bradley since.

Mathews thought it odd, but whatever.

He shoved his gun in the corner behind the stack of boxes. Charlene must have fallen asleep downstairs. All night, he only heard footsteps, the refrigerator opening and closing, no signs if that red-headed fuckwad stayed. He'd plant more bugs in the house soon. The two weren't cutting it.

A couple days ago when he sat in this very spot, he overheard Charlene's one-sided phone call that she'd plan to stay at Greenwood Manor on Halloween. He had everything planned: the laced wine, a warm bed. Bile rose from his stomach and perched in his throat. "Big fuzz...That cocksucker!" Mathews banged his fist on the wall. His well-thought-out plan of getting Charlene to fall into his arms had gone up in flames because of that redheaded dipshit. He'd blow the fucker's head off the first chance he got.

"I hope I'm worthy of a *yes* one day," a masculine voice drifted over the receiver.

Had he been so far into his head, he hadn't heard them?

Her voice was so low, Mathews' couldn't hear. "Son of a bitch!"

He turned up the volume on the metal box.

"I want to take what we have between us further," the fuckhead said.

"No fucking way!" Mathews shouted. Rage rose from his stomach to his face.

A door slammed, the walls in his hideaway shook.

"Shit!" He turned off the receiver and pulled the chain to the overhead light. "Who the fuck was here?"

****

Reeling on the fact Charlene wanted to go alone to Greenwood Manor, Larry parked his Suburban in the driveway of Jake and Pamela Gibson's two-story, brick house. Realistically, he didn't have the right to demand or expect her to listen to his advice. Still, he couldn't stop his primal instincts from going further where she was concerned. He wanted her to count on him with every aspect of her life. The sensation landed him in unfamiliar territory, a feeling he didn't know how to handle.

Hs sucked in a deep breath to get a handle on his wayward reactions. The scent of her peach shampoo, lingering on his clothes, inundated his senses. His groin tightened.

Frustrated for letting his guard down even a tiny bit, he hit his hand on the steering wheel. He wasn't relationship material. The few times he counted on women they ripped his heart out. *Never again.*

An old saying played through his mind, one that he'd repeated over and over to himself to give him hope. *Time heals all wounds.* His jaw tightened. If only the proverb had held true. Scars from emotional wounds inflicted on him years ago stayed fresh and refused to let go.

Yet… He stared at his knuckles whitening on the wheel as his insides gripped with need. When he'd looked into Charlene's eyes for the first time six months ago, magic cast a spell over him. That day, he'd lowered the wedge between him and the world a fraction. The reckless act scared the crap out of him.

He hadn't called her when his fingers itched to, didn't stop by her house when his car wanted to drive by. He kept his distance, keeping his desire at bay.

Last night, the first taste of her overpowered him, urging him to lower the barrier. As much as he yearned to kick the protective wall away, he knew keeping the wall erected to its full height, or even higher, was safest. The quandary was like a pebble in his shoe, shifting around and poking him. Not a good position for an agent whose clarity saved lives.

Frustrated with self-reflecting, he climbed out of his Suburban and gazed across the sparse wooded land to Jake, pitching a stick into the Rappahannock River for his Labrador, Willis, as he'd done countless times while they'd discussed cases.

"Hi, Larry!" Pamela stepped out the side door of the house with a small cooler in her hand. "I figured you guys might want some refreshments."

"It's barely past noon."

She smiled. Her face glowed, the sun reflecting off her dark hair. Signs from the kidnapping had disappeared. "But it's five o'clock somewhere. Besides, you guys always have a beer when discussing a case on the 'thinking rock'." She made quote fingers to express her point.

"Thinking rock?" His question slipped out clipped. Irritation with Charlene, himself, and fatigue from not getting much sleep last night sneaked into his tone.

"That's what it is," Pamela snapped.

Charlene had him in knots. He needed a distraction, something to take his mind off the chemistry flying between them. Maybe, he should talk to the Director into sending him overseas, plenty of high profile cases needed attention…

"Larry." Pamela's gentle voice snapped him out of his self-loathing.

...Or, he'd just apologize to Pamela and seek out his friends. "Sorry. I didn't mean to be short," he said. "Long night."

Her features softened. "No offense taken."

He received the drinks and kissed her cheek. "Jake's a lucky guy."

She laughed. "Remind him, would you? Hearing a man complimenting his wife does a guy good."

Larry snorted. "And get one of his glares? No thanks."

"You have a point." She wiped her hands on her jeans and nodded toward the water. "Steve's lingering near the river, too. Tell the big lug he'd better say hi before he leaves."

"That, I'll do."

Larry watched his best friend's wife head inside before he headed toward their office without walls.

The crisp, cool breeze rustled the leaves on the trees and his hair. Fallen leaves covering the boarded walked way crunched under his feet, the perfect time of year, not too hot and not too cold.

The walkway ended and he made his way through the noisy ground covered in dead leaves and twigs to the large rock, near the water's edge.

"Hey, buddy." Agent Steve Anderson stepped from behind a tree, a furrow marring his brow. "You okay?"

Larry looked between his past and present colleagues, realized from the concern lines etched in their faces that he wore his turmoil on his, and quickly schooled his expression. "Why wouldn't I be?"

Steve studied him.

Not wanting to give a reason to discuss his inner thoughts, he maintained the blank expression.

"No reason." Steve shrugged, letting him off the hook by not questioning him further.

Clean-shaven, blond hair, and a powerful force in the field, Steve was known around the office as the all-American boy, a perfect field agent. "Heard you kicked ass overseas."

"The team did, yes. We're lucky. A few times the guys ended up in a tight spot."

Larry patted him on the back. "Glad everyone's intact."

"Me, too," Jake said, tossing a stick into the water.

Willis scurried after the stick, kicking dirt and leaves behind him, and jumped into the water.

"Exhaustion must have stolen your covert skills," Larry said to Steve. "Pamela saw you from the window."

Steve glanced toward the house. "Jake, you'll have to plant a tree or two to conceal our rock cave."

Jake snickered. "Rock cave. Is that anything like a man cave?"

"Yep." Steve shuffled and leaned back against a tree.

"Beats thinking rock." Larry chuckled.

"Thinking rock?" Jake and Steve asked in unison.

"Pamela's words, not mine," Larry assured them.

"You can't hide from my wife."

"I'm not trying to. You know she's like a sister to me." Steve said, "I'll talk to her after we're done." He faced Larry. "So, you have the hots for Charlene and came close to ruining the case."

Steve was direct, but his meaning was lost on Larry. "What are you talking about? What case?"

"Get it right, Steve."

73

Larry appreciated his former comrade's support.

"By him playing footsy with Charlene," Jake said, "he didn't come close to wrecking the case, he crippled it."

Larry's jaw dropped. "You're shitting me. Your brother calls on Charlene to stay the night alone on Halloween, at an old house no less, after enduring a kidnapping, and somehow, I managed to cripple a case I know nothing about?"

"Paul had no choice but to call Charlene," Jake said. "I was tied up on a case."

"Same here," Steve added.

Jake petted Willis's head and picked up the wet stick his dog dropped at his feet. He tossed it into the water. "She could have said no."

Steve darted his gaze toward the cooler in Larry's hand. "Do you have a beer?"

"Thanks to Pamela," he said, passing the container.

Steve set the cooler on the ground next to the rock, handed an open can to Jake and popped open another for Larry.

"Crippled a case? No way in hell." Irritated, Larry snatched the beer from Steve's hand, downed a few gulps, and enjoyed the robust taste.

"You didn't cripple the case," Jake said. "I'm messing with you, man."

Willis returned and stared at Jake with beady eyes, waiting for the stick to sail through the air again.

Steve rested his back against a tree and sipped his beer. "Your dog never tires."

The river's steady flow, gentle and inviting, sent a peace over Larry, hypnotizing him. He breathed in the woodsy scent, letting his worries slip away. "I wish I could say the same. I'm beat."

"Debrief us," Jake said. "Then I'll fill you in on the Director's phone call."

Larry's eyebrow arched. The peaceful moment vanished. Was more happening than a few odd lights? "As you already know, I went to Greenwood Manor to check on the mysterious glow per Paul's request. Before I could investigate, I came across an Allen Mathews staring at Charlene through the kitchen window."

"Did you run his history?" Jake asked.

"I did, and confirmed he worked on the manor. There's no information before this year."

"Not a lot to go on. Hell, he could be a spook." Jake drank some beer. "As long as you have a positive ID that it's Mathews and not her ex, Andrew Smith. By now, he knows Charlene received a reward for helping with the recovery of the bonds. He's a piece of work, capable of anything."

"Even so, by now he would have made a move," Steve said.

The rage that roiled through Larry just by thinking how Smith left Charlene and Henry in a dire mess had the ability to turn him into a loose cannon, something he'd best heed and control. "Any sign of Smith since he bailed on his family?"

"Negative," Jake said.

"He's too yellow to come back," Steve growled. "Hell, any man deserting his family is a douche bag,"

"Don't count on it." Uncertainty flashed over Jake's expression, and the pulse in his neck ticked. "Stranger things have happened."

"If he's smart, he'll stay away," Steve said. "They're better off without him."

Steve had a point, yet Andrew Smith was Henry's father. The boy deserved to have his dad in his life. Larry grimaced… maybe not. If Larry's dad hadn't been part of his, he'd been a lot happier, his mother, too.

The niggling sixth sense that had kept him out of harm's way shouted loudly in his ear that nothing was as it seemed where Charlene was concerned. *What am I overlooking?* "Why bring up Smith?"

A loud splash and they watched as Jake's dog chased after a Mallard duck.

"Has he ever caught one?" Steve asked, walking closer to the bank's edge.

"Once." Jake tilted his head. His expression went dark briefly. "Pamela had a premonition."

A momentary shock silenced them.

"Really?" Steve stepped toward them. "Since when does she have them?"

"Willis! Get back here!" Jake yelled and whistled until the lab climbed the embankment and shook. "Can't say She believes someone is after Charlene. I asked her not to act like a mother bear. If she did, Charlene would never relax."

"Which brings us back to, why did you drive Charlene home?" Steve's gaze narrowed and sharpened.

"Are you interrogating or debriefing me?" Annoyance filled Larry's tone.

"Whatever it takes?" Jake picked up the stick and tossed it. "Last time, boy."

Willis flew into the water two feet below the bank.

He didn't like the tone in their voices. "Both of you are assholes," Larry said, butting up to the rock.

"We know," Steve said, "and you're easy prey, man-by-the-book. But seriously, why'd Charlene leave her car at Greenwood Manor?"

"Because of her shaky equilibrium. She couldn't drive."

The dog jumped onto the bank, dropped the stick, and shook.

"Whoa. Willis, not here," Jake commanded.

The dark-eyed lab looked at his owner, walked in a circle, and lay down.

"Equilibrium?" Steve raised a questioning brow. "Is that code for drunk?"

The laced wine more than likely caused her loss of balance, but with her hitting her head on the ground, he wasn't certain. Either way, the wine was the root of her abnormal behavior. Still, he didn't want to go into details concerning Charlene's behavior. If she wanted it known that she drank a bottle of wine by herself, then it was for her to tell, not him. "It's not that simple."

"Let me take a stab here. Charlene drank to deal with ghosts and you think by not spilling what happened, you'll protect her virtue." Steve squeezed the empty beer can and tossed it beside the cooler. "Wonder if she saw the Madison Hand we heard about recently?"

"Come on," Jake said with a that's-ridiculous tone embedded in his voice. "Who believes in ghosts?"

Larry lifted an eyebrow. Steve must have done the same.

Jake snorted. "You guys can't be serious. No facts, no proof. Hell, the witnesses who thought they observed the renowned hand, doesn't even believe their lying eyes."

"I'm not saying I believe in them," Larry refuted. "Incidents happen that I can't justify."

"The manor made a ghost-believer out of you?"

Steve's snarky question irritated Larry. "That's not what I said."

Steve held up a hand. "As much as I hate to admit it, not everything can be explained. I'm surprised Greenwood Manor shifted your way of thinking. The last time we talked about a phenomenon, it was you two against me."

Larry still didn't know if he believed in spirits. "My way of thinking hasn't changed. I'm just admitting that not everything has an explanation."

"Well, that's progress." Steve nodded toward Jake, "You?"

"Nope. There's a reason for everything."

"You'll see the light one day." Steve snickered. "Back to the case: I have a nagging suspicion one of you guys hasn't coughed up the whole story with Greenwood Manor and the magic lights. I can locate either of you via satellite, but I don't have the equipment to read your minds. Now spill."

"A call came across the FBI tip line." Jake plopped down on the rock, his voice turned serious. "An illegal drug trade run by a small outfit, The Impalers, is thought to have a manufacturing plant at the manor."

This was the first Larry heard of an outfit. "Wait a minute. Why in the hell wasn't I informed before I went out there to check on the verity of the lights?"

"Did you see any?" Jake asked, igoring Larry's question.

Fireflies, Charlene had called them. "Yes."

Jake cleared his throat. "You needed a partner. Why didn't you call?"

"Excuse me?" Larry seethed. "Since when do I need a babysitter? And how the hell did you know where I was in the first place?"

"Steve," Jake said.

Larry didn't have to ask how Steve knew. The man had eyes everywhere.

"I might not be in the FBI anymore," Jake's voice rose, matching Larry, "but you damn well better cough up what's going on. How else can you have backup?"

Larry sighed, raking a hand through his hair. Jake and his demands didn't add up. "Are we talking about the same job? Paul called, told me Jed Bradley, the overseer of Greenwood Manor, had received a phone call about strange lights. Given the nature of the call, Bradley elicited your brother's help. I can't say why Paul called me and not you."

Jake dropped his arms, a smile stretched across his face. "You've been had."

Steve laughed.

A bright, sunny day and Larry felt like he had been in the dark since he arrived. "What the hell is so funny?"

"Brother Paul set you up," Jake forced out between breaths.

Jake's words took a moment to sink into Larry's brain. Jake just proved his earlier suspicions. Paul had set the stage for him and Charlene.

Larry jabbed his hands on his hips and stared at the water as another thought plunged into his mind. *Had Paul laced the wine?* Given Paul's character, he shook his head and immediately dismissed the notion. "No way."

"Having a private conversation with yourself?" Steve asked.

Larry ignored Steve. "So you're pulling my leg about not calling you."

"Sort of," Jake said and finished his beer.

"I'm not. An agent is always prepared, has backup," Steve kept on.

"Anderson, you're a pain in the ass."

"You need standby for those tight spots, like a blind date blind-siding you." Jake tossed his can to the cooler. "What irony. Damn, this is better than fishing."

"How'd you handle yourself, agent?" The corners of Steve's mouth twitched. "Given your fear of women, did you nosedive or deliver?"

Larry couldn't stop the anger blazing through his veins from his friend's teasing. He didn't want to explain his behavior toward the female race to clarify Steve's misconception.

He opened his mouth to tell Steve to go to hell when Jake's face switched to agent mode, dead serious. "Back off, Anderson. Untouchable territory."

Steve glared at Jake and then took in Larry over his beer can, swallowed, and nodded at Larry. "Sorry, man."

Outside of Jake no one knew the truth about his past. He planned to keep it that way. "It's forgotten."

"Back on topic," Jake said. "Do you have any more to report?"

"No. With Charlene's appearance my investigation stopped before it really got started. What do you have?" Larry asked Jake.

"Late last night after the Director filled me in on the tip, he requested I work on the case on the down-low. He suspects a modest operation that can be taken out easily."

Steve eyed Jake. "You can't get away from the FBI, can you?"

"Not from the Director, I can't. I'm doing side work for him under Old Town Investigations all the time," Jake said. "I'm betting one of the Impalers invented the factitious Madison Hand and flying ghosts to ward off suspicion from what's actually happening on the manor."

"Hoaxes to remove suspicion off the illegal drug trade," Larry mumbled, speaking the ridiculousness out loud. "Lights dancing on the horizon."

CAIT JARROD

"Poetic," Steve snickered.

"Shithead," he retorted and finished his beer. "When the lights flashed, the length of each light varied, similar to Morse code."

Jake stood and picked up a stick. "A signal."

"Sounds like the worker bees were busy," Steve said.

The stick in Jake's hand snapped. "Larry, you have any idea how far south things could have gone last night? Next time notify me."

Larry spotted the disappointment in his friend's face, understood it, but held firm. If he had to do it again, he would. "You're newly married. I didn't want to pull you away to take a ride. Remember, I didn't think anything more would happen. Hell, you went through enough with Sanjar and his men shooting you."

"Maybe so, but this shit's going on in our backyard," Jake said." If I'd known, I would have prevented Charlene from going."

"I didn't even fucking know!" If Larry had, he would have taken Charlene home immediately. Peculiar lights were a whole different stakeout than illegal drugs. "I handled it."

Jake chuckled. "I supposed you did. You've had your eye on her since you met. Paul did you a favor."

Larry never considered himself an open book. "I'm that easy to read?"

"Not for the average person you're not" Jake said.

"A stone sculpture tells more than you," Steve interjected. "I didn't know."

"See, the average person can't tell." Jake grinned and turned his head toward the water ignoring Steve's glower. "From six o'clock last night until three this morning, I surveilled Ellis Goldberg's house. His alias is

Roach. He's not high on the totem pole. I hoped he'd lead me to the 'go to' guy."

"I take it, you came up empty," Larry said.

"Yes."

They needed eyes on the land. "Let's meet at the manor in an hour for a search," Larry said.

"Do you have any idea how big the farm is?" Jake asked. "We'd need a team of a hundred to cover it."

Jake was right. Over six hundred acres embodied the manor, which required more man power than they had for a case that was supposed to stay low-key. "I'll fill the Director in that we're looking into it," Larry said.

"He already knows I'd drag you and Steve into it if I needed extra eyes and hands," Jake said, petting Willis.

"I'm heading to the house to see Pamela." Steve tossed the empty cans in the cooler. "She'd kick my ass if I don't. Larry, can you give me a lift? My wheels are at the office."

"Will do." Larry stared out at the water, the sick feeling that things were about to get worse crept down his spine. "Damn, I hope this case doesn't escalate into something more than the obvious."

Chapter Six

The schoolhouse haunted Charlene—everything that happened last night did. With Larry's help, she'd muddled through some of it. Still, she needed to put eyes on the land to determine what was real or fake.

After careful consideration, she changed her mind about taking her son to Greenwood Manor with her. He'd enjoy running around the open land and seeing the animals. Not that any livestock inhabited the land that she was aware of, but a cat or two roamed the area, maybe even kittens.

An image of a witch flying on a broomstick visualized in her mind. She squeezed her eyes, warding off the apparition. If going to the manor to rid the oddities didn't work, she didn't know what she'd do.

Charlene dressed in a cotton shirt, jeans, and tennis shoes, and headed downstairs. "Mom! Henry!" She set her purse on the hallway table and froze.

The normally active house lay quiet. Her mother had said she'd fix something to eat. *Where are they?* An odd thought ricocheted across her mind: *Andrew's back.*

Adrenaline spiked, raising her senses to high alert. She scanned the area: umbrella stand—without a habitant—a pair of flip-flops, nothing to use as a weapon.

"Charlene, dear." Her mother's voice sang with the clicking of the back door.

Tension whooshed out of Charlene on a puff of air. "I'm here." She headed toward the kitchen as Henry barged through the back door. "Mommy, can I go? Can I? Huh? Huh?"

Charlene took in her mother's casual dress and Henry's shirt and slacks. She knelt in front of him, slid the tendril of sandy-colored hair off his forehead, and took in his excited face. "Where do you want to go, sweetie?"

"To the movies with Grandma's friend. Her grandson will be there." Henry's eyebrows lifted. "He's ten, Mommy!"

Charlene smiled, wishing she could bottle up at least some of his energy, and glanced to her mother.

"We'll go to an early movie and be back before dinner." Doris moved closer and placed her hands on either side of Charlene's face. "You look like you've seen a ghost. Are you okay?"

Henry blinked and tilted his head.

A feeling of failure purged her veins from the 'kick ass' adrenaline that pumped in her blood moments ago. She couldn't let her son see her cowering. "Nope. I haven't seen a ghost. I wanted to ask Henry if he wanted to go to Greenwood Manor today." She focused on him. "You're such a lucky boy. You get to pick what you want to do. Whichever you choose is fine with me."

His nose and mouth twisted as he gave the choices due consideration, but she had a good idea he already had his mind set on going to the movies with a bigger kid.

When he took too long in responding, she answered for him. "You want to go to the movies, don't you?"

He nodded.

"I think that's a wonderful idea. You'll have so much fun." She leaned in close to him, in a conspirator way. "You can make sure your grandma behaves, too. You know how she gets when she's with her friends."

Henry grinned and looked up at Doris. "I do. She giggles a lot," he whispered and directed his attention back to Charlene. "If I need something, I'll use Grandma's phone to call you."

"Sounds like a plan." She squeezed him tight, rose, and kissed her mom on the cheek. "Thanks."

"No problem, me and my hooligan friend will enjoy his company." Doris laughed and guided Henry to the back door. "Pancakes are in the refrigerator."

"Thank you." Charlene followed, locked the door, and watched them skip to her mother's car. *Skipping?* Her mother cracked her up.

Fear that Andrew, or anyone, could possibly break into their home urged her upstairs and to the bedroom. She swung open the closet door and grabbed the baseball bats she'd stashed in the corner.

Until today, considering that an intruder could invade her place had never entered her mind. *Why?* Chills covered her skin. She ran downstairs and put the bats in the empty stand beside the door and said a little prayer she'd never use them.

The movie would take a few hours. If she left now, she'd have enough time to drive to the manor, look around, and return to spend the evening with Henry. She snatched her purse and stepped outside. The warm sun and crisp, fresh air heated her skin and relaxed her muscles.

She stopped dead.

Where's my brain?

Larry drove her home last night. She flopped down on the porch steps of her white brick rambler, grabbed her cell from inside her purse, and searched through the contact lists. On a weekday, in the middle of the afternoon, who'd have it off? A few of the neighbors were school teachers, but today was a work day. Maybe one of them would give her a ride.

Her cell rang. Celine Marx's name flashed on the screen. *Perfect.* "Hi."

"I'm so pissed at Steve right now. What are you doing? Want to have a beer?" Celine was the only member of the BOFs that rambled.

"Sounds like a plan, but first, I have a favor to ask. Could you give me a lift to Greenwood Manor?"

"Okay, but…" The phone went silent before Celine said, "You stayed there last night, didn't you? I should have come out after work. How'd it go, or should I even ask?"

If Celine had called and offered to stay, Charlene wouldn't have spent time with Larry. "No worries. Can you give me a ride?"

"Not a problem. I can rant about Steve on the way. I'm turning onto your road."

Charlene disconnected and stared at her phone, amazed how each member of the Band of Friends would do anything for each other. She'd never had friends like them.

A horn honked. Celine's blonde hair, blue eyes, and sun-kissed skin out-shined the new red Camaro.

Charlene slid into the car. "You were fast."

"I was almost here when I called. Pamela told me you were off today."

Before she fully shut the door, Celine sped off.

"Why are you driving like the car is a bat out of hell?"

"Steve and I broke up."

"I'm sorry," Charlene said, trying not to sound like a broken record.

"He's never here. At a moment's notice, he flies off to who knows where, leaving me behind." The car's signal flashed, and she left the subdivision and turned right onto a four-lane road. The speed increased. Celine whipped in and out of traffic.

Charlene grasped the armrest, her head growing woozier with each jerk. Leaving the house might not have been a good idea. Nope, Celine driving when she was ticked off was the epitome of bad ideas. She twisted her lips, trying to hold back the bile wanting to rise. "You have to slow down or your car's beautiful black leather interior will soon have spots."

Celine slowed down before turning onto a road with two lanes. "Sorry. He pisses me off. I can't think straight. I want to wring his neck."

"I don't understand why you get upset. He's doing his job. It's not like he has a choice when he leaves."

The glare Celine gave smacked Charlene in the face. She rested her head back on the headrest and closed her eyes. "I didn't mean to snap, but you two fight all the time."

"No, we don't."

"Ever since I joined the group, you have." From the corner of her eyes, Charlene spotted tears trembling on the end of Celine's thick lashes. For several miles, Charlene remained quiet, thinking of a way to make up for her curtness. "I know you love each other," she said tenderly, "but not everyone belongs together." Her life with Andrew flashed in her mind. "Fighting is not healthy," she spouted, her tone laced with anger. "How can you date when you argue? I can't...I *won't* stay with another man like my ex. He yelled, manipulated, and didn't trust me to make the right decisions."

"I didn't say I don't trust Steve. He doesn't yell or question my decisions."

Guilt steamrolled over Charlene. She had no right to lecture Celine or make her doubt her relationship. "No, that's my hang up filtering its way into this conversation. Sorry."

A pop sounded and the car swerved.

The surprise sent a shock of adrenaline through Charlene. Her pulse raced and breathing released in gasps. *Had someone shot at them?*

A thud, thud, thud noise resonated in the interior of the car.

"Crap, I have a flat." Celine white-knuckled the steering wheel until the car reached the dirt shoulder and stopped. She put the gearshift in park and looked at Charlene. "Hey, it's okay. I blew a tire."

Charlene unclenched her fists. "Sounded like a gun."

"More like a cherry bomb, but—" The skin between Celine's eyes wrinkled. "Blown tires can create the same sound…sometimes."

Celine's attempt to reassure Charlene failed. Her mind whirled with someone trying to harm them. "What if…"

"No one shot at us. Why would they?"

Good question, which made her wonder. Had her jumpiness since the kidnapping been her imagination after all, or was there a reason for it? She thought back on the last several months. Being taken against a person's wishes would make anyone jumpy. Still, the gut feeling that a deeper reason was behind it caused her to have unsettled nerves. What the reason was, she couldn't quite put her finger on.

"I need to check the tire." Charlene shoved the door open.

"I don't have a spare."

Charlene's eyebrow shot up.. "You don't have a spare?"

"Didn't buy one. I figured, I'd be close to town and could call the auto service if I needed."

"For the love of…" Charlene climbed out of the car, looked at the flat rear tire, and shook her head. A minute later, she sagged against the seat. "Do you have a jack?"

"Um, I don't think so."

Charlene swallowed the lecture she wanted to give Celine. "We need to call someone."

Celine stared ahead. "I don't want to call Steve. Do you have someone we could call this time of day?"

The question didn't require any thought. She yanked her phone out of her purse and called Larry.

"Hi, Charlene," he answered. His hot voice soothed her like a gentle breeze. She pressed the receiver closer to her ear, wanting him near, and caught Celine watching.

"Hi, Larry. Celine and I had a flat tire. She doesn't have a spare."

"Where are you?"

What she'd say next wouldn't go over well. "Heading to Greenwood Manor."

The silence that followed rang loud with his anger. He cleared his throat. "You went? You ignored my advice?"

His tone along with the unspoken order from this morning got under her skin.

Larry didn't yell. Still, memories rushed back: Andrew making demands, ordering and manipulating her to do what he wanted. Larry's tone made her feel like a heel, as if she'd stepped over the proverbial line…the same manner Andrew had forced upon her.

"Charlene?" Larry said, snapping her out of her deluge of thoughts.

And she'd believed he was different. "Sorry to bother you." She moved the phone away from her ear, waiting for a horn or some odd creature to appear and stop her from making a huge mistake. Nothing happened. She hit the disconnect button. "Men."

"They're scum." Celine pushed her bottom lip into a pout. "I love them, but they are."

Disappointment and a healthy dose of shame flowed through Charlene.

"I don't know what's between you and Larry. From where I sit, the driver's seat by the way, you called him quickly, too quickly for just acquaintances."

Charlene needed to think of something fast before Celine took what was not going on between her and Larry too far. "Noth—"

Celine held up her hand, stopping her. "Let me finish. Larry didn't respond the way you wanted, so you hang up on him? And you question me and Steve arguing? What's up with that? What's good for you isn't good for me?"

With no words to explain her behavior, Charlene shifted her gaze from the empty road and gazed at her friend. Feeling ashamed and mixed up, she slowly lifted a shoulder.

Celine studied her a few moments, her expression shifting from frustrated, to concerned. "Don't worry. I still love you." She pushed the blue-tooth button on the steering wheel, and said, "Steve Anderson."

A ringing sound filled the air. "Anderson." Steve's commanding voice thundered over the speakers.

"Steve, I have a flat."

"You never bought a spare, did you?" he asked, his voice tight.

"No."

"Where are you?"

While Celine gave him their location, Charlene stared out the window at the cows grazing in a nearby pasture and thought about her flippant behavior toward

Larry. With him, she stayed in emotional turmoil: Wanting a relationship when she didn't trust anyone with her heart proved difficult to handle and made her lash out.

"Thanks." Celine hung up and squeezed Charlene's hand resting on her knee. "You okay?"

"Yeah."

"Steve's on his way."

"I thought you two were broken up."

Celine forced a laugh. "Well, we have our moments. He doesn't like for anyone to be stranded. If a BOF member broke down, he'd come running. That is, if he was in the area."

"I shouldn't have yelled at Larry."

"You won't get an argument from me."

Charlene gave a half smile. "What do you know about him?"

"Not much. He's a decent guy, cute actually if you like redheads, and loyal to Jake and Steve. That's about it."

"Auburn."

"Huh?"

The memory of Larry's hair, disheveled, and gorgeously hanging over his forehead, crossed in Charlene's mind. "His hair is auburn."

Celine slanted her head. "Back to my question…why is he getting to you? You two have a thing?"

"Not a thing…more like a moment."

"Obviously, you won't share, so I'll change the subject. Is Paul coming to Cocktail Hour?"

Celine knew more about the group's comings and goings than she did. "I haven't heard."

"It's funny how we never know where Paul is. Now, he's a man that'd be hard to date…at least with

Steve, I have half a clue when to expect him in town. Paul leaves at the last minute for parts unknown, to compete in some sort of race that he just found out about. I think there's more to his story."

Not knowing him well, Charlene had similar thoughts. The few months since she joined the group, Paul had been the one who wasn't around much, not Steve.

"Makes me wonder, is all," Celine said as a black SUV stopped behind them. "The Cavalry has arrived."

Charlene eyed the driver's door opening in the rearview. Larry filled the mirror. "I didn't think he'd come."

Steve closed the passenger door.

"Hmm…I wonder how they got here so fast." Celine raised a brow, watching the men.

"Do they have a tracker on your car?" Charlene teased.

"On our phones, I'm sure."

"What?"

"They mean well."

Celine's soothing tone and comforting hand on Charlene's arm didn't stop her irritation from gaining momentum. Charlene shoved open the door and came nose to nose with Larry. Her hands landed on his chest.

The specks of gold shining in his honey eyes tugged an awareness low in her stomach and convinced her nipples to stand at attention. It was all she could do not to lean forward, like he'd done to her this morning, and kiss him.

Her pestering negative side raised its ugly head, insisting she not allow Larry to have influence over her. She moved her fingers to shift away, but the side of her that wanted to be loved and to believe in Larry's trustworthiness fought back. She fisted his shirt and relished in the contour of his chest.

"There's a nail hole," Steve said from somewhere in the distance.

Neither Larry nor Charlene responded.

Larry covered her hand. His deep soul-searching scrutiny cut right through her, the kind where a decision was made if you want the person or not. The gaze stole her breath.

For a beat of time, he let her see deep inside him. A place she believed no one was allowed, a place of doubts and fears.

He blinked.

The moment disappeared, replaced by a confident, mysterious front that wouldn't allow anyone in.

He released her and walked to the rear of Celine's car.

What had he seen when he looked into her eyes? What decision had he made? Did he want her?

Did he decide he didn't want her?

The pings shooting through her from him walking away stung, tightening her chest, then grew stronger, seeking to grab hold of her essence and let loose her tears. A part of her she refused to let anyone touch.

With the car held up by a jack, Steve removed lug nuts. Larry knelt beside him. The jeans strained, cupping his muscular thighs and butt. She had to look away, and moved to the boarded fence to watch the cows grazing in the pasture.

By Larry silently making demands, all the vices her ex possessed crashed with a sensation of doom, her weakness. A place she promised she wouldn't go again.

She wanted to yell at Larry for telling her what to do, for tracking her by phone—if indeed he had. A piece of her felt violated while a small portion, a minute part, had to admit to liking the attention.

"I don't know what you expect from me."

She flinched. Larry's low masculine voice surprised her.

The sound of a motor neared. Celine and Steve climbed into a truck, with 'McDowell Brothers' stenciled on the side, and drove away. She shifted her gaze to Celine's car, still propped up on one side.

"They're heading to a garage to patch the tire," Larry said.

She nodded and locked gazes with Larry. "I don't expect anything."

He stepped closer. Incredible heat rushed to her stomach. "Yes, you do."

The innuendo of his comment mixed with the sensual overtures of his voice flooded her face. She dug deep to dismiss the erotic feeling. "Not only do you tell me what to do, you also know what I think." The belligerent words flew out before she thought twice. She meant to confront him, but not in a harsh tone.

Hurt tore across his face before his grim features lessened and his expression went deadpan.

"I didn't mean what I said."

He remained silent, his face neutral.

Once again, she wondered if this was his way of saying he made a choice. He had given her a second chance by saying she knew what she wanted, and yet again, she blew it. Reading his mind was impossible. Understanding hers was worse. She didn't know what she should or shouldn't do.

Charlene stared at his incredibly attractive face, wanting him to say something, anything so she might have an inkling of how to field his reaction.

"When they return, I'll give you a ride home," he finally said.

Holding onto the board like a lifeline, she stared after him walking toward Celine's car. The cold, flat tone of his voice reminded her once again of Andrew. Wanting a reaction out of him, she hissed, "More manipulation."

His body went rigid.

Moving on from stupidity and fear, she latched onto anger, and shoved off the fence. Time to get this over: the quicker the fantasy was put to rest, the faster she moved on with her life.

Her irritation picked up velocity. Love was a freaking waste of time. People got hurt too easily. She swallowed, preparing for his onslaught of words, expecting him to handle their argument the way Andrew did. By the time Andrew would finish his rant, he'd have stirred up her feelings of incompetence, doubts, and guilt. This time, she'd be stronger. She dug her heels into the ground, determined not to show a sign of weakness and to keep her wayward body parts in check.

Larry turned. His eyes narrowed as he approached. She assumed he'd stop a few feet away to yell, but his imposing body came closer. The passion reflected in his eyes surprised her and shocked her, convincing her feet to move backwards until she hit the fence.

Again, she'd lost control.

She had to restrain herself. Setting her hands on her hips, she jutted her chin upward in a way that dared him to come closer.

It didn't work.

He eliminated the distance between them and grasped the fence on either side, caging her in. The heat of his body seeped through her thin cotton shirt. Her resolve weakened.

"Andrew…manipulation…You used words to hurt me?" The annoyance in his voice was measured. "Why? What have I done to you? I'd think you would be grateful for someone staying with you while the narcotic in your blood stream weakened, rather than tossing allegations like stones."

She stared, dumbfounded, but his voice didn't rise. He didn't throw words to get even, just said what mattered.

He hesitated and angled his head. She wasn't sure what he would do next.

"Do you think for one second accusations would stop me from doing what I know is right?"

She imagined he waited for an answer. Andrew never did. He yelled, did what he wanted, and never asked her opinion about his actions.

"I don't know what's going through your head right now," Larry said, his voice stern, yet quiet, "but I deserve an answer if we have any chance to remain friends."

She'd put this argument into motion, so why did it hurt when he pulled the 'friend, not lovers' card? "What are you saying?" Her voice broke more than she liked, exposing how much he got to her.

"Simple. You think so little of me you compared me to your ex-husband. Saying I'm manipulative…" He rammed a hand through his hair and looked away, the movement stretching and flexing his muscles under the camel-colored shirt. His scowl locked on hers. "Your impression of me is the opposite of what mine is of you."

A car passed. She blinked and remained quiet.

His gaze slipped to her mouth.

She wanted to be mad, tried to stay irritated to break off the thread of a relationship they had left, but was so enamored, her mind ceased to work. Any corrupt emotions vanished and more of her resolve chipped away. "I know."

His eyes bore into hers, and an expression she couldn't identify skimmed his features. "Careful what you say." Heated breath brushed across her face. Shifting closer, his chest brushed her breasts, causing her nipples to do the happy dance. "Say only what you mean." The authoritative tone lowered to a conspiratorial whisper. "Or say nothing."

Again, he told her what to do, but the yearning in his eyes stole her strength to call him on it.

His scrumptious lips gave her no choice except to nod.

"I protect, Charlene. It's what I do. I damn well will protect you." His mouth came down over hers. His taste, the gentleness of his mouth…the swooning she experienced earlier replayed. A moan broke the connection a moment before his gaze flicked to hers. An odd, yet exhilarating spark passed between them, leaving her with a sense of emptiness if she didn't kiss him again.

He lowered his head, giving her the king of all kisses. Her legs turned to mush. Larry slid his hands around her back until they settled on her rear. Hard muscles and other interesting features she wanted to become intimate with skimmed her legs.

The sound of a motor defused the moment, splitting them apart. A black Chevelle parked behind the car.

"Understand?" He cocked an eyebrow.

No way was he using his slick moves to convince her to listen. Ready to tell him what she thought, she jabbed her hands on her hips.

Grinning, he kissed the tip of her nose and slid his fingers down her neck, lower, toward the swells of her breasts. "I want to finish what we kicked off," he whispered, moving his hands to her waist, and nibbled on her ear lobe.

A knot formed in her throat. "Kicked off?"

"Larry, we've got to go." Jake's voice interrupted. "Charlene, drive my car. I'll get it later." Jake tossed her the key to his car. She snatched the ring out of the air a second before it hit her.

"Quick hands," Larry ribbed.

She smiled and looked at Jake. "You sure? It's your baby."

"My *baby* works at The Memory Café." Jake winked.

Larry placed a finger on her cheek and nudged her until she locked gazes with him. "Okay if I come by later?"

The promise of what was yet to come lingered. Her insides boogied. "Okay."

Chapter Seven

Larry disconnected the call from the FBI office manager, Missy, and set his phone in the console. His grip tightened on the wheel. "Another anonymous tip."

"What's it this time?" Jake asked from the Suburban's passenger seat.

"Illegal plants at Greenwood Manor," Larry said, his brain wanting to stay fixed on Charlene and not the case. Her confusion, hurt, and then her desire detained his attention. Watching her expressions change so vividly spoke volumes for her mental state. *Damaged*, like him. He wanted to pull her into his arms, shield her from the bad in the world, and comfort her to make her troubles disappear, the thoughts tempted and daunted.

"Wonder if the tipster is calling out of revenge." Jake's voice pulled him from profound thought. "Or perhaps they want to take over the operation, or something else more sinister."

"The *something else* has me concerned," Larry said.

A half mile from Greenwood Manor, Larry pulled into a country store parking lot next to a McDowell Brothers' Construction truck. Mark McDowell sat behind the wheel, Steve next to him.

Larry rolled down his window and propped his arm on the door. "Hi, Mark."

"How's it going?" Jake called out to his longtime friend.

Mark pushed up his Panama hat with a finger. "Hey, guys! You ready to go on a fishing trip?"

Larry pressed his lips together. With the workload sitting on his desk, and now with the manor situation, he doubted he could take time off. Truth be told, he didn't want to leave Charlene. A few days' fishing trip, with little to no cell service, wouldn't work. His gut demanded for him to stay close. "Not anytime soon, I can't."

Jake leaned forward and turned down the chattering police radio. "Ditto, Panama Jack."

"Told ya they wouldn't take off," Steve said and slid out of the construction truck. "Thanks for the ride."

"You bet, buddy." Mark focused back on Larry and Jake. "You guys are sticks in the mud."

"Not everyone can take time off whenever they want."

"Jake, did you forget you're the boss?"

Jake chuckled, halfheartedly. "The detective agency is trying to find its feet. If one of these guys," he nodded toward Steve and Larry, "would join, then I can take off."

"Well, hell, that won't work," Mark said, looking in his rearview mirror. "We're all supposed to go. Paul, too."

Larry looked behind Mark's truck. A woman with brown shoulder-length hair approached.

"Gotta go. You guys call me when you get a life." Mark saluted and drove off before the woman reached him.

"Another woman bites the dust." Jake laughed. "One day, he'll stop running."

Steve smiled at the woman and climbed into the backseat of the Suburban behind Larry. "I have the key for the lock on the side gate. Take the next right."

Larry put the Suburban in gear. "Did you get the tire patched?"

"Yes. Mark helped," Steve said. "Celine's employee at Fredericksburg Tourist called in sick. She had to go in."

Jake snapped his fingers. "What's the employee's name?"

"Hell, if I know," Steve muttered.

"He's always hitting on her," Larry chimed in, trying to rile Steve.

"Didn't they go out once?" Jake asked.

"Shut up." Steve bristled. "You don't know what you're talking about."

"Or do we?" Larry laughed and turned off the road to a dirt path leading to an entrance.

With Steve as gatekeeper and Larry and Jake watching the area for anything that might stand out as strange, they passed through the entrance quickly.

Steve slipped back into his seat. "Park behind the rows of trees."

Larry drove through straw grass, followed a path made by a vehicle, and parked the Suburban behind the trees. In front of him, woodland stretched out separated by patches of grass. Off to the right, woods; to the left, an open pasture.

Larry opened the door and slid out. Smell of grass, manure, and mud assaulted his senses. Knee-high grass brushed his legs and crunched under his steel-toe boots. "Have you guys been back here before?"

"Not this far back," Steve said.

"Nope." Jake unclipped his magazine, looked at the bullets, and clicked it back in place. "Heard coyotes run wild. Keep your eyes peeled."

"What's up with you?" Steve moved a branch out of his way. "Why would you have to check to see if you had bullets in your gun? Where'd you think they went?"

"Never know," Jake slipped his gun in the back waistband of his jeans.

"Say it's not so." Steve paused. "Is Pamela not letting you load it before you leave the house?"

Jake chuckled. "Don't be ridiculous."

"Your routine's broken," Larry said. "Messes with a guy."

"It is, but not because she won't let me load it."

"Ah, she's letting you load something else, distracting you." Steve chuckled and shifted before Jake's fist connected with his shoulder.

"The tip insisted a trailer held illegal drugs. It's supposedly located in the wooded area close to the main road." Larry pointed to the grove of trees fenced off from the open pasture. "Let's check it out first."

"Damn, that's a hike." Jake unlatched an aluminum gate. They followed.

Larry took in the cows scattered across the field. "Where'd the livestock come from? They weren't here last night?"

"Don't know," Jake said. "Paul mentioned the land wasn't ready for livestock. He's anxious to get his horses over here. There's more riding area here than on the farm where he boards them."

"Paul still rides?" Steve asked. "When does he have the time?"

Jake shook his head. "Beats me."

The bright sun had Larry slipping on his sunglasses. "I hope a bull isn't nearby." Jake and Steve had been around farm animals, but not him. He wasn't sure what to expect, but knew they'd charge when scared, hell, for any reason.

"You think the sunglasses will hide you?" Steve teased as a crow cawed overhead.

"Ass-wipe."

Grinning, Steve set his shades on the bridge of his nose. "Watch the herd. If they get aggressive, duck behind a tree. They can't turn well." Steve took the lead, following a narrow path the cattle had made. "Have either of you two talked to Jed Bradley?"

"He's out of town at a funeral. We keep missing each other." Larry thought back to the message Jed left on his cell a few days before. Said he and Mr. Scott, the guy that owned the manor, were okay with whatever he needed to do and left both of their cell numbers. Larry thought it odd at first, but given Paul and Jed's friendship, he understood. "I left him a voicemail that we're checking on the lights and a suspicious tip," Larry said. "Did the same with the owner, Orville Scott."

"Son of a bitch." Steve hopped around on one foot then slid his boot through tall grass. "You'd think the cows would crap where they don't walk."

"They're not the smartest animals. Then again, they don't care if they walk in manure." Jake laughed.

Larry chuckled. "At least I know not to step in cow shit."

Steve glared. They laughed harder.

"Glad I entertained."

"I appreciate it." Larry smirked and moved toward the trees, which put them in the open.

"As many times as I've visited this place with Paul, it amazes me the stuff I still haven't seen," Steve said, nodding toward a large sawdust pile with bones poking out.

"A cattle cemetery," Jake said. "What's the story with Jed? I've met the man a few times and Paul's good friends with him, yet he's a conundrum. He's supposed to oversee this manor, yet he hires someone else to look after it. What's up with that?"

Larry had asked the same questions when Paul called about the lights. "I can answer some of it. Jed Bradley runs another farm."

"Yeah, the place where Paul keeps his horses," Jake interrupted.

"That's right. The owner of Greenwood Manor and Jed Bradley knew one another as kids. When Scott decided he wanted the manor to be operational again, he hired Bradley as the overseer with the condition that Bradley wouldn't start full time for another six months. Hence, the reason Bradley hired this guy Mathews."

"You received confirmation on Mathews's employment?" Steve asked.

"I did," Larry said.

Nearing the fence row where the trailer was located, Larry removed his sunglasses, hooked them on the front of his shirt and drew his weapon. Jake and Steve lifted their guns.

Fallen leaves and twigs covered the dirt. Through the sparse woodland, a rusty trailer butted a dirt slope, the front tires buried in the soil. Old, metal doors stood propped open by mounds of dirt. Faded signage covered the side.

Gun in one hand, elbow bent, Larry motioned with his other hand to Jake and Steve to advance. He progressed to the right, while Steve, gun at the ready, advanced to the left. Jake covered them.

Stepping closer to the opening, a pungent odor drifted toward him. Larry reached the door and peeked inside. Dirt and plants covered what once was the floor of the trailer.

Steve joined him, shoving his gun in the front waistband of his pants. "Weed."

Jake walked inside and knelt. He nudged the greenery with the barrel of his gun. "Tops are gone."

"Wonder what's getting high," Larry said as clattering echoed on the tin roof.

"There's your answer." Steve tugged out his gun. "Better make sure it's not a decoy."

Larry aimed his gun to toward the ceiling, twisted in a circle, and looked for indentations in the metal, judging the weight of the intruders. There were none.

"Just animals," Jake muttered.

"On three," Larry whispered to Steve across from him, Jake a foot behind. He held up one finger...two...they charged outside and turned.

"Baa-aa..."

They pointed their guns at two goats: one brown and the other black, both with horns.

"I can see the headlines: FBI takes down goat marijuana ring." Steve chuckled, lowering his weapon.

"The uncatchable catch." Larry grinned.

The goat shook its head, mocking them.

"How'd he get up on the roof?" Steve asked, sounding dumbfounded.

"Darn, if I know," Jake said.

"The slope in the back." Larry put the safety on and shoved his gun in his holster.

"More goats magically appeared, too?" Steve reached for a baby, a kid.

"Nah, Paul mentioned Bradley bought goats to clean up the brush," Jake said. "Cute kid."

Steve arched a brow. "I've never seen one up close."

Jake crouched next to him and petted the silky hair. "Baby goats are called kids."

Larry eyed the five goats surrounding them. The largest one's dark eyes fixed on Steve. Long hair grew under its chin, simulating a beard. It was stained yellow against its white and black hair. Horns grew from his head at an angle, giving him a wicked presence.

"Think they ran over when they saw us?" Larry studied the area.

"They had to protect the marijuana investment," Jake said, amused.

"Looks like the young'uns have gotten into the sauce." Steve tilted his head to a medium-sized goat separated from the group. It kicked his heels and pranced.

Larry chuckled. "There's a first."

Steve grasped the kid around the neck and belly and lifted. "Wild plants?"

Larry stroked the kid behind the ear. "Cute."

The brown goat clicked off the roof and down the mound of dirt, baaing.

"The mother's getting pissed. Better drop the goat," Jake warned.

Steve knelt and set the baby on the ground. It ran away, bucking. The rest followed.

"This was a waste of time." Larry shuffled the dirt with the toe of his shoe. "There's black stuff on the ground that looks like raisins."

"More like chocolate-covered raisins, but I wouldn't eat 'em." Steve chuckled. "They're goat droppings."

"Delicious." Jake laughed.

"Come on. Let's find Larry's sparkles," Steve jested.

"The lights came from the hilltop." Larry motioned to the field bordering the road and replaced his sunglasses.

Steve slipped his sunglasses on and asked Jake, "Where're your shades?"

"Left them at home, and don't give me any shit." Jake's voice was tight, leaving no room for discussion.

Eyes peeled, senses on alert, they walked through the field in the direction Larry had seen the lights. They climbed over a stock fence, dividing the fields, and stopped in the shade of a tree line.

"What's with the fence?" Steve asked.

"I don't know." Knowing nothing about cattle, he had heard horses should be careful where they stepped. Maybe the same conditions that could hurt a horse would injure a cow. He nodded toward the bottom of the hill. "Looks like uneven terrain around the creek. I guess the cattle could break a leg."

"What'd they, shoot it, like a horse?" Steve asked with mischief in his voice.

Larry ignored him and faced Jake.

"At twelve o'clock, twenty yards up, a piece of metal." Jake pointed to a reflection with the branches of the maple tree.

A flat piece of metal, nailed to a tree, had creases to divide it into thirds, giving a tri-fold appearance.

Larry scanned the tree line. "Yep. Two trees down is another. I saw three to four different lights sparkling at the same time." He stepped backwards to see the trees on either side. "Do you see the…"

The earth disappeared. He dropped. "F-u-c-k!" His stomach fluttered. Darkness greeted him. Abrasive material hit his thrashing hands. Dirt jabbed under his fingernails. Panic clawed its way into the pit of Larry's stomach.

He was falling…bouncing from side to side, the interior wall taking bits of his skin with each bump.

His body jolted to a stop.

Air escaped his lungs. Pain shot through his back, legs. His heartbeat boomed in his ears.

"Damn," he groaned.

A coarse surface scraped his cheek. Dirt kissed his mouth. He twisted, spit, and looked toward the sky.

Two forms blocked the light. Faint garbled noises drifted toward him.

Larry sucked in a gulp in air filled with mold and mildew. He gagged.

Anxiety threatened to control his thoughts. Another fortified breath, and he slipped into survival mode, steadied his nerves and focused.

"Lar-ry!"

The thumping of his heart lessened. Words became clear. The owner of the voice did not.

"Ye-ah!" His voice was weak. He hoped they heard him respond.

Snakes…rats hid in wet, dark places.

Anxious to see his surroundings, he stuck his hand in his pocket, grabbed the penlight, and pressed the button. A small, yet bright beam lit the confined, clay space. He shifted to test his legs.

A rattle echoed.

He stilled. For a fraction of a second, his brain couldn't decipher the sound.

Another rattle, hollow scales beat against each other.

The originator of the noise sunk in. He tensed.

Wishing twisted hope that he was wrong, he lowered the beam. Ice tendrils of dread snaked down his spine.

A snake's head rose several inches from the dirt floor. A rattlesnake eyed him. Its tongue snapped out and in rapidly, ready to strike.

Oh, shit!

Larry reached for his gun and came up empty. Passing the light over the dirt, he spotted his gun halfway between him and the venomous reptile. Any sudden moves, the snake would strike.

"Larry!"

Jake's voice reached him loud and clear. He didn't answer. Gaining strength and courage was the only thing he could manage. Faced with this poisonous reptile, Larry landed on the outside of his comfort zone. He hated snakes. Give him a thug any day over one of these creatures.

"On the count of three," he said to himself. "One…two…" He snatched the gun.

The snake lunged.

He shot.

Ringing boomed in his ears. Matter splattered in every direction. The snake, less than an inch from his arm, collapsed.

"What the hell? Are you okay?" Steve yelled.

Larry stuck his fingers in his ears to turn the damn noise off and gave up. He ran his hands over his arms and body, waited for the sting to scorch his skin. *No pain, just ringing.* "I'm all right. Snake's not."

"Larry," Steve's low tone warned what his friend said next Larry wouldn't like. "If there's one, there're probably two."

Larry rolled his eyes. *Snake 101.* He wiped his face on his shirt and checked his surroundings: the piece of grass he stepped on, the snake's remains, and lots of dirt. He slid backwards to the wall, a gun in one hand, a flashlight in the other. The other snake lay motionless. He took the butt of his gun and hit it over the head before it could strike. Another shotgun blast would give him permanent hearing loss. "Only one. It's dead."

"You all right, buddy?" Jake asked.

Muscles ached, and he had the beginning of one hell of a headache coming. "I'm good."

"Do you have rope in your truck?" Jake's head loomed above him, blocking the light.

"Yes."

"Throw up the keys," Steve said from the opening. "Or I could break a window."

"Nah." With the wall's support, Larry straightened. "You better catch them on the first go." Larry slipped the light into the waistband of his pants and pulled out the keys. "Coming up."

"Toss them." Steve stretched out his hand.

Muscles strained, but Larry managed to get enough *oomph* into the throw.

Steve, the former baseball player, snatched them out of the air. "Got'em. Be back shortly."

Larry slid down the wall until his butt hit the dirt.

"What do you see?" Jake asked.

Larry shined the light again at the ragged walls. Dirt, his broken sunglasses, and pieces of roots stuck out from the sides. The room looked like it had no purpose, except...oh, shit.

"Son of a bitch!" Jake disappeared from the edge of the hole.

"Except to keep people out." Larry rested his head against the wall. "He fell in a fucking trap. Idiot!"

Jake returned. "Steve almost bit it."

"Whatever the Impalers are involved in, they're going to great lengths to stop people from finding it. Man-made holes...lethal snakes..." He didn't know if Jake heard everything he said, but he was sure his friend thought the same.

"We need a team here," Jake insisted.

"Can't." Larry stretched his achy legs, groaning. "Too many agents botch a case."

"Hell, the Impalers will know we've been here."

"Not if we cover it up..."

Steve dropped to a knee beside the hole, panting. "Are you up for this?"

"Have to be." Larry straightened, holstered his gun and lifted the lump of grass, covered in Astroturf, which had caused his fall. The piece was different, like real grass, but had the thinness of a piece of carpet.

Steve tossed down the rope. It dangled a few feet above his head.

"Can't reach."

"Wait a sec. Steve's tying it around his waist."

The rope lowered. "You better walk up that wall," Steve ordered.

"Yeah, yeah. Done it before." Larry stuck the penlight in his pocket, tucked the grass in his flannel shirt, and tied the rope's end around his waist. He needed another surge of energy to get out.

"Ready?" Jake asked.

He sucked in a deep breath. "As ever."

Thoughts of Charlene and the kiss from this morning sent adrenaline surging through him. He gripped the rope with both hands. Steve and Jake pulled. With men, stout as mules, pulling him, he walked the sides easily. He reached the top, collapsed, and rolled onto his back. "Damn."

"You're one lucky SOB," Steve puffed and sat beside him.

A momentary shocked silence settled between them.

"What held the grass in place?" Larry asked, huffing to regulate his breathing.

Jake flopped down on the ground beside him. "A spider web of sticks in each corner."

"This is more than a small operation," Larry groaned.

Chapter Eight

Jake's car drove like a dream. The motor purred, lulling Charlene into 'daydream-land': dreams of Larry, her thoughts alternating between fantasy and reality.

The confrontation with Larry on the side of the road boggled her brain. Charlene wanted him, yet knew it was best to stay far away. Still, she couldn't avoid him. The instant draw of her attraction to him wouldn't let her.

She parked at the mall and headed to the lingerie store.

Tonight when he visited, perhaps maybe she and he could sort out the newbie relationship issues without having to date for months to learn about each other. The conversation would be a little unorthodox, yet the perfect plan. She'd didn't want to waste time on another asshole.

After a quick intimate purchase, she headed back to Jake's Chevelle.

Excitement from what possibly might happen later put a bounce in her step. She smiled at the words, 'kick-off', Larry had used: so different, yet poetic in its own way. She should talk to him about their relationship first before they resumed the kissing, but—she peeked into her lingerie bag at the black, silk nightie—maybe not.

Arriving home, she parked in the driveway beside her mother's gold Hyundai and grabbed her bag.

She unlocked the door and waited for the usual onslaught of questions and hugs from her son and mother.

Like earlier, they didn't rush to her. This time, the silence raised goosebumps on her arms. The same type she experienced when she first met the treacherous Jameson at her restaurant in Colonial Beach. Back then, by ignoring instinct, she'd put her son's life and hers in danger. Now the same unnerving awareness returned, smacking her between the shoulder blades and putting her on guard.

Gently, so as not to make a sound, she dropped her purchase and purse on the foyer table and snatched her weapon of choice from the umbrella stand. Gripping it the way she had as a teen hitting a homerun, she peeked into the living room.

Empty.

She tiptoed down the hall toward the kitchen.

A voice she'd hoped never to hear again burned her ears. A knot of anger swelled in her chest. She dug deep to steady her nerves and approached the threshold.

Mousey brown hair peeked from beneath a red cap with a darker red brim. An 'I' embroidered on the front with a halo. Dark eyes studied her. Sitting next to Henry, her ex- dipped a cookie she and her son had baked, in a glass of milk, as if he belonged there. Her mother sat at the end of the table, her eyes stern.

Doris sat, stiff-backed. The anxiousness in her gaze spoke volumes to how nervous she was. Henry dipped two cookies at once into the milk, leaned over the plate, and ate without looking at anyone. Liquid dripped down his chin.

Tears stung Charlene's eyes. Henry hated having food on his face. She often thought he was obsessive with neatness. Only reason for him to ignore it, he was scared.

The atrocious, selfish behavior of her ex scorched her insides. He'd left them fighting for their livelihood, ultimately their lives, *and now he thinks he can just show up?*

Never again would he hurt her family.

She raised the bat, ready to knock Andrew across the head. Her son's watery, questioning gaze landed on the bat and chipped at a piece of her soul.

He's Henry's father.

For that reason alone, she lowered her arm. "Came for a little visit, did ya?" The heat of her anger covered her face and body. The pulse in her neck ticked. Her eye twitched. The son of a bitch dared to come into her home with the illusion a visit was okay. She tapped the bat against her palm and waited for what lame brain excuse he had. This time, she wouldn't recoil or cower.

"Honey. Is that any way to act toward the father of your son?"

Henry squirmed and shifted closer to his grandmother, his eyes sad. Her happy little boy, who'd made a hundred percent recovery after the abduction, looked more scared of his father than he had that awful day. What had Andrew said before she'd arrived? "Did you threaten him?"

"Char, come on. I wouldn't dare." Andrew covered Henry's hand with his. "We're having a great time, aren't we, kiddo?"

Henry's gaze didn't waver. He didn't move.

Her mother clasped Henry's waist and pulled him closer.

Charlene knew Andrew's ploy. In one simple move, he conveyed he had controlled what would happen to Henry if she didn't heed. "Answer my question," she said, taking Andrew's focus off her trembling son.

Andrew stood so quickly the chair fell backwards, spilling milk over the brim of the glass and making Doris and Henry flinch, but not her. She stepped a foot away from the side of the table, hit the bat against her hand, and met his glare.

"You won't use that on me," Andrew stormed. "If you try, I'll beat the shit out of you with it." Spit sprinkled her face.

With all the indignant, hateful acts Andrew had committed in the past, he'd never threatened or hit her. The menacing look in his expression said this time was different. She caught her mother's eyes then slid her gaze to the door, trying to tell them to leave without Andrew realizing. If Doris and Henry walked quietly, they could get out the back door before Andrew noticed. "What do you want?" she asked, to lure Andrew's attention away from them.

He stepped around the table and raised his hand as if to touch her face. She tipped her head backwards, out of his reach. With her glare fixed on him, she raised the bat behind her, ready to hit Andrew like a softball. He used his son as a bargaining chip...a pawn. No dad behaves that way. He was fair game.

Doris slipped the keys from the table, grasped Henry's hand, and moved toward the door. It creaked when it opened. Andrew twisted to look.

"What's it gonna be?" she asked before he noticed they'd left. "Want to challenge me?"

Please say yes.

Freeing her body and mind from the pent-up anger with the bat hitting a part of Andrew's body would be criminal and disgusting, yet therapeutic.

He squared his shoulders and faced her. "You were never a challenge. You came easily when we were together."

The 'I'm master of the universe' grin he plastered on his face was disgusting. He thought she'd loved their intimate time together. In the beginning, when she conceived Henry, she had. After that, he changed. She pretended to enjoy their time in hopes to halt his verbal abuse.

She laughed. "You're so gullible. Didn't you ever wonder how I got off so quick? Think about it. It wasn't because I was so enamored of you. I wanted to eradicate your presence as quickly as I could. How better than to fake an orgasm, so you'd follow suit and get the hell off me." His glare turned dark. He was close to the boiling point. She pushed a little more. "I played you. You're not the charismatic lover you thought." She fought with fire and didn't care. Let him bring it on.

"Bullshit. You're not that good of an actress. You're not good at anything."

"By your own admission, I am…I was."

He lifted his head and looked down his nose at her.

She pushed his buttons and expected him to come after her. Instead, he regarded her as if deciphering what she said.

"I'll prove how good we are together."

No!

The etched lines in his face turned soft, a glint of desire passing over his gaze.

One too many times, she laid with him, not wanting to ever again. Her shaky legs moved backwards. She hated that she showed a sign of weakness and reached behind her to touch the counter to steady her nerves.

The curve of his lips repulsed her.

A step closer, and the scent of his aftershave drifted. The manly scent that once excited her now made her nauseated. "Chicken?" he asked, his voice low and seductive.

The iron-clad resolve she developed after he left shot forward. Adrenaline gave her the courage and strength she needed. "Take another step and I'll swing."

"Really? Bet ya won't." He moved.

She swung.

He caught the bat. The expression on his face grew fierce. She raised her knee, ready to knock his package into next week.

He shifted, snatched the bat, and shoved her to the wall. Cold metal pressed against her windpipe. She grasped the bat to push it off her throat. He held firm.

Her heart boomed, tripping in her chest and flooding her eardrums. The air in her lungs swooshed. Her vision blurred.

"Stop," she wheezed.

"Here's the deal," he hissed and eased the pressure off her neck a tad. "I want the money from the award. You give it to me or never see Henry again."

"Money," she puffed. "You threaten your son's welfare over money?"

The pressure returned. She sputtered.

"Don't be a fool, Charlene."

The only option she had was to agree in hopes he'd remove the weight. She nodded.

"That's my girl." He backed up a step and held the bat at his side like a club. "See, kiddo, your mother isn't unreasonable like you thought."

Charlene waited for him to realize Henry and Doris had escaped.

"You don't want to live with a weak parent, do you? You could have a better life with me," Andrew said. "I would protect you. Not let someone take you from my home."

When gang members had abducted her son, they'd also beaten her mother. All this time, Charlene thought Andrew hadn't known the kidnapping details. The monetary award was a detail easy to find out. The case had been publicized in the local newspapers.

Andrew was scum. She'd never realized to what extent until this moment. His son had been in danger, yet he hadn't come to see him…until now, when he wanted their money. What kind of sick person was he?

Andrew peered over his shoulder toward the kitchen table. His jaw went slack along with his grip on the bat.

Bingo!

She snatched it, backed toward the counter, glimpsed at the driveway through the window above the sink. The car was gone.

They're safe.

"You bitch! You'll regret this," Andrew snapped.

The venomous tone, at one time, would have had her withering. But not anymore. "Pig!"

He charged toward her, eyes wild, nostrils flaring.

She swung, faking high and going low. The bat connected with his stomach.

"Fuck," he puffed and clutched his gut. "You'll pay." He straightened and snatched the butcher knife from the block on the counter.

Crap!

The shiny blade glistened above his head.

It was her or him. She dug deep, seizing strength from all the wrongs Andrew had inflicted on her family, fortifying her with the power for what she needed to do. She raised the bat behind her head and went for the homerun...for her...her mother...and most importantly, her son. She struck his arm. Bones cracked. The knife flew out of his hand. He stumbled backwards, holding his wrist, and fell backwards into the wall. She raised it again, aiming for his head.

The bastard's Henry's father, her conscience screamed.

At the last second, she pulled back and clobbered him square in the ribs.

Yelping, he collapsed on the floor. "You bitch!"

She lowered her hand, clasping the handle, ready to swing. "Not another word. Get the hell out of my house!"

"I'll be back!"

She raised the bat. "You asked for it."

"No!" He held up his good hand and sidestepped.

Jerking back, she readied for him to come after her.

He didn't. He hobbled toward the foyer. A second later, the door slammed against the jamb.

Charlene slumped against the counter and sucked in deliberate breaths, slowing her pulse. Her world spun and exhaustion plagued her muscles.

A loud crash sounded. She gripped the edge of the counter and rose to peek out the window. Andrew swung a bat at the hood of Jake's car and left a dent in the fender.

"No…no…no," she chanted, racing out the door.

Andrew jumped into his car in the neighbor's driveway and left, tires squealing. She looked at Jake's prize Chevelle, his baby, and wanted to throw up. The hood and fender, dented. The windshield and grill was cracked. The rearview mirrors hung by wires. She didn't know much about cars, let alone the year of this one, but knew it was a classic. Finding parts to repair the antique car would be a hardship. Seeing the damage would tear Jake up. Hollowness invaded her. Once again, she brought grief to the BOFs.

Sirens sounded in the distance. A moment later, blue lights streamed across the landscape. Her mom had called the police—not the local police, the FBI—namely, Larry.

He hopped out, didn't pay much attention to the damaged car, and rushed toward her. His hands roamed over her head and shoulders. "Are you hurt?"

Physically she wasn't, but inside she was as beaten as the car. "No."

"Ah, babe." He exhaled, slid his arms around her, and held her like a precious gem. She relaxed into him, absorbed his comfort and warmth, and fisted his shirt. The edginess she possessed in Andrew's presence diminished. Tears stung her eyes.

"You're safe," he whispered with the same tenderness in his voice she'd heard when he helped her and Henry after the kidnapping. For a brief moment, Charlene wondered if he used the same voice whenever he consoled victims, but then, he tightened his embrace. His breath releasing on a ragged sound showed he cared...for her.

She flattened her palm against his hard chest, wished she could touch his skin, and settled for searching his eyes. The sweet man gazed back. Unlike earlier, he didn't shield his emotions. They were written all over his face. So much so, she pressed her lips to his and kissed him. Their mouths mated, revealing what they wanted to do in a more intimate setting. The tug in her groin scooted her hips into his. She wanted to climb his body, feel him filling her.

He grasped her arms. "Babe," he said on a puff of air. "Not here, not now. Not when you're on emotional overload."

Charlene pulled her lips inward and recoiled. The sexual fog had her thinking irrationally. He was right, not here, not now, not...just not. Emotional overload had her acting crazy. Embarrassed, she shifted and watched the approaching car. Steve and Jake sprung out of a vehicle.

She stiffened. Larry slid a comforting arm behind her back.

"Charlene." Pamela hurried from a red car parked in front of her house and hugged her.

She appreciated Pamela's support, yet sadness weighed heavily. She stepped back.

Larry went to Jake, who surveyed the damage.

"Son of a bitch!" Jake yelled.

"He's blowing off steam," Pamela said, placing a hand on Charlene's arm. "He's not mad at you,"

"I screw up everything." She gave a defeated sigh and approached Jake, ready to meet the consequences.

His stern gaze stayed on his car, his face a deep red.

"I'm so sor-ry." Charlene's voice broke. Her energy left with the last swing she inflicted on Andrew. If that hadn't done it, Jake's anguished expression would have. He'd done so much to help her, and this was how she repaid him?

The crinkles around the corners of Jake's eyes softened. He hugged her and kissed the top of her head. "There's no reason for you to apologize. I'm glad you're okay."

He locked gazes with Pamela. A silent conversation passed between them before he gave a weak smile. Pamela returned it.

She'd love to know another person so well that thoughts were relayed telepathically...

"Hey." Steve drew her into his chest. "Celine couldn't make it.," No one was available to work at Fredericksburg Tourist. She mentioned, she'd kick everyone out and would close the store early if you wanted her to."

"There's no reason. The word spread like wildfire, huh?" Charlene gave a weak smile.

"Yep. It's what we BOFs do. Larry called Jake for back-up. Jake phoned me and Pamela, and so on. You get the picture. "

Charlene nodded. The family the BOFs gifted her, Henry, and her mother with was irreplaceable. She cherished it and hated anyone or anything that tried to come between them or cause them harm.

Jake crouched, examining the car's broken grill before he lifted the hood. "The radiator is busted!"

"Andrew will pay," she pledged under her breath.

"Be careful," Larry said, stepping beside her. "He's dangerous."

She raised an eyebrow. "Are you telling me what to do again?"

Larry shook his head and ran a hand down his face. When he dropped it, he looked weary. "How can you be sweet one minute and so defensive the next?" He held up his hands. "Never mind, I get it." He pulled her against him and kissed her lips. "You have my number."

She nodded, folded her arms under her chest, and gazed unfocused across the street. The bitch in her came out twofold when it came to Larry, like a defense mechanism. His sweetness and the desire she had for him scared her, causing the worst in her to surface.

Larry started his Suburban. The back and forth emotional stuff between them grew old fast.

Her body wanted him. Her psyche fought it. She had an accepting inner voice and a scared one. The positive one insisted she stop him. The negative, afraid side, demanded she protect herself and let him go, not allowing anyone in to her personal space to witness her feelings.

The scared side won. In the past, her kind disposition had caved too many times. Look where that kind of behavior got her…fighting her ex-husband with a baseball bat.

She slid her gaze to Larry. *Look at me, she willed ,let me know you genuinely care.*

He waved and winked.

Warmth radiated over her body and she smiled.

The tension she experienced seconds ago evaporated. She struggled to find her own balance with life. Life's burdens rained down, threatening to destroy the last bit of strength and willpower she had.

And him…well, she didn't know what was up. As charming as he was, she believed a checkered past motivated his possessiveness and need to tell her what to do. She recalled the discarded lingerie purchase in her foyer and hoped Larry would return later to pursue 'kick off.'

"Mommy…mommy." Henry bumped into her legs.

She spotted her mother's car beside Pamela's as she smiled at Henry. "Hi, sweetie."

"Mommy, where'd Daddy go?"

"I'm not sure."

Her mom approached. When Henry moved off to hug the BOF's members, Doris asked, "Was Andrew arrested?"

"He was gone by the time they arrived."

Doris stretched her arm around Charlene and gazed at the car. "I wonder if Andrew has any idea the wrath he set forth today. Not only did he come after a good friend of these men, but he damaged Jake's car." Doris shook her head. "Andrew will wish they'd arrested him."

Charlene watched Jake, talking to Steve and Pamela. What her mother said was true. Andrew would pay, but not at the hands of her friends. They'd been through enough because of her. She snatched the bat Andrew used to damage the car from the pavement. "I'll handle it."

Doris gasped.

Chapter Nine

Parked in an empty driveway in Charlene's subdivision a block from her house, Mathews punched the dashboard, a bucket of fury slamming into the center of his chest. To the right of the steering wheel, the hard material cracked and fishtailed a line to the glove compartment. "Goddamn it!"

Pain stung his knuckles, matching the throbbing in his left hand, the burn over his bruised ribs, and the ache in his heart. Charlene swinging a metal bat at him had been a setback in his plan for a happy family.

When she struck his wrist, ligaments popped. He knew his bride could play ball. He'd just never thought about how hard she could swing. Her newly acquired aggression was another item to add to his, 'Why I hate the fucking Band of Friends' list.

A black Suburban approached, and Mathews ducked down in the seat before 'big fuzz' saw him. Discovery would ruin his chances to win Charlene.

Surprising her by having milk and cookies with Henry, Mathews assumed she'd remember what they once had before he left. He expected she'd ask him to stay with open arms and a warm bed. The bat in her hand told him differently. Immediately, he devised a new plan to wiggle his way into her life and pushed aside the image of her hot body wrapped around his...for now.

Getting off wasn't his issue, Rona's petite hands did the job perfectly. She'd proven it last night when she showed up at the manor unexpectedly. He'd escorted her to his secret room and banged her until she could no longer stand. Letting Rona into his world, even just a little, was more than he wanted. She'd become a liability. One that he'd use to his advantage, until she no longer had a purpose. Blowing her brains out didn't set well.

Nope, he'd dispose of her with a little more grace than what he had planned for the big fuzz.

A lethal dose of the Columbian herb 'devil's breath' would do the trick. He knew just the place—in the babbling spring below the barn. Rona often cupped a hand in the clear liquid to drink the water whenever she had the chance.

Andrew scooted against the back of the seat until he could see out the windshield.

Charlene walked into the house, carrying Henry, his head resting on her shoulder. An emptiness filled Mathews's chest. He missed his family. Only one more day before big fuzz and his partner would be out of the picture, and he could claim his family again.

The Black Scorpions were due to arrive. The rattlesnake traps he set failed. He'd use the posthole digger to construct the holes for anyone who thought they'd try to take over the operation. The added snakes told the Impalers he was not a man to cross.

Earlier, Mathews had peer through his binoculars at the gaggle of agents walking toward the traps from a window on the second floor of Greenwood Manor. He'd nearly come from the thrill of watching big fuzz disappear into the hole. If only he'd died.

He twisted the key to his worn out Celica. The engine roared to life. Time to work off his excitement. He put the car in gear and headed back to his hideaway to find Rona.

****

A sphere of guilt played havoc with rationale, or what Larry perceived was the right action to take. As much as he wanted to hold Charlene close, feel her heart beating against his, he listened to his internal alarms that said by staying he'd do her more harm than good, and dragged himself away. Staying at a distance was best for both of them. So, why in doing so, did he feel like shit?

Charlene needed her friends. People who could listen to what happened to her this afternoon and not let rage take control. His knuckles whitened on the steering wheel as he turned out of her neighborhood onto a main road.

Her ex taking his anger out on the car told Larry all he needed to know. Andrew was out of control. The simple solution to keep her safe would be for her to stay with him, or vice versa.

He shook his head. She'd never go for it. She'd see his motives as controlling and not him protecting someone he cared for.

Charlene's mood swings compared to that of Jake's after his car was mangled. One second, she acted like she'd melt in his arms. The next, she took the warpath approach by not letting him know how she needed him. Hell, he wasn't any better. With their trust issues, they'd kill each other before revealing their feelings.

When Doris Weber had called, he'd just stepped from the shower to assess his body for bruising and scratches. As soon as Charlene's mother said Andrew Smith was at Charlene's house, blood roared through his veins, steam rolling all common sense. The continued ringing in his ears from shooting his gun in close quarters intensified. He'd dressed and flown out the door to his Suburban, ready to kick ass.

Larry looked at his reflection in the rearview mirror for abrasions. Not a sign.

The adrenaline died down as he made the last turn on the route home. His muscles ached. Soon bruises would darken his skin. Tomorrow, he'd be stiff, but he was alive. The fall could have been worse.

Great lengths had been taken to keep people away from the fenced in area on Greenwood Manor. Digging fifteen-foot holes and putting rattlesnakes in them made it first-degree murder if anyone died. Jake and Steve had walked the fence row, found four more holes, rattlers at the bottom of each. By the size of the reptiles and their alertness, no doubt they were well taken care of. The million-dollar question was: who, and why?

Known for keeping their activities on a small scale, the Impalers had never done anything more elaborate than selling drugs or taking things they didn't have a right to have. They called it borrowing. The police called it robbery. Still, they never set traps with deadly consequences. This thought brought forth the question: what type of activity were the Impalers involved in, or by chance, was the FBI mistaken? Did some other outfit run the show?

Larry's gut twitched. Somehow, some way, Mathews was behind this. The sixth sense that said nothing was as it seemed roared to life.

His cell rang from the cubbyhole beside the police radio.

Kathy Newman.

Sweet ol' Mom. The only time she called was when her husband used her for a punching bag. Larry cleared his throat to try and keep the irritation out of his tone. Why a woman would stay with a man when he beat her was beyond him.

"On my way," he said instead of hello.

She managed to say, "Thank God," before the line went dead.

Rage shot through his veins as he stomped on the gas, made a U-turn, and flew down the highway with the police light flashing and siren blaring.

His muscles tensed as he zigzagged around cars. The number of people who didn't move from the path of an emergency vehicle frustrated him. In minutes, he pulled onto the gravel road where his mother and her present husband lived.

Her second husband was no better than the first. The piece of shit he had for a father beat him and his mother one too many times before Larry retaliated. The mistreatment from the man who was supposed to give him unconditional love still gave him nightmares.

After Larry went through the FBI academy, he assumed his father would back off with the antagonizing catcalls, baiting him. He hadn't. One day, the taunting went too far.

Larry parked, and unloaded his guns from his hip and ankle holsters. He stashed them in the console and locked the doors on his way out. The last time he went to a fistfight with a gun, it ended badly.

The cedar siding house had seen better days, but at least it still held up. The jackass wouldn't put a dime into anything of value. Afraid if he did, too much attention would be directed toward it—and by default, his mother—his stepfather did everything in his power to keep the property just barely this side of the Health Department condemning it. He treated his mom the same, hence hitting her in spots that he could cover up by saying she was just clumsy.

Despite his mother's past pleas, this was the last time he'd only break up the fight, next time he'd arrest his stepfather or worse—he'd end up with the same fate as his father…buried in the ground.

Larry opened the squeaking screen door and shoved the wooden one back. Screaming mixed with his mother crying blasted his ear drums. Red-hot fury tackled his muscles, pumped adrenaline into his veins. He rushed through the kitchen to the living room. The TV lay on the floor, screen shattered. The coffee table was overturned. Soil scattered across the room. A broken potted plant crumbled in the corner as if it had been used for a weapon.

Roger, his uncle turned stepfather, pinned his mother on the floor with a knee in her stomach. His hands wrapped around her neck.

Larry felt like he'd blow his mind and steam would rush out of his ears and nose. "Get off her!"

The asshole applied enough pressure to frighten her, but not cut off her air supply. A sick joke his father and uncle both enjoyed.

"Now!"

Roger twisted and glared. "This. Is. Not. Your. Business." Spittle flew with each syllable. He stood.

Men who beat their wives…children…couldn't be reasoned with. Only one thing they understood…an ass-whooping. He charged the last two steps.

"Think you're gonna do me in like your old man? Better think again."

Larry hit him in the jaw and stomach. The younger and bigger version of his dad grunted but didn't waver.

"Bring your gun this time, pussy?" Roger's hand flew backwards. Larry ducked.

Each time they fought, the dialogue was identical. Roger making petty comments thinking it'd rile him up. It did, but he shoved it back, not letting the man's pathetic words interfere with logic.

Larry tagged Roger's nose, then his gut. The old fart had too much body weight to move fast.

From the corner of his eye, his mother moved. With her, he never knew if he was the good guy or the bad one. Sometimes, she'd come after Larry to stop him from hitting his father, or in this case, his uncle.

When she sat on the couch, he blew out a sigh of relief. He wasn't the bad guy this time.

Bent at the waist, Larry rammed his stepfather in the chest, lifted him off the floor, and forced him backwards until Roger's back collided with the wall, Then slumped onto the floor, moaning.

Larry stepped backwards, flexing and closing his hand. He wanted to knock the living shit out of his uncle, but knew he shouldn't.

Blood covered Roger's face, and he cradled his stomach.

Larry turned to his mother, who stared at her hands in her lap. "Are you pressing charges?"

She shook her head no.

"Then, I am."

"Please no, Benny, *please*," she cried.

How could he not arrest him? By law, he had to. Personally, he wanted to throw him in prison and let the other inmates take care of him. They didn't like people who beat on women, especially women the same age as their mothers.

"Ben-ny, don't." Her crying deepened into sobs. She played the card he couldn't resist. The name she called him when he was a boy.

"This is the last time." He wanted to tell her the next instance, he'd bring an officer who would have no choice but to make an arrest, but if he did she might not call. A chance he wasn't willing to risk.

Family screwed with his judgment. As far as he was concerned, she was his only blood relative. Yet, she caused more grief than all the other agents' families in the department put together.

After a fight, Roger usually behaved for a while. At least, Larry had some sort of consolation and would breathe a little easier without worrying about his mother's safety for the next few months.

"Ben," she sobbed.

He held back and didn't swear at the name she called his father. "It's Benjamin or Larry, but never Ben."

"It's your name."

"Don't call me Ben if you expect me to answer." The man was dead…gone…buried in the ground, and still made his blood boil. He turned to leave, but stopped. The love he had for his mom outweighed the craziness. She was a victim.

Numerous assault cases he'd worked had the same pattern, battered women refusing to leave their spouses. A helpless feeling ate at his gut with each circumstance. With his mom, he felt downright hollow. He remained helpless, not able to do anything to stop the atrocious events in her life, until she decided to help herself. Why women thought they had to tolerate the agony, he didn't know. Shelters, family members, friends, and several different organizations would help abused women. Now, like previously, he offered support. Until she made up her mind, his options were limited unless he wanted to cut ties with her. Something he could never do.

Sitting on the couch, holding his mother's hand, Larry's mind drifted to an event that altered the course of their lives. He shot and killed his old man. When it happened, he didn't experience elation for their troubles ending. Felt no sadness. The act left him numb and would forever scar his soul.

After years of dealing with his father's abusive behavior and not able to convince his mother to leave, Larry left home, signed on with the FBI, and was trained at the highest levels. When he returned, the beatings his father inflicted on his mother still occurred. After trying to make him understand reason to no avail, he gave a warning: hit her again and it'd be the last thing he did.

His dad had nodded and understood Larry would do whatever he needed to do in order to keep his mother safe. When Larry arrived at his parents' house the next time, he ended the life-long battle. In the process, he'd lost the affection and admiration of his mother.

Black, blue, and bleeding from every orifice, Kathy had yelled at Larry, saying she disowned him. A year later, she married her husband's brother. It disgusted Larry, but he supported her despite her disowning him. Here they were again, in the exact same predicament.

He knelt in front of her, covered her hands with his, and took in her black and blue face. A lump formed in his throat. If only he could throw her over his shoulder and take her to his home. "I wish you'd leave." He couldn't stop his voice from cracking.

"I will. Take me to my friend's house. I'll stay with her for a while."

His mother believed being away from Roger for a few hours would solve the situation. "I meant, leave him for good."

She gazed with the same color eyes as his. Lines etched her face, making her years older than she was. "I can't. Where would I go?"

The identical conversation they had on numerous occasions. "Live with me."

"But you have a life of your own. Besides, you're gone all the time. I'd be by myself. I can't…" She shook her head. "I can't be alone, Benny. You know that."

He did. His mother suffered from autophobia. "Have a friend stay or I can hire someone."

A groan from Roger broke off his futile argument. He eyed him across the room, hunched against the wall, to make sure he wasn't moving. He didn't want any sneak attacks or another man would be dead, this time by his hand and not a gun. "What if I hire a nurse or someone to stay with you?"

Before he finished, she shook her head. She truly believed this type of life was her destiny. But no one deserved this treatment.

Unless Larry declared her incompetent, his hands stayed tied. Arresting Roger would only add fuel to the fire and push her further away from him. At least, he had the comfort of knowing his father didn't have any more brothers who could draw her into their sick web. If his mother agreed to leave Roger, he believed he could convince her to stay away from other destructive personalities.

One thing he discerned to be true, Roger, like his father, would only go so far with the beatings. If she wasn't here, they'd lose power. But, damn the beatings. Larry pressed his fingers into his eyes. He couldn't do this anymore.

He cleared his throat, removing the lump before his eyes stung more. Damn, he wanted her free.

Kathy patted his hand. "You go. I'm okay. Roger's hurting too much and needs my attention."

She'd changed her mind about going to her friend's house. Larry dragged a hand down his face, feeling absolutely and utterly worthless. "Mom—"

She held up a hand, cutting him off. "Don't."

He dropped his chin to his chest. Next time, he'd follow through with his previous thoughts and bring Jake with him. His comrade would stay focused and not become as enraged as Larry. He didn't want to kill another father figure. If Roger laid another hand on her, he would. "You know where to find me." He kissed her cheek. "You don't need an invitation to come to my house."

She smiled. "You are a good son. I wish you'd stop hurting people."

He grimaced. "I defend. Huge difference."

"Use your words," she said with a pat on his cheek, bringing him back to when he was a boy and had a fist fight in school.

"Yes, ma'am." Nothing else could be said to get her to understand he wasn't the bad guy. "I love you, Mom."

"I know you do."

Larry left the house with the sense he was stuck in a movie that replayed over and over, the same dialogue, the same fight, the same dismissal. He climbed into the SUV, retrieved his guns and holstered them, and waited in the driveway hoping Roger would come after him, yet praying the ignorant fuck would magically straighten up.

Through the picture window, he watched Roger slump next to Kathy on the couch and lay his head on her shoulder.

"Same shit. Different day."

Larry stuck the gearshift in reverse and stomped on the gas. Tires spun. He flew onto the side road, caught his behavior, and breathed in a deep breath to calm down before he wrecked. Two things he wished: to hear his mother say she loved him, maybe say she was proud of what he accomplished in life despite his odds, and most of all, that she loved herself.

Back on the main road, he glanced at the time. Nine o'clock. The day got away from him. When he and Charlene spoke on the side of the road, he mentioned he'd come by later. After the episode with Jake's car, he wasn't sure she wanted company.

She was another person who had been abused. Maybe that's why he was so drawn to her. A person battered at any age had a hard time coping. No matter how irritated Charlene made him with her mixed signals, he would never lay an angry hand on her.

The drive to Charlene's didn't take long. He hoped she wanted to see him since he parked in front of her house. Tired and sexually frustrated, he slid out of his truck, grabbed the flower he picked from the manor that afternoon, and prayed he knew what the hell he was doing.

Chapter Ten

Resting in Henry's bed, Charlene's back against the headboard, Henry's head in the crook of her arm, she lifted the book from the table beside to start their nightly tradition.

She loved this time of day, Henry snuggling and talking about whatever was on his mind. Tonight, he'd remained quiet. His silence worried her. Afraid Henry would withdraw like he had at the table earlier, she asked, "Sweetheart, do you want to talk about anything?"

He shook his head and twisted his hands in the sheet.

Charlene's heart clenched for her baby. Andrew putting their son in this position, of not knowing what he should say or do, was unfair. The thought sent a new wave of anger through her system. Tomorrow, she'd search for and deal with Andrew. She gazed at the blue wall and then to the ceiling and lassoed in her anger before she tried to talk to Henry again. Hearing her taking crap shots at his dad wouldn't help her baby.

"Sweetie, you can talk about your father. Remember how we used to sit in bed and discuss how Andrew left?" She hated bringing up the past. It was like tearing open another scab, doubling the pain, but her goal was to help him understand that talking about what upset him was okay.

He shifted from staring at his fingers, twisting in his blue and red Spiderman sheet. Big brown eyes looked up at her. He nodded.

"We worked through a lot of hard stuff. We can do it again."

His face softened a fraction.

"Would you like that?"

"Yes," his sweet voice broke. "Mommy, why did Daddy come here today?" He paused.

She wanted to answer him quickly, but knew he tried to gather his thoughts and waited.

"He left me."

Charlene let out a long breath and tried to remember what her mother had said to her in this same situation when she was a little girl and couldn't remember. No explanation for why a parent disappeared could make a child feel better. The unloved and unwanted feeling never left.

Instead of making up excuses for her ex like she had for days after he disappeared, she spoke what she knew. "He wants money."

Right? Wrong? She didn't have a clue, but she was done trying to smooth things over for Andrew where their son was concerned. She wouldn't bash him and wouldn't sugarcoat what Andrew did, either.

"Money?" Henry's bottom lip stuck out. "When he held my hand, it didn't feel right."

She wouldn't say Andrew used him as a tool to get to her.

"Not the way you and Grandma hold my hand. He felt...cold." Henry straightened and faced her, sitting cross-legged on the bed. "Do you think he feels we don't want him? Is that why he left?"

Maternal protectiveness clutched her chest and expanded into out-and-out fury. She wanted to take the baseball bat to Andrew again, but taking care of Henry's tender heart was what mattered most. Once again, she shoved down her fury. Soon, her cup would runneth over, as the saying goes, and she'd explode. "No, sweetie, that's not why. You showed him with every hug and smile you gave him."

Henry's gaze drifted to his wooden dresser on the other side of the room. The last gift Andrew gave him, a stuffed bear, sat in the middle of comic books. "You did, too, Mommy."

She smiled at her son's comforting, reassuring words. He was growing up fast.

His gaze snapped back to hers. "Do you still get scared?"

The question, asked with such a solid tone, surprised her.

"It's okay if you do. You can say so."

She drew Henry into her lap and smiled at him coaxing her into talking. "I think I'm better. Staying at Greenwood Manor helped. I haven't been jumpy since."

When she'd walked into the house earlier that day instinct had told her someone was there. From the earlier conversation she had with her mother, she learned that when Andrew arrived, he wasn't surprised Charlene hadn't been there. Now, knowing Andrew was in the area and obviously watching them supported why she'd been so jumpy.

"Why'd Daddy hit Uncle Jake's car? It was really mean."

"I agree. I don't know why. I guess, he thought the car belonged to me."

Henry glanced up at her and like the man he'd become at his young age, he nodded as if she made perfect sense, and yawned.

"Are you ready for a story?"

"If it's okay with you I'd like to think a while before I go to sleep."

"You never cease to amaze me." She hugged him and kissed his forehead before sliding out of bed. "You're a very, very, good boy. I'm proud of you."

"You have to say that, you're my mommy."

"Nope, there's nothing in the handbook that says I have to."

He rose, pecked her cheek, and climbed under the covers. "I'm proud of you, too."

Tears formed in her eyes as she turned on his bedside lamp. "I love you." She flipped off the ceiling light switch. A glow flitted over Henry's face.

"Love you more," Henry said and closed his eyes. His steady breaths told her he'd already drifted into a slumber. They'd had a long day. Too bad she didn't feel tired.

In hopes to quiet her active mind from Andrew's atrocious behavior, she poured a glass of red wine in the kitchen and went back upstairs. She set her glass on the nightstand and changed into a nighty. . Thoughts of Larry swathed her as the cotton slid over her skin, bringing her girlier parts to life, and wishing Larry had stopped by.

Settling into bed, she lifted the glass and sipped the wine from Lake Anna Winery. The rich, robust taste soothed the tension in her muscles.

She couldn't stop from thinking about the destruction she brought to the Band of Friends' lives, from the kidnapping to Jake's car. She'd do anything for each one of them and hated that indirectly she'd brought grief. A hollow sensation filled her.

Not liking the direction of her wayward musings, she swallowed more wine and snatched the remote from the nightstand, turned on the TV, and flipped through the channels. Reality shows, movies, comedies…nothing sounded appealing.

Everything led back to Larry or the chaos Andrew dumped on her family. She emptied the glass and slid out of bed.. She padded down the hardwood corridor, and peeked in at Henry. He slept soundly, the bear having found its way into his arms. She smiled, eased the door closed, and remembered having to bake new cookies to replace the ones that Andrew had touched after her mother had tossed them into the trashcan.

Her stomach growled. She zipped down the steps to the new batch of cookies they made this evening and rounded the corner toward the kitchen. If the food didn't fill her belly and make her sleepy, she'd pour another glass of wine.

A knock sounded on the front door. A jolt of electricity shot through her veins, freezing her nerve endings a second before her hand hit her chest. Anxiety that Andrew returned induced her to grasp the bat.

"Charlene, open up."

Larry's smooth voice created a craving from within. Her girl parts reacted, boogying and chanting, *'I'm gonna get some.'*

She released her grip, letting the bat fall back into the umbrella holder, and flipped the porch light on and cracked open the door. His hair mussed, eyes heavy-lidded, and his five o'clock shadow teased her girl parts more. "I didn't think you'd come," she said, keeping her voice neutral, and moved back.

He stepped inside. Grim lines contoured the corners of his mouth. His eyes flashed with...worry...concern? "Sorry, I was detained."

She debated on asking what kept him, then figured if he wanted to talk about it, he would. "Um, would you like a drink or something to eat? I'm heading to the kitchen. You're welcome to join me."

Eyes drifting over her, he closed and locked the door. "Where's Henry?"

"Asleep. I tried to, too p, but couldn't."

"Why not, Charlene?" His voice was a seductive caressed and awoken each nerve cell.

She diverted her gaze from his alluring one to the stairs. *Should she ask him to her room?* "Do you want some milk and cookies?"

His chuckled was low and sensual. "That's not what I want."

Every erogenous zone in her body went on alert. "Oh?"

"I'm having a problem."

Not what she expected. From what she knew, which wasn't much, Larry didn't discuss private matters. "What's wrong?"

"You see—" He reached behind him, pulled something out of his back pocket, and presented a rose. It looked suspiciously like the one from the rosebush at the manor, like the one she believed he'd stroked over her body, her mind was still fuzzy about that night

"This flower—" He twirled the stem between his fingers before moving closer.

As much as she wanted to stay grounded, reflexes made her take a step back. Her butt hit the wall.

He followed. With the touch of a feather, Larry slid the flower over her forehead...nose. "—needs attention." The soft petals touched her lips, chin, lowered to caress her neck. "It needs TLC."

Her nipples tightened. Liquid heat tugged low in her belly.

His gaze lowering followed by his low masculine groan reminded her that she hadn't put on her robe.

"You sure Henry's asleep?"

"Yes," she breathed, her body humming.

He tucked the stem into his shirt pocket. His hands flattened against the wall, caging her in. For whatever reason, her defensive armor didn't come out when his body surrounded her. She liked this...feeling his heat…knowing she drove him crazy. "I want you. More than I want my next breath."

She sucked her lips inward. Wanting this man and acting on it were two different things. Her focus needed to stay on motherhood, on removing Andrew from her life, but around Larry, an unnamed awareness ruled. A need so strong it took her away from the usual chaos her life had become and plunged her into the surreal fantasy of vacationing on an exotic island.

"The thing is—I'm in unfamiliar territory." He paused, his face pinching. "I'd like to set ground rules."

His comment stung. Going into a relationship with rules would hinder the chemistry flowing between them, not foster the feelings. She searched his eyes, wanting a glimpse into figuring out his comment. *Nothing.* "You're giving me conditions?"

"I am, just one."

"Which is?"

"No expectations."

A smile curled her lips. She couldn't stop from giggling. Was he referring to their relationship or sex? "No worries." She scooted away from the wall and headed upstairs. If he wanted to follow…fine; if not, she'd deal.

He cleared his throat and asked. "Am I supposed to tag along?"

Half way up the stairs she paused. *Yes, please.* "Suit yourself."

Footfalls approached fast behind her. She raced up the stairs, into her bedroom, and closed the door, laughing.

He caught the door with his foot before it shut and eased inside. His heated gaze found hers.

"Do you still want to give me conditions?"

****

"Conditions? To hell with conditions," Larry said, his out of control organ speaking for him.

Since this morning, he'd wrestled with a boner. As soon as he lassoed his dick's urges, his mind's eye would produce her image and put him in a fix, an uncomfortable one. Taking matters into his hands only worked momentarily. He'd already tried in the shower this afternoon after his plunge into the pit and made the issue worse. Thoughts had escalated of her warm flesh touching him, soothing him from his fall.

Either they'd take the lust shooting through their veins and manage their desires or end up hating each other from denying what they both craved. He wasn't willing to risk the latter and removed his shirt.

Her eyes heated, the intense gaze giving him warmth he hadn't experienced or wanted in a long time. With the thoughts running through his mind, he'd better speak up before he admitted feelings neither of them was ready to hear. "Nothing's changing between us. No attachments. We're friends with benefits."

The intensity in her gaze didn't waver. "Friends." She pulled off her nightshirt.

He unbuttoned his jeans, shoved them down, and kicked them to the side.

The distance between them closed. They were on each other like white on rice. Hands grabbing and groping, mouths demanding and needy. Arms twined and legs twisted. They knotted together into a pretzel until they fell apart on the bed from lack of oxygen.

"Jeez," he breathed, regrouping. He expected when he'd touched her the encounter would feel good, but the fact it was this fantastic stunned him. His blood hummed with pleasure.

Charlene lay on her back, studying him. Her chest rose and fell, beautiful rosy nipples rising ever so slightly with the action. She was perfection, a natural beauty. A woman he could do the unthinkable with by losing himself into her warmth, into her softness, forever. Warning bells sounded: *pursue with caution.*

"Larry." Desire dripped off her words.

A freight train of lust roared into his brain, tossing the alarm aside, and imbedded a feverish arousal low in his belly. He wanted to devour the sight of her, take his time to spoil every inch of her, yet his hunger wouldn't hear of it. More than a year had passed since his body had enjoyed the tight pleasure of a woman. Even then, he wanted them for a fix, not the same as what his body and soul wanted with Charlene. "I need to be in you…now."

She lifted her hips and ground her sex against his arousal. The friction almost caused an instant explosion.

"Strip," she said, mischief written all over her face. Her hair fanned out around her. Her breasts tilted to the sides from her position. Man, she was a sight.

He inched back, kissing her jaw, her throat, and latched onto a nipple, licking, sucking, and tugging on the erected bud.

She moaned, slid her hands into his hair, and gave a gentle tug.

He moved his hand downward, caressing her heated skin, and cupped her core. A thin piece of silk separated their skin. "Jesus." He rested his head on her breasts and enjoyed the excitement spiraling through his body.

She mewed.

Her excited thrill tightened the already tight knot low in his belly, reminding him he'd better move before he embarrassed himself by behaving like an overzealous teen.

He backed up until his feet touched the floor and stood.

There was no turning back after he removed the barrier of clothing between them. Not that he wanted to, but he had a niggling the world as he knew it was about to change.

In one fluid action, he shoved his briefs down and kicked them to the side.

Charlene let out a needful whimper.

He met her gaze, slid his hands up her smooth, silky legs, and grasped the edges of her lacy panties.

With her arms above her head, Charlene's eyes bore into him as he admired what he unveiled.

"Magnificent," he breathed and wished he had more time to explore her crevices and curves with his hands, mouth.

A flush covered her body from her belly to her neck. "Come here." She stretched out her arms to him and wiggled her fingers, motioning him to her.

Skin to skin, he blanketed her with his body, savored the feel of her warmth, and braced his elbows onto the mattress on either side of her. He consumed her mouth, pouring every bit of his desire into the mingling of their lips.

From his neck to below his knees, his body tingled. *Tingled.* Not a word he used, but it described what he experienced best. "You're beautiful," he murmured around the side of a kiss.

"You're gorgeous," she said, moving her head further into the mattress to look at him. Her face glowed.

He chuckled, cupped her face, and kissed her. Warm, soft lips stroked his, stirring up a freight train of lust. The last bit of his sanity waned. He'd go mad if he didn't have more of her.

She tightened her hands behind his neck, holding him close and urging him on. The part of him that craved connection brushed her clit. She bucked. Their hips aligned perfectly. The next act came so naturally, he had no time to think. He thrust into her.

She clutched his butt and whimpered. Moments ticked where neither of them spoke, then she squirmed and lifted her legs higher, giving him better access.

He eased out and pushed in further, penetrating deeper.

"Oh my god, Larry!"

Oh shit!

He covered her mouth with his, absorbing her scream, and hammered his hips into her. Her body tightened around him. Dizziness tossed his consciousness out the window. He thrust, picked up momentum, ready to come when he realized what he'd forgotten. Putting a Herculean grip on his libido, he stopped.

Double shit!

With the strength of an elephant, he pulled out of her delicious body. "I don't have a condom." He shifted to move.

She wrapped her arms around his neck. "Where ya going?"

Spilling his seed on her skin wasn't an option. Running out to his SUV to retrieve a condom from his wallet wouldn't work either. "Ah."

She brandished a condom packet from the nightstand and ripped it open with her teeth.

Holy, shit!

"I hoped you'd come by."

As if she'd done this a million times before, she rolled the protection onto his shaft.

A skim of sweat covered his body.

"Get back in me."

It wasn't a request but an order. One he didn't mind obeying. He pushed inside. She moaned and tightened the wonderful muscles women had to drive men crazy.

Rising onto his knees, he gripped the back of her thighs. He pulled out and surged forward, his tempo hard and fast. The movements of a man so far on the edge with want, he became frantic for her.

"Oh, God! Larry! I'm going to come!"

Another stroke, she released on a scream.

He wanted to quiet her with a kiss so as not to wake up Henry, but when the power of her orgasm freed, it rendered him unable to do anything but concentrate on his own all-consuming release. Her legs tightened around him. He collapsed on top of her and laid his head on her chest, their breaths heavy and winded.

They stayed in that position, her fingers running through his hair, him listening to her slowing heartbeat, for what seemed like hours. The shock of what transpired between them rendered him speechless. Not only the explosion from their bodies connecting, but the one he feared would occurred between them did. Their souls joined.

Perhaps if they'd do it again, the sizzle would fade and he'd be able to reclaim the piece of his heart that slipped around the edge of his barrier.

Her hands dropped to the mattress.

He raised his head, moved a strand of hair off her face. Her eyes were closed, her breathing shallow. Was she asleep or avoiding eye contact? Had what passed between them thrown her off kilter as much as it had him?

They needed to keep the relationship as agreed, friends with benefits. He eased off her, disposed of his used condom in the adjoining bathroom, and picked up the forgotten rose. When he picked the flower from the bush at Greenwood Manor earlier, he planned to seduce her with the memory of what they didn't get to pursue the other night.

The rose wasn't the opening act, but it definitely would have its scene. He flipped off the ceiling light and slid the flower along her cheek, neck, breasts, letting the silky petals caress her supple flesh, the moonlight aiding in his ministrations.

Her eyes opened. "Larry?"

"Any more condoms?"

Her laughter washed over him, settling a blanket of comfort over him.

"You bet."

Chapter Eleven

Charlene stretched and smiled. Larry had slipped away in the wee hours to avoid the accidental chance of Henry seeing him, leaving Charlene's muscles loose as if under anesthesia. Their first connection had been so fast and so explosive, her feelings from deep inside rushed forward. Between wanting to cry, professing she had strong feelings, and the urge to flee she remained quiet with her eyes closed. Then, he'd done the unexpected, turned off the light, and caressed her body with the rose's soft petals. She sighed, reliving the moment.

"Mommy," Henry yelled. Her bedroom door thudded against the wall.

"Hi, sweetie. Ready for school?"

He jumped on the bed and curled beside her. She hugged him close. "There's no school today. It's another teacher work day."

She knew. "Another one? Wow. You're so lucky."

"What do you want to do today?"

"Are you working?"

"Nope. This is my long weekend off. I'm off until Monday."

"You know Aunt Pamela."

A week after the kidnapping, Henry had picked up the habit of calling the members of the BOFs his aunts and uncles. "Yes, I know her." Charlene smiled, wondering where this conversation headed.

"I like her. She gives me cookies like her grandmother used to do for her after school."

The picture became clear. "You want to go to The Memory Café today?"

"Can I? Please, Mom." He pulled out the Mom card, to show how big he was. "You could drop me off there. Grand Ann and Grand Ben are going to be there for lunch. Can I go?"

Pamela's grandparents spoiled Henry rotten with their stories of the past and making him feel special. She wouldn't dream of keeping them apart. "Of course."

"Yes!" Henry's fist pumped the air and he jumped off the bed. "Oh, yeah, Grandma's here."

"Here?"

"Yep. She's here. I let her in while you slept." Henry's stocking feet barreled down the hall.

Charlene's skin crawled. What if Henry opened the door for someone else? "Henry, would you come back here?"

The pounding of his feet against the wooden floor stopped and then she saw an eyeball appear at the edge of the door. "Did I do something wrong?"

Charlene straightened, the covers falling into her lap, and thought about last night. She glanced down at her covered body and sighed. She barely remembered putting on the nightie when Larry left.

"What's wrong?"

"Oh, nothing. I just sat up too fast." She patted the mattress beside her. "No, you haven't done anything wrong. I want you to open the door for Grandma, or any of the other BOFs."

His face twisted. "Does that include Larry?"

Especially him. "Yes."

"Do I start calling him Uncle Larry?"

"Uh, no." She hadn't considered what her relationship with Larry would mean to Henry. "Let's just leave it at Larry."

He nodded.

"But, and this is a big but, don't open the door for anyone else, regardless of how nice you might think they are."

"You mean Daddy. You don't want me to let him in."

"No, sweetheart, I don't."

His face dropped. "Okay. Can I go now?"

Charlene breathed in a gulp of fresh air. She didn't want him to leave, not with him having such a remorseful expression. Making him stay wouldn't do any good either, that much she knew. "You can go."

He kissed her cheek and ran off, probably to her mother and pancakes, she thought as the buttery scent drifted up the stairs.

Charlene rested back and thought about her to-do list. Larry had said he'd drive her to Greenwood Manor later today to pick up her car. That gave her time to use her mother's second car that was parked in Charlene's garage, to drive out to Colonial Beach to visit a friend, the lone connection she still had to Andrew. If Andrew had been watching her and was near, he'd recognize her new car. She wanted the element of surprise on her side, so as not give him a chance to formulate a plan or be able to talk his way out of the list of questions she had.

She threw the covers off her. The remains of the rose scattered across the fitted sheet. The things Larry did with the petals brought back memories from Halloween: the way he caressed her face and neck. Then he introduced new uses for a rose. *Heaven.* Heat, followed by need, bloomed to the juncture of her legs.

She scooped up the wilted petals, and placed them inside a potpourri dish in the center of her dresser. The stem tucked behind a leg to the nightstand. She tossed it into the trashcan and headed for the shower.

"Mommy, Uncle Jake and Aunt Pamela are here," Henry said outside the bathroom door as she finished drying off.

"Be right out," she said, opening the door, and glimpsed the heel of Henry's shoe. A moment later, the front door banged shut.

With the towel snuggling around her, she peeked out her bedroom window.

Jake stared at it, his head shaking back and forth. Pamela rubbed his back.

Battered and beaten, the car looked to have taken part in a demolition derby. Charlene quickly changed into slacks and a blouse, dried her hair, and headed downstairs.

"Would you like some pancakes, dear?" Her mother asked, approaching.

"I didn't know you were coming over this morning. I would have gotten up earlier."

Her mom looked at her with the expression that 'mothers know all' and nodded. "That's why I didn't mention it. I knew you needed to sleep and Henry would have you awake at ungodly hours."

She couldn't hold back her smile from replaying what she'd been doing at the ungodly hours.

A roar of an engine alerted them to the driveway.

"I bet that's the tow truck. I better find Henry." Charlene scooted outside.

Pamela stood off to the side of the driveway, holding Henry's hand. Their eyes glued to the driver hooking the Chevelle to the back of the tow truck.

Charlene joined them, stopping beside her son. He laced his fingers through hers, a flat-line smile dimming his usually cheerful face.

Pamela released Henry's hand and hugged Charlene. "This isn't your fault," Pamela said, stepping back.

"It feels like it, though."

"Hi, Charlene." Jake waved. "Hey, little man, want to help?"

Henry's eyes grew round. "Can I?"

"Go ahead."

He raced off.

Charlene folded her arms over her chest and brought her gaze back to Pamela. "I know that look. Might as well tell me what you think."

"Just remember if I didn't care, I wouldn't say anything."

That much, Charlene knew. Pamela was the most sincere person Charlene ever met.

"Are you planning on chasing after Andrew on your own?"

Damn straight, she was. Telling Pamela her plans for revenge didn't seem right, like it was a conflict of interest considering what her husband did—*does*—for a living.

Pamela touched her arm. "Don't worry about answering. I already know you want to get even with him. I'm asking you... please don't. Think of Henry, think of us. We don't want to lose you. He's a dangerous man."

Puzzled, Charlene narrowed her eyebrows. How'd Pamela know she planned to get revenge? Yesterday, she didn't even tell anybody she'd hit Andrew with the bat. Why would anybody think she'd take the initiative to go after him? Then she remembered her mom gasping after Charlene had said, *I'll handle it.* "Mom said something to you?" Now, she knew the real reason her mother dropped by unannounced. Charlene eyed the front door and found Doris watching from the porch.

Charlene faced Pamela. "I understand and appreciate your concern, but you know as well as I do I need to convince him to leave me and my family alone." She looked away to check on Henry. He rattled away to Jake, but shadows had formed over Jake's face. Clearly, his mind was elsewhere, other than listening to the ramblings of a six-year-old.

"That's why I'm here. I do know you and I care. I saw how you came to life to make sure we got out of the cabin alive. That day changed us. Well, *several* days did it to me."

Charlene nodded. Her friend had been through pure hell.

"We're fighters, but we can't take the law into our own hands. Promise me you'll talk to Jake. He can offer advice. If you need him to investigate, he will."

Jake approached, holding Henry's hand. He kissed Pamela and faced Charlene. "Are you doing okay?"

Charlene knew why Pamela fell hard for Jake Gibson. The man oozed *badass*. Sunglasses covered his beautiful blue eyes; a permanent five o'clock shadow covered his jaw. "I am. Listen—"

"Are you mad at my mom, Uncle Jake?"

Jake knelt in front of Henry. "I'm not. I'm mad at the person who did this."

Henry scuffed the toe of his shoe against the pavement. "That'd be my dad."

Jake nodded. "I know."

"My dad's an asshole."

"Henry," Charlene chastised.

"I'm not a little kid, Mom. I'm almost seven. I can say those words when I really...really mean them."

Charlene sucked in a deep breath. How could she argue with such wisdom?

Jake saved her from responding by tugging on Henry's shirttail. "Are you free to go to lunch today? Aunt Pamela and Marge are making your favorite."

"Spaghetti?"

"Second favorite." Jake chuckled.

A toothless smiled stretched across Henry's face. "Mac and cheese?"

"You got it." Pamela smiled. "Charlene, if it's all right with you, I'd like to take Henry with me when I leave. He can run errands and then pick up Grand Ann and Grand Ben with me."

Henry squinted against the bright sun to look up at her, his sweet face beckoning her. "Can I go?"

She squeezed his hand and smiled. "Yes."

"Henry, breakfast is ready," Doris hollered from the front porch.

Henry rubbed his belly. "I have to eat first. Will you wait?"

"I drove separately from Uncle Jake, so whenever you're ready."

Charlene looked at the two vehicles parked along the street. Pamela's red Toyota and some ugly looking car.

"I'll hurry," Henry said, rushing into the house.

Charlene had no doubt he'd suck his food down way too fast. "Don't rush."

"I'll see you this afternoon, buddy," Jake said.

Henry grinned and jogged up the steps.

"Work waits." Jake kissed Pamela's lips. He pulled Charlene into a hug and kissed her cheek. "This is not your fault." His voice lowered. "I'll see that he pays."

She nodded, yet thought: *Not if I see him first.*

He kissed Pamela again and left.

Pamela studied her. "Please consider what I said."

****

Larry stormed into the ranch-style building that housed Old Towne Detectives. After leaving Charlene's this morning, he'd given up on the idea of sleep and went to the FBI office to search the databases. "I can't find the SOB anywhere," he spouted before realizing Jake's office was empty. "Hell." He spun on his heels and observed the empty reception desk.

"Can I help you?" a dark-haired man with an earring in his left ear whose hair touched his shoulders asked.

The man gave Paul a run in the height department. "Who are you?"

He squared his shoulders and crossed his arms, puffing out his chest.

Must be military.

"You're in my place of business. I'll ask the questions."

"You're in Jake Gibson's agency," Larry challenged back.

"I work here. You don't."

Respecting the guy for watching out for Jake's agency, he gave a slight nod and offered his hand. "Larry Newman."

The man relaxed and grasped his hand. "Pleasure. Jake's told me a lot about you. I'm Quigley."

"Quigley? Your parents have something against you?" Larry chuckled.

"Did yours? Only Larrys I know are simpletons."

Definitely military. "Got a last name?" Larry asked, releasing his hand.

"Collins, Quigley Collins."

Larry had heard of him. Navy Seal, forced into retirement after a bad drop. The man had an outstanding military reputation. "Good to meet you. Where's Jake?"

"Right here." Jake kicked the door shut and carried a box into his office. "What's up?

Larry followed while Quigley walked back down the hall and disappeared inside another office. The space looked like a living room more than a workplace with a couch, recliner, and TV. "I've searched all the databases for recent information on Andrew Smith. It's like the man has vanished." Larry slumped onto the couch. Wrapped so tight with need for Charlene, he hadn't given any more thought to the reason Smith stopped by her home. He hadn't probed her for more information when he should have.

He may not know exactly what happened, but he did know Charlene possessed enough grit to get her mother and son out of the house before Smith showed his wrath.

The gleam in her eyes spoke volumes for the strength she possessed, a look he recognized all too well. He rubbed his jaw and wondered what the hell happened inside that house to make Andrew Smith furious enough to take a bat to a car.

"I need to find him before he makes contact with Charlene again." Larry's gut instinct said if Charlene saw Smith again, the man's life would be in danger. Not something that concerned him, but Charlene did. If she threatened his life, she could pay for her actions behind bars.

"What's his angle?"

Larry thought back on past conversations and the details the FBI had learned about him when Charlene and Pamela were kidnapped. Other than Smith realizing he was a putz for walking out on someone as breathtaking as Charlene, he didn't have a clue. "Don't know."

Jake set the box on the desk and lifted a figurine.

Larry raised a brow.

"It's a wedding present," Jake said defensively. "I gave her one, so she gave me one. Enough said." He placed the sculpture of a couple holding each other in the center of his desk.

"Damn, you're soft."

Jake glared and tossed the box into the corner. "How are you feeling?"

His brain went right to last night. Charlene's touch had given him a temporary moratorium to his turmoil and pain he'd endured every day. Each soothing caress had ratcheted up his desire to the point of no return. Arousal shot through him. He shifted, cleared his mind and took in his friend's worry lines on his face. "Little sore, not bad."

"You're one lucky SOB."

I am. Charlene was a treasure. He narrowed his eyes. No way had Jake known what he did last night. "Why exactly am I a lucky SOB?"

"You weren't bitten by a venomous snake." Jake dropped into the chair behind the desk. "What the hell did you think I was talking about?"

"That."

"Uh-huh. More like Charlene. I've seen the connection between you two. Only stands to reason, you're seeing her."

Larry said nothing.

Jake's stern gaze landed Larry's. "Are you telling Charlene?"

"What?"

"You know what I'm talking about."

Larry groaned. The unspoken subject was clear and didn't need mentioning. When he remained quiet, Jake said, "If you're dating or even contemplating dating her, she deserves to know. Otherwise, she'll never understand you."

Digging into his past, telling his secret, exposing a side of him that Jake alone knew wouldn't benefit anyone. Charlene would have empathy for him and their friends with benefits relationship would become cluttered. He wanted and needed simplicity. "We're not anything." His throat tightened on the lie.

"You're not?" Jake leaned forward, bracing his elbows on the desk. "Well then, you must be sick. Whenever she's around, you turn red, like either you're pissed or in heat."

"If you're noticing that much about me, then Pamela isn't keeping you busy enough," Larry retorted.

"Maybe the relationship I have with Pamela allows me to understand what's ailing you."

"Ailing? Damn."

Jake relaxed against the back of his chair. "I'll drop it."

Before Jake brought it up, the idea had already been planted in Larry's brain. Should he or shouldn't he confide in Charlene?

"Let's talk shop," Jake said, interrupting Larry's musings.

Larry straightened. "Let's have it."

"Once Smith left the area, there's no history." Jake tossed a folder onto the center of his desk. "How in the hell did he vanish from the techno world?"

"Don't know, "Larry said. " The FBI has no information."

Quigley propped his shoulder against the doorjamb. "No record?"

The man had soft feet. Larry didn't hear him approach.

"Sorry for eavesdropping. I blocked out the girly parts." Quigley focused on Jake. "Wonder if he assumed another identity to disappear off the radar."

"Like a Navy Seal." Larry arched a brow. "You guys are ghosts."

"We drop from the sky, dressed, and ready to kick ass," Quigley chuckled.

"By the way, how's the coccyx?" Larry teased.

"You've done your homework on me," Quigley said. "It's fine. Wanna check?"

Larry held up a hand. "I'm good. We have no leads, no address, what about his friends? People he hung out with while he and Charlene were married?" Speaking of Charlene and Andrew's past relationship felt like acid on his tongue. "Maybe someone has been in contact with him."

"I'll do some digging. See what I come up with," Jake said. "If I find anything, I'll follow up."

Larry's gaze snapped to Jake. He knew exactly what Jake was up to. "Man, don't go there. You can't take revenge. The authorities will have no choice but to take your PI license."

Jake's grunt was his only response.

Shit. Another person to worry about.

"Switching cases, I talked to the Director concerning the lights."

"Yeah, I got my phone call early this morning." Larry had just pulled out of Charlene's driveway when the Director called, demanding a full report. He wanted the case solved ASAP. "What's the rush on this case?" Before the Director had given Larry all the details, he received another call and had to disconnect.

"The owner of Greenwood Manor is a childhood friend of his," Jake said. "He's doing it for a favor."

"Again?" The case involving Charlene and Pamela had Hal Kennedy asking for favors because of a war buddy. "He's friends with everyone."

"Small community." Jake's lips pressed into a flat line. "We should do surveillance on the manor, especially in the area of the man-made holes. By the way, I sent Quigley out there yesterday to check for more traps."

Larry twisted to look at Quigley who shifted from one side of the doorjamb to the other. "Find any?"

"Yeah, there's one about every twenty yards, just inside the fence row."

"Sounds like we're dealing with an underground operation."

Jake propped his elbow on the armrest. "That's my guess."

The front door squeaked open.

"Hey, Q," Steve said walking past to Jake's office. "What's the word?"

"Not much on either count. The little we have on Greenwood Manor concerning the lights is in here." Jake handed Steve the folder.

"What's next? Are you setting up surveillance?" Steve asked, thumbing through the few pages.

"I thought you had an assignment in another country?" Jake asked.

Steve lifted a shoulder. "Not at the moment. Looks like I'm homebound for a while. I told the Director to cut me some slack. I need to work out issues with Celine. Still, if the FBI calls, I'm gone."

"Damn, another guy's talking smack," Quigley chuckled, turned toward the sound of the door opening, and whistled. "Gotta go."

"Want to head to the manor this afternoon?" Larry asked Jake.

"Sure."

"Hi, I'm looking for—" a woman's nervous voice drifted in from the outer office, "Jake Gibson."

Larry bolted upright. "Charlene?"

Chapter Twelve

Charlene didn't expect to come face to face with Larry so soon. Still reeling from the surprising, intense feelings that slammed into her last night, she tried to keep them in check to get through the day and to get done what she planned without falling victim to fantasizing about him. Knowing firsthand the incredible feeling of having Larry touch her made the task difficult.

His masculine scent mixed with his clean-shaven face aroused her in such a way she could hardly breathe. But it was his dress pants hugging his butt and thighs, and his button-down shirt stretching across his broad shoulders, that yanked on the knot that resided low in her belly, threatening to make her come just by looking at him. "Hi."

He grasped her arm. The unusual gentle grip contrasted with the hardness of his muscles bunching under his shirt.

"Is everything okay?" His gaze locked on hers, and crinkles of worry appeared on the corners of his eyes.

The sweetness of his voice, his concern, touched her, yet tartness seeped its way into the sensation, making her a little nervous. Dragging Larry into her personal vendetta would cross the non-committal, 'just friends' line.

The only reason she came to Jake's office was to appease her friend. What Pamela had said about losing Charlene would have made sense if her goal was to obliterate Andrew. The mere thought of killing someone ran chills up and down her spine. Despising somebody was on a different playing field than not wanting them to breathe.

Larry lifted her chin with a finger. "Charlene."

"Everything's fine." His intoxicating, charismatic grin that had probably stolen its fair share of hearts nipped at hers. Larry had no clue how incredibly handsome he was.

He kissed the tip of her nose. By tenderness in public, he'd crossed over the non-committal friends' line.

Baffled and not knowing how to respond, she latched onto her purse strap to channel her awkwardness and adjusted the piece of leather on her shoulder. "Pamela convinced me to come by to speak with Jake."

"Charlene, come on back," Jake yelled from his office.

Larry escorted her into the room, stopped at the doorway, and whispered. "Do you want me to stay?" A hopeful expression crossed his face. In such a short time, he stopped schooling his features around her and let his face reveal his feelings, another epiphany she didn't know how to manage.

"If you don't mind, I'd like to speak with Jake alone." And then she did something that felt like her normal day-to-day routine. She kissed his cheek.

With his eyes fixed on hers, he pulled in his bottom lip and nodded. She wondered what Larry thought. The mix signals of kissing him, yet not wanting him to sit in on her and Jake's conversation, had to confuse him.

He placed a hand on the curve of her waist and kissed her lips. Without a word, he walked out of the office and closed the door behind him.

Charlene stared at him, mouth agape. "Is he for real?"

Jake's chuckle caught her attention, making her realize she spoke out loud. "Oops."

"No worries." He crossed to the front of his desk, rested against it, and motioned to the couch. "Have a seat. What can I do for you?"

"Pamela insisted I stop by. She's afraid I'll do something that will put me in trouble with the law. I won't, but I do plan on talking to my ex-husband by myself."

Jake studied her for a long moment. Finally, he said, "Okay. It's your call."

"Really? No lecturing to tell me I'm making a huge mistake?"

He stopped halfway back to his chair. "Why assume I'd give you a lecture?"

Why indeed. She was used to them. Andrew gave her one after the other. "It's what—" she stopped short of saying, "I expect." Enough was enough of her assuming other men would mistreat her based on Andrew's behavior. After all these years, the light bulb turned on. If she wanted to move forward with her life, she had to stop assuming all guys were jerks. "I'm mistaken. You wouldn't have."

Jake winked. "I'm glad we had this talk."

Her heart filled with gratitude for having the BOFs in her life. "Thank you, Jake, but nothing's changed. I have to talk to Andrew alone and I appreciate it if you'd keep that bit of information quiet."

He slumped into his chair, the leather squeaking from the contact, and knocked his knuckles on the desk's surface, his eyebrows narrowing to frustrated slashes. "You want me to keep this from Larry?"

"Yes."

"Ah, Charlene," Jake said on a sigh. "You're asking a lot out of me. Larry and I have been friends when I didn't have anyone else to trust. Asking me not to tell him something is like suggesting I don't tell Pamela."

He paused and rubbed a hand down his face. "You want to keep this from her, too?"

She nodded.

"You're killing me, woman. Flat out killing me. Might as well put a gun to my head. That's what's going to happen, you know, if either of them suspects I know something concerning you and don't tell."

"Well…it's not yours to tell. It's mine. You're not telling because I asked you not to, not by choice."

"You've never been on the receiving end of Larry or my wife if they think they've been kept out of the loop, have you?"

She'd seen Pamela upset a time or two but couldn't imagine she'd had it in her to be that mad. As far as Larry was concerned, he may be a redhead, but she'd never seen him yell at someone. "No, I guess not."

"Good. Let's keep it that way. Tell them just what you told me. That it's your choice and you don't need them hovering."

"I didn't accuse you of hovering."

"No, but adding that bit in there will get their attention." He stood. "I'll get Larry. We can discuss what happened at your place. It's your choice if you tell him anymore. But know, if he straight up asks me, I will tell him the truth, the same with Pamela. Honesty is always best."

"Do you talk about your other cases?"

Jake released the doorknob. "I'm not investigating a case for you."

"What's your fee?"

He jabbed his hands on his hips. "I can't and won't take money from you."

"Will you take my case?"

"What is that, exactly?"

"Find out any information on Andrew. Where has he been since he left?"

"That's easy. He has no history. It's like he vanished for the last couple of years."

"You've already investigated?"

"Of course, so has Larry."

Men like them, naturally they investigated. So then, how could she convince Jake to stay quiet?

"Can I let Larry in now?" Jake grabbed the doorknob again.

She slipped a five out of the side pocket of her purse and laid it on Jake's desk. "Consider yourself working for me."

His head fell forward. "You play hardball. Will you report to me? Tell me every action you make where Andrew is concerned?"

"Yes."

"Know this, if I think you're in trouble, I will tell Larry."

"Agreed."

Jake opened the door.

Larry leaned against the wall, hands in his pockets, eyeballing them.

"Come on in," Jake said. "Steve, Q, wait a sec."

Larry strolled into the office, plopped down next to Charlene and without any questions grabbed her hand.

She smiled, loving the sense of safety and comfort she felt in his presence. "I want to fill you in on what happened at my house yesterday."

Jake closed the door and returned to his cushioned chair.

"Your mom filled me in on what she witnessed when she called," Larry said. "So after Henry and Doris left, what happened?"

"Andrew demanded money. He knew about the award and wanted me to give it to him." A lump formed in her throat and her eyes stung as she remembered his next words. "He said if I didn't, I'd never see Henry again."

"Do you think he'd follow through with the threat?" Jake's tone was firm.

"I don't. He's talking out of his head, idle threats." She shook her head. "Taking him from me…no way…he wouldn't."

"You're sure?" Larry asked, squeezing her hand.

"I am. Henry would get in his way. Andrew showed me that we weren't worthy of his time." Whatever criminal activity Andrew was caught up in, it was more important than family.

Larry rubbed a circle with his thumb over the back of her hand.

Her nerves went on alert. The soothing action meant either he had bad news to share or the question he was about to ask she wouldn't like.

"Do you know what caused Andrew to hit the Chevelle?"

She thought back to the fight, the bat hitting his ribs and wrist in particular. Acid burned her stomach and rose to her throat for the brutality of her actions. He left her with no alternative and she'd do it again if he backed her into a corner.

"After he threatened Henry—" she paused and fought back the mountain of rage forcing its way to the surface, "—I hit him."

She looked from Jake chuckling to Larry pressing his lips together as if trying to hold back a smirk. The gold specks in his honey-colored eyes sparkled, easing the tension knotting in her shoulders. "What?"

"Now, I'm getting the picture," Jake said. "You got the best of Andrew so he took his frustrations out on my car."

Was that what she'd done? Gotten the *best* of him? "I didn't think of it those terms."

Larry lifted her hands and examined them. "Are your knuckles bruised?"

"Oh, no. I didn't use my hands."

"I'll take a guess, you used a bat?" Jake asked, a grin still stretched across his face.

She nodded.

"I understand why you believe Smith won't come back." Jake looked at Larry and nodded his head toward Charlene. "Slugger here is a force to reckon with."

Larry's all-knowing sigh created prickles on her skin.

"In more ways than one," he said, next to her ear.

"All right, I'm out of here." Jake rose and crossed to the front of the desk. "Don't forget what I said." He kissed Charlene on the cheek and gave Larry a nod. "I'll catch up with you later. Oh yeah, Pamela called. There's a party coming to The Memory Café tonight, so Cocktail Hour has been pushed from four to five."

"Does she need help?" Charlene tugged out her phone and checked for any missed calls. "She hasn't phoned."

"She and Marge have it covered."

A little ping rushed through Charlene that she couldn't help. One of the things she missed most about running a café was the party planning.

When Jake walked out of the room, she stared at the closed door and tried to think of how to tell Larry she needed to leave. If Andrew was at his friend's house in Colonial Beach, the earlier in the day she arrived, the better chance she had of catching him. "I should probably—"

Larry threaded his hands through her hair and tilted her head back and devoured her in a hot, demanding kiss, sending a thrill of excitement straight to her core. On a breathless moan, her lips parted and his tongue slipped inside, stroking and reliving what their bodies did earlier that morning. He tasted of coffee and sex. She wanted more.

"I could do this all day," Larry said around the kiss.

"Me, too." Nose-to-nose, mouth-to-mouth, she opened her eyes and gazed into his. Hope, belonging, and desire stared back at her through cautious eyes.

He pecked her lips, the tip of her nose, and eased back. "Do you have a minute to talk?"

She scraped her teeth over her lower lip. She wanted to give him a whole lot more than a minute.

"There's a detail about my past you should know."

Her mind churned on what possibly turned his features so serious. Had he been married? Did he serve time in jail? "You're leading a double life?" Instinctively, the question spilled from her mouth.

"No." He shifted to sit on the coffee table, his legs straddling her knees, and linked their hands together. "Ah," he sighed. "Not in a million years did I ever consider divulging what I'm about to say with another person." He spoke in a low tone, keeping his gaze on hers.

Warmth spread through her veins, and in unison worry crept in, dampening her surreal moment. She slid her hand from his grasp and stroked a finger down the side of his smooth face. Last night, the euphoria she experienced with him shocked her, leaving her unsure whether she should stop herself from feeling what came naturally. It made her doubt the need for rules she created to protect her heart.

Had he had a similar type of experience, one that had him acting outside the norm by confessing secrets?

She wanted to hear what he had to say, yet by him doing so, the stepping over the line of non-committal friends toward a relationship was becoming a habit. A pattern they needed to beware of.

His impossibly handsome face studied her.

"Your hands are distracting." He moved her hand from his face and kissed the back of it.

She arched a brow and smiled. "I like getting to you."

He chuckled. "You get to me more than you know; that's why I have to say this."

"I'm listening."

He slid her hair off her face and knew he eyed the bruise from where she hit the wall yesterday during the fight with Andrew. "I can't stand violence."

The meaning of his words and the kindness in his gaze weakened her self-imposed rules more. "Odd considering you're in the FBI."

"It's the reason why I'm with the Bureau. I'm defensive when warranted."

"So, you're saying you don't hit, yell, or manipulate to acquire what you want?" Yesterday, she promised herself not to let her relationship with Andrew interfere with her future, but she had a hard time not questioning Larry.

"Charlene, we're a pair."

The slow drawl of his voice and the tenderness in his tone tugged at her heart.

"You're scared to let me in because of how your husband—"

"Ex," she said.

"—treated you. For me, I have difficulty letting someone know me because of how I was raised."

"Raised?"

"My father didn't treat me or my mother well."

What had his father done to make a grown man cautious, especially one who was trained to fight and protect? Horrible thoughts crossed into her mind: had he touched him inappropriately...? She shook her head and stopped her wayward thoughts.

"My father," he swallowed, "was mean. Not just when he had a few drinks. My mom and I were punching bags."

Charlene gasped—a hand flew to her mouth and the other her chest. "Oh, no."

"As a child I didn't have the ability to fight him much. When I became a teen, I fought more, but when I did he retaliated on my mother. Often she told me she didn't want or need my help. When she did, I'd blow off my anger by running the streets of the neighborhood. Clearly, I was in a no-win situation."

Charlene thought back to her situation and how hers wasn't that much different, except she sheltered Henry from Andrew's emotional cruelty. A mother not protecting her child left her feeling sick.

"I joined the FBI and went through training. The first day I visited my parents afterwards, my dad came at me. He wanted to show me who was boss. He as much as said so."

Larry's face turned beet red as if he relived the experience. She wanted to touch him, but knew he needed to finish telling the story without interruption.

"I beat the living shit out of him. I'd hoped what happened taught him a lesson and he'd leave my mom alone." Larry stared at the spot of floor between his legs.

"I cracked his ribs, gave him a swollen eye, and a fat lip. My behavior was not becoming of an FBI agent. I could have lost my job." When his eyes met hers, anger raged behind them. "A few months later, my mom called, crying my father attacked her. I rushed to the house. When I arrived, I learned he hadn't laid a hand on her." Larry shook his head. "She had lied."

What Larry said was unheard of. Why would his mother play such an awful trick on her son? "What?" Her voice quaked. She didn't want to show any emotions, knowing it'd be harder for him, yet couldn't stop them from encroaching in her voice. "Why?"

"Maybe he wanted to see what I'd do. In his sick mind, he probably thought he did me a favor. He enjoyed testing my control, my integrity. No matter what I did, he said I fell short of behaving like a real man."

"A favor?" With her forefinger and thumb, she pinched her lips together. "I'm sorry," she mumbled. "I'll stay like this."

His smile lightened the tension in his expression. "Don't worry about it." Larry removed her hand and held it. "That night, I warned him. I told him in no uncertain terms that the next time he hit her, one of us would end up in the hospital, in jail, or the morgue."

"The next time? You didn't throw his ass in jail then?" She grimaced. "Darn it, I interrupted again." She resumed holding her lips.

Given that he didn't remove her hands this time, the next part of this conversation was probably hard for him to say.

"No one knows what really happened except for Jake. The Director knows only what he needed to know to keep me out of trouble, at his request, not mine."

She lowered her hand and held his.

"My mom phoned. This time, the call came from the house I purchased just after I graduated from the academy. For a brief moment, I thought she'd left him. Her voice was angry and firm, not shaken or scared like the other times. When I arrived, I spotted three cars. My mom's…dad's…and my girlfriend's."

An eerie feeling went through Charlene.

"I came into my home…heard odd noises. Found my mother withering in the corner in a chair in the living room. Her clothes had been torn, face black and blue. The sound grew louder. I pulled my gun from the holster and edged my way toward my bedroom."

Charlene closed her lids against the pain in his eyes and voice. When she opened them, moisture formed in them. "And," she said gently when he made circles on her hand with his thumb.

A muscle ticked in his jaw. He sucked in a deep breath, released it. "And…I found my father banging my willing girlfriend in my bed."

Charlene gasped, froze. She didn't know what to say, how to react. How did someone move past such a betrayal?

"Dad was an evil man." Larry made a scoffing sound. "When he noticed me, he sneered."

At a loss for words, she managed, "I'm so sorry."

"My father nodded toward me and got off. My so-called girlfriend screamed his name. The sick fucks!"

Outraged for what Larry suffered, her eyebrows slashed downward and her mouth fell open. "Oh my god…?"

"I must have been in shock, since I don't remember him putting jeans on, but he had before he lunged at me. I had the sense to holster my gun and fight him, but then the situation grew worse. My supposed girlfriend came after me. My mother went after my father. I grabbed the girl, handcuffed her to the staircase banister in the hall. Hell, I don't even want to say her name."

Charlene knelt on the floor in front of Larry and rested her hands on his knees. "You don't have to."

"When I returned to the family room, my father was clutching my mom's throat. He and his brother have this sick game where they try to make a person submissive by pretending they're choking them. They apply pressure, but not enough to make the person pass out. This time, his grip was tight. I yelled, ordered him to release her. He wouldn't, so I pulled my gun."

Her mouth opened and closed. She couldn't think of anything to console him.

Larry waved his hand. "The end—I shot and killed my dad."

Charlene cupped a cheek and kissed him. "I don't know what to say."

"Nothing can be said to alleviate the burden. It is what it is."

"You're such a strong man." She kissed his eye, then the other one. "I've dealt with crap…I can't imagine what you went through."

"I have battle scars, but I'm okay."

Charlene gave into the nurturing and compassionate emotion that tightened her chest. She wanted to help him like she did when Henry needed someone to understand what he went through. She slid her arms around his neck, pressed her breasts into his chest, and held him.

He squeezed her so tight and for so long, she started to think they'd stay that way for the rest of the day.

The first brush of his lips against the curve of her neck sent an electrifying current throughout her system.

A powerful force within her demanded him closer. She eased back to gain access to his mouth.

Larry kissed her hard…the glide of his tongue, against her lips, demanded her to open. She did. Remorse, sadness, happiness from their pasts, the present, went into the mating of their mouths until the lack of oxygen forced them apart.

"Wow," he said, his intense gaze flicking between her eyes and mouth.

A crushing need to have him, to be a part of him, slammed into her chest, embedding Larry in her soul. She let out a long breath to relieve the tightness threatening to shut off her air supply. "I shouldn't have interrupted you," she said, in an attempt to reduce the passion throwing her heart against her ribcage.

His eyebrows arched, his hands gripping the curves of her waist. "Oh yeah, you should have."

She laughed and kissed him again before scooting backwards onto the couch. "I feel like you have more to say."

"You're perceptive."

"Go figure."

"Unlike what you have with your mother, I don't have much of a relationship with mine," Larry said. "The only times I hear from her is when her new husband is beating her. She holds me accountable for my dad's death, her true love."

When she thought Larry's story couldn't possibly continue in a more tragic way, it had, dumbfounding her. "Your mother's second husband is beating her, too? She blames you?"

"Yeah." He nodded. "Here's where you'll want to run. My mom married my uncle."

Charlene slumped against the leather couch. She thought she'd heard everything. The crap Andrew put her through didn't compare to what he survived. "Your father's brother?" The question was rhetorical, but with the craziness he voiced, she had to hear him say it.

"Yes."

"After dealing with one husband who beat her, how could she marry a man who does the same?"

"It's a vicious cycle."

The front door clicked shut. They remained quiet, watching a squirrel using a nearby tree as his playground.

Charlene replayed what Larry had said: the beatings, the gun, his girlfriend, and his mother's pattern for getting involved with abusive men. A nagging thought hit her then it settled into a full-blown concern. "Are you worrying that your uncle…stepfather, will make a move on me?"

He shook his head, his mouth in a firm line. "No. I'm not."

She didn't want him to feel worse than he already did, but questions flew through her mind. "Did your mom follow your dad…to the house that day?"

Larry leaned an elbow on his knee and rubbed his forehead. "Evidently, my dad had a fling with Chelsea." He groaned. "I didn't mean to say her name. Doesn't matter," he said with another wave of his hand. "Mom overheard their conversation on the phone and followed him. When mom walked into my house, he hit her and forced her to stay in the corner until he finished."

"Gross!" The word came out a yell rather than a comment.

"The whole situation is twisted. See, this is why you need to run for the hills."

She eyed him and saw a genuine, caring man. One that would protect when necessary, not control her like she first suspected. Her battle scarred conscience wanted this, him. "I'm not going anywhere."

As if the sun appeared for the first time in days, relief washed over Larry's features then flicked to seriousness. "So," he said, moving to sit beside her on the couch. "Want to tell me why you didn't come to me?"

Honesty, Jake had told her. She wanted to confide in Larry, yet dealing with Andrew on her terms was necessary for her to attain closure that she desperately needed. If she shared with him, he would no doubt want to help and offer advice. She expected no less from a man of his character. "Pamela insisted I talk to Jake about Andrew."

Larry curled his arm around her and stayed silent.

Every instinct screamed she'd be lost if Larry wasn't in her life. Unknowingly, he gave his support by the integrity he possessed, showing her that decent people did exist. Learning about Larry's past today cemented her first opinion of him. He was honorable and was sincerely compassionate. Given these traits it made what she needed to tell him harder to say. "Larry."

"Uh-oh, I don't like the sound of this."

She forced a smile. "I have some things I need to take care of on my own."

Refusing to meet Larry's eyes, she stared at his chest and clutched his shirt. "I don't know if I can do what you want, not until I resolve issues with Andrew."

"And what is it that I want?"

"Have a relationship," she said.

"Huh? You want to be fuck-buddies?"

While the question was vulgar, it's exactly what she wanted. "To start. Actually, I call it non-committal friends."

"Same thing I said last night, friends with benefits."

He had, but what he shared today put their relationship on a different playing field. "Friends with benefits don't worry about what's going on in the other person's life. If they do, then it becomes a relationship." She waited for the impact of her words to hit, hoping he wouldn't be offended and wouldn't pry for more information about the issue she had with Andrew. Larry was smart: if he hadn't already figured out that in order for her to move on with her life, she'd have to deal with Andrew, he would soon.

His grip tightened. "Makes sense to me. One more thing."

Had her determination dissuaded him?

"Yeah?"

"Know this, I will protect you and at times you will probably think I'm controlling. I'm not. I'm looking out for my interest."

She split her gaze back and forth between his eyes.

Mirror reactions coursed through her brain. Admiration that Larry would do anything for someone he cared for, and anticipation for when others' decisions didn't impact their relationship. "I can live with that. While we're friends with benefits, I promise to be exclusive."

His chuckle turned to an outright laugh. He kissed the top of her head and held her to him. "You phrase what we have any way you want. I'll say okay."

"Wuss."

He laughed again. "Only to you, sweetheart. Only to you."

Chapter Thirteen

Driving her mother's decade old, white interior plush car that rode like she'd imagine a tank might, Charlene turned out of Old Towne Detective Agency and headed toward Colonial Beach to talk to Andrew's best friend. The secret Larry had shared meant a lot. She understood his need to protect her, actually loved the idea. Her mother had called it right: Larry was a keeper.

If he knew where Charlene headed, his face would turn red…sweat would bead on his brow….and his eyes would darken. She sighed. Excitement from picturing him above her in the throes of passion sent a thrill through her blood. Her center clenched.

She'd have to put aside her lustful thoughts of Larry. With any luck, she'd finagle a way for him to come by tonight after Henry went to sleep. Letting her son know she and Larry were seeing each other this soon could give him false hope. She'd rather wait until her feelings reached the point of no return. Though, the strong sensation she experienced but tried to bury deep inside her came close to the dangerous 'love zone'.

Nearing the outskirts of Colonial Beach, her thoughts turned to Andrew. Her anger boiled, remembering what he'd taken away from them. Her beloved Café, and her home. Her prize belongings lost due to his inability to manage money. His insistence on doing the restaurant's books when she wanted to hire an accountant should have flagged something was amiss. Andrew had hated math in school.

Those possessions were near and dear to her heart, but they weren't what cut her to the quick. Andrew's behavior toward their son sliced through her as if a butcher knife had torn her heart to shreds.

The new lengths Andrew used to achieve what he wanted flabbergasted her. To threaten their son... An ache shot through her, stopping her from completing the thought. Any possible sentiment she had toward him dissolved into a puddle when Andrew touched Henry's hand, indicating he had more regard for money than his only child's life. In a million years, she didn't think Andrew could stoop that low.

She had no words...no tears, just blazing fury.

Charlene passed the familiar 'Welcome to Colonial Beach' sign. Nostalgia struck with the sight of her restaurant and placed a heavy weight on the center of her chest.

"The son of a bitch!" She whipped the wheel. Tires squealed and she screeched to a halt in the parking lot in front of the café and shoved the gearshift into park.

Andrew may have ripped her heart out, stolen her foundation, and made her life a living hell...but damn it, she would reclaim it.

She bolted out of the car, ready to speak with the new owner. A sea of churning memories surged into her brain, faltering her steps and throwing a cold bucket of water over her anger.

The decorations around the atrium structure looked the same as when she left. *Impossible*. The wooden chairs and tables she purchased from a retailer in Lancaster, Pennsylvania, stayed fixed in the spot she placed them five years ago. Balloon party lights she received for a wedding present dangled from the canopy. They'd have to go.

Scooting along the cement sidewalk flanking the restaurant, she dragged her fingers over The Café's swaying sign, and took in the picturesque view of the Potomac River. A soft breeze drifted from the water, gently tossing her hair and brushing her cheeks. The river's scents drifted toward her: briny, algae, musty. On their own, they'd reek. Together, they were a memory. She tilted her head up and closed her eyes, letting the sun warm her face as she had done a thousand times before, and enjoyed the moment until seagulls squawking drew her attention and had her opening her eyes.

She looked from the people lounging alongside the Potomac to the people sitting under the awning on the Riverside Deck and glimpsed a piece of yellow. Time stopped. Near the kitchen door, a yellow plastic baby swing suspended from the rafters by four pieces of rope…Henry's toddler swing. The swing hadn't moved from the spot from where she had spent countless hours pushing him. When he outgrew it, she didn't have the heart to take it down.

Why would the new owners keep it? Questions engulfed her. Why did they not change the décor? Why not make the restaurant theirs?

Emotions roiled through her as she marched toward the front, climbed the steps, and pushed open the door. Customers filled the rows of picnic tables, covered in brown paper for all-you-can-eat crabs. Servers, carrying trays, weaved in and out of the chaos. Bartenders split their attention between two counters on either side of them, one facing the water, and the other opened up to the inside of the cafe. *Identical to before.*

"Miss, how many for lunch?"

Charlene turned toward the voice of the woman she helped after her husband died in the war. She'd given her a job and friendship. "Gloria."

"Charlene! How are you?" Her words escaped on a high pitch.

Gloria Heart jumped up and down, her long, blonde ponytail waving behind her, before she crashed into Charlene to give her a hug.

"I'm okay," she managed to say through Gloria's tight grip.

"I've missed you so much."

Funny, if Gloria missed Charlene, why hadn't she called? Once after the kidnapping, she had while Charlene had left messages for her friend a few times, but Gloria never returned her call.

Gloria shifted, her expression changing from happy to a scowl, thanks to slashing eyebrows, and she played with the cloth belt draped around the waist of her black, ankle-length dress.

Bracing for the worse, Charlene folded her arms and stared at Gloria. "What's up?"

"Nothing much. I've been working nonstop. Between Todd and working here, my time is pretty much booked. I'm sorry I haven't called. We should get the kids together for a playdate." Gloria's voice ended on a high note and rounded eyebrows.

Why was Gloria acting strange? "I'm glad life is treating you well. What else has been happening?"

"What do you mean?"

"We worked together too long for me not to pick up on the indicators that you're hiding something."

"Oh." Gloria waved a dismissive hand. "I'm wound tight, trying to get the schedule covered for next week. Nothing more."

"You are?" Charlene's manager, Dean Wilkens, had managed The Café when she owned it. "Is Dean not working here anymore?"

Gloria pressed her lips together. "No. He left when the new owner wouldn't let him be partner." She reached out, looking as if she wanted to touch Charlene's arm, then withdrew her hand. "I'm sorry the bank foreclosed on your café and home."

Charlene didn't want to discuss what happened. She was here to figure out a way to get her business back. "Is the owner here?"

"Yes." Gloria gave a slight nod, but didn't give any further information.

"May I speak with them?"

"What's this in regards to?"

The question shot irritation through her body. Charlene gave her a sideways glare. "Excuse me. This is between me and them."

The door opened and a party of four stepped into the foyer. Charlene moved aside and waited for Gloria to seat them.

"Come on," Gloria said, when she returned and motioned with her hand to follow.

Charlene trailed behind her through the throng of tables, waving and smiling at familiar faces. She didn't slow to chat, though. Another day, she would have. They passed by the bar toward the back of the restaurant. Gloria opened the door to Charlene's old office and waved her arm, signaling for Charlene to step inside.

Again, the furnishings stayed from when she ran the café. She moved toward her old desk. Her planner, sticky notes that she had scribbled, even a cup a customer had brought her the last day she worked sat on the aluminum desk.

Gloria closed the door and raised her hand, palm forward, a silent gesture for Charlene to listen. Tears filled Gloria's eyes. "Here's the thing. I didn't call you, 'cause I didn't know how you'd take what I did."

Charlene's gut tensed. "Which is?"

"I bought the café, hoping you'd say yes to be a partner with me, but when you remained working at The Memory Café in Fredericksburg, I didn't know what to do. I was afraid you'd see me as controlling.."

Shame washed over Charlene. She'd made her friend feel bad and hadn't realized it.

"In essence, I was. I did something without your knowledge, expecting you to jump at the chance to at least own half the restaurant." Gloria blew out a choked breath. "There, I said it. Go ahead and kill me."

Twin reactions raced through Charlene. One, she wasn't happy that her friend made a decision for her. And, two, she was numb from her fingers to her toes from Gloria's generosity. And here she had a blip of a moment where she questioned her friend's motives. "What would you have done if I said no? And when were you planning to contact me?"

"I don't know and I don't know. After I made my decision, I had fundraisers. I've used the money raised to pay for your half of the mortgage. The town's people love you. They hated that you went through such hardship."

"I'll pay them back."

Gloria acted like a jumping bean again and her eyes widened. "That means you'll do it? You'll be my partner?"

Charlene loved this place too much to turn it down. She tucked her hair behind her ear and nodded. "If you stop jumping, yes."

Gloria grounded her feet and stared at Charlene's forehead. "Oh my god, what happened?"

Charlene touched the bruise on her head and decided not to share that Andrew was in the area. If Gloria saw him, she would have mentioned it.

Thinking about her current dilemma, she didn't want anyone to know she had ownership of The Café until she'd sorted out her troubles with her ex. Her ex would manipulate and do whatever was in his power to sell it out from under her and keep the money, not caring who was involved. Gloria didn't need to be sucked into Charlene's troubles.

Until then, the celebrating would have to wait. "Gloria, there are things that I can't share yet. I would appreciate keeping our agreement quiet for now. If anyone asks, please tell them you didn't get a chance to talk to me about it."

A watery-eyed Gloria stared, a questioning expression shooting her eyebrows into her bangs. "He's back."

Panic that Gloria would do something crazy tripped her heart. She coughed to plunge it back in rhythm, but it wasn't enough to stop the sour taste from reaching the back of Charlene's throat. "I don't want to discuss him. Not now. Later. Okay?"

Gloria nodded but her hazel eyes kept questioning.

"Thank you. I'm sneaking out the back door. I'll be in touch."

"I'm glad you're back…almost back." Gloria smiled, reminding Charlene that the BOFs didn't corner the market on good people.

****

"Hey, Missy." Larry stopped beside her desk and picked up his messages. Other than a note from the Director, keeping him up-to-date on the 'need to know case', the rest were junk. "Thanks for covering for me."

"No problem. A Rona Thomas is waiting to speak to you. She's sitting in the chairs outside your office."

Larry glanced over his shoulder to the back wall to a light-skinned female in her early twenties with pink and purple hair. She gripped a red baseball cap in her lap as if it was her lifeline. The toe of her tennis shoe lent leverage for her bouncing leg. She embodied nervous energy.

He turned his attention back to Agent Missy Richards. "Did she give a reason for wanting to speak with me?"

Missy tilted her dark hair toward the girl. "She mentioned that she hoped you'd hurry before anyone notices she's missing. About that time you entered the office, I directed her to the chairs."

He lifted the message in his hand. "Thanks."

"Anytime."

As Larry approached, Rona's eyes grew wide and she sat straighter.

"Hi, Ms. Richards, I'm Special Agent Newman," he stretched out his hand. "How may I help you?"

"Can I talk to you in private?" she said, her voice quaking, and she diverted her gaze to the floor.

"Sure. Come into my office." The minute he turned his back to open the door, Rona took a gulp of air and wiped her hands on her jean-clad legs.

Someone or something had her running scared.

He stepped into the office, breathed in the aroma of his morning coffee, and waved his arm to the chair on the opposite side from his desk. "Have a seat." He balled up and trashed the Director's message, and parked himself in his chair, the faux leather groaning under him.

Rona's gaze flicked over the few organizers he kept on his desk for files, his closed laptop, his empty coffee mug that read, "Work Sucks," a departing gift from Jake, and bare walls. "Man, your office is boring."

Larry braced his elbow on the armrest of his chair and leaned his chin against his hand. A person who'd made the effort to come to him wasn't concerned with his office furnishings. "What can I help you with?"

Her gaze flashed to his, her body vibrated in way that let him know she risked a lot by being here. "I don't want anyone to know I came here." She plopped her cap on her hand and rubbed her hands together between her legs.

Larry got a good look at the hat. An 'I' stitched in the center, the Impalers' insignia. "Got it."

"I have this friend. I think he's in trouble…eh….going to cause trouble."

Larry picked up a pad, clicked his pen, and jotted down Rona Thomas and Impalers. "This friend, he have a name?"

She sliced a hand through the air and gave a quick shake of her head.

Friend, Larry noted.

The Impalers' gang Rona was mixed up with was a small-time outfit that engaged in the run of the mill crimes in the Northern Virginia area. From the information Steve dug up, only a few members had branched out into violent crimes. Given her small stature and soft features she didn't look like she'd participate in anything more than growing weed. "What type of trouble?" he asked when she didn't give a name.

Expression serious, her gaze did a constant tour of his virtually empty desk. "Mouse is threatening people."

"Mouse, is he the friend?"

She nodded, her eyes drifted to his. "He's threatening the guys, saying they'll regret crossing him."

"Does Mouse belong to the Impalers' gang too?"

Her mouth dropped open, shock registering in her features. "You know?"

He pointed the end of the pen at her head. "You're wearing the hat."

"Oh, right."

"I'm not sure what you expect or want from me," Larry said. "Without details, I can't help." His cell vibrated. "Excuse me." He tugged it out of the holder on his belt and looked at the image Jake sent him. A newspaper clip of Charlene and Andrew Smith's wedding party. Larry brought the phone closer. The image was fuzzy. Other than seeing a white dress, dark suits, and a splash of purple, he couldn't make out anyone. He pressed his middle finger and thumb on the screen to spread the image. In the caption, Randy Millstone of Colonial Beach was circled in red.

"Huh?" Why would Jake circle this guy's name?

An address followed.

Impatience and urgency ripped through his gut. Jake and Charlene must have talked about more than what he was informed, for Jake to send him this info. "Ms. Thomas, something has come up and I need to leave." Larry stood.

Bolting upright, she flashed a palm. "Wait, please! If you'd come to Greenwood Manor and talk to Hulk, he could give you more information."

Larry dropped back in his seat. "You have my attention."

"Mouse has confided in him. Every morning Hulk and I check the fences and feed the…" She scraped her teeth over her lower lip then the upper one. "Arrest us for trespassing, bring us in and interrogate us. He'll break."

"You want me to arrest you?"

"Well, I expect you'll release me after you find out the information you need."

Larry eyed her, his senses on high alert. "An Impaler wants to work with the FBI?"

"To stop Mouse from acting stupid. He wants to bring in other gangs."

Larry arched his brows. "What gangs?"

"I don't know, that's why you need to question Hulk. Listen, I got involved with this gang. I was bored with my life, wanted a little excitement, so I dyed my hair, and joined. I don't want anyone hurt." Her words rushed out in a hurry, desperation lacing them. "Please!"

Either she witnessed true hostility and told him the truth or The Impalers had upped their game to target agents. "Where and when?"

"On the corner around nine o'clock. Remember, you don't know me."

Larry penciled it on the notepad. "I'll be there."

****

As Charlene turned onto the familiar side street lined with fishermen's homes, she regretted not seeing Randy Millstone since she'd moved away.

Half way down the street, she slowed in front of the box-shaped house. The turquoise trim identified the house from the rest on the block, Randy's home. She parked the car on the dirt and gravel shoulder.

Randy, bent over with his back to her, weeded a chrysanthemum bed. A white lattice, enclosing the crawl space, acted as a backdrop and made the already rich colors of the red, purple, and yellow blooms more vivid.

Charlene watched him for several minutes, working up the guts to question him, before she turned off the engine.

Gravel crunched under her feet as she made her way to the sidewalk. Seagulls squawked and the light scent of fish floated through the air. She never understood why Randy stayed friends with her ex. The well-mannered, kind man outshined Andrew in every aspect as a human being.

Closer she moved toward him, the more her nerve cells jumped, similar to how Gloria couldn't stop bouncing. A man that she'd known for years, who was best man in her wedding, shouldn't elicit a nervous reaction from her, yet here she was. Guilt had a way of making her uneasy.

Before she reached him, he stood and faced her.

Olive-skinned with crinkles at the corners of his eyes, enhanced by the time he spent in the sun… Graying at the temples of his dark hair, revealed the tough life he led, and added to his fisherman's charm.

He looked good.

"Charlene."

The lilt in his voice eased the tension building between her shoulders and slowed the fluttering in her stomach. "Hi, Randy, it's good to see you."

"You, too." He pulled her into a massive bear hug.

Memories of how well he treated her and Henry surfaced. She shouldn't have stayed away. Andrew may have been a jackass, but not Randy, never.

He released her and stepped back. "What do you need?"

"You were always direct and to the point."

"No other way to be."

She'd take the same tactic. "I'm looking for Andrew."

He folded his arms across his chest, stretching the cotton material over toned muscles. Dirt covered his hands and sleeves. "I figured."

Her skin prickled, not from the water's continuous breeze this time of year, but from his watchful eyes. She diverted her gaze and skimmed the houses and colorful yards bordering his. In the middle of autumn, flowers in this neighborhood flourished. "I don't know how everyone keeps the blossoms looking so beautiful this late in the year."

"Tender loving care." His powerful gaze toured her as if he read her mind. "You're stalling."

"Have you seen him?"

"I have."

She waited for him to be forthcoming. When he didn't, she asked, "Would you elaborate?"

"No."

She rolled her eyes and gazed at the water a few blocks over. Coming here wasn't a good idea. While Randy's loyalty to Andrew puzzled her, she'd respected it and wouldn't push. "Okay, Randy." She turned toward her car and hesitated, debating the wisdom of walking away from the only link to finding him.

When Andrew left her and Henry with no money and a pile of bills, Randy had contributed. Not having much money himself, his actions had said a lot about his character. Coming from a turbulent background, he couldn't stand for people to be mistreated. She twisted to tell him about Andrew's latest stunt and flinched.

He'd moved closer. "Where'd this come from?" He pointed to her face, and something dark flashed over his features. The pulse in his jaw ticked.

The turmoil of reactions that kept her stomach in an uproar lodged in her throat. She blinked back the tears, fighting to emerge, and remained quiet. "You know where."

"Is there any more?" His intense gaze lowered from the bruise to her neck and lower, as if inspecting her for injuries.

A lone tear broke through. She wiped her cheek. "No."

"I'll kill him." His tight monotone reinforced the molten rage flickering behind his dark eyes. His fists clenched into massive lumps at his sides. "Is Henry okay?"

"He is." She shook her head and gulped down the growing swell of emotion. "Andrew wouldn't touch him."

"I didn't think he'd ever hurt you either."

Her gaze locked on his and her breath hitched. He was right. When she and Andrew married, the thought of him harming her emotionally or physically hadn't been a possibility.

"Damn, when he split the way he had, I figured he'd lost it. Him hurting you puts him on the all-time-low, shithead lists." Randy placed his hand on his hips, his face twisting between anger and frustration. "I gave my word not to give his whereabouts. I can't renege. I owe him."

She scraped her teeth over her lower lip. "You've always had a peculiar loyalty to him I've never understood."

"Yeah." Randy pulled her into his arms.

Chapter Fourteen

On his drive out to Colonial Beach, Larry tried to think about Greenwood Manor's case and what his visitor had told him earlier, to no avail. Charlene and the issues she was having with her ex along with wondering why Jake felt it necessary to send him Randy Millstone's address ran rampant in his head.

Fifty yards from his destination, he slowed the Suburban to a stop on the shoulder of the rural road and scoped out the area near Millstone's residence.

Ranch style houses lined the road. Identical chain-link fences separated yards and at the rear of the perimeter, the sandy beach and the Potomac River. A barking dog paced the length of the fence.

He tugged out his binoculars from the console between the seats and scoped out Millstone's home. Green shutters, flower beds, and a man and woman hugged. From the information he compiled at his office before heading out, Millstone was of Italian descent. Dark hair and tanned skin confirmed the chances the man he looked at was the best man in Charlene's wedding. He focused on the woman. Long, brown hair reached her shoulder blades.

An unsettled feeling plunged into the pit of his stomach. He lowered the lenses…trim waist, oh so perfect butt.

Charlene?

Anger and jealousy spiked. He wanted to reach through the distance and shove the guy off her. Grinding his teeth, he dropped the binoculars to his lap and his fingers curled around the steering wheel as he tried to remove the barb that stabbed him in the chest.

Irregular situations often led to measured anger he handled every day, but the annoying emotion of jealousy streaming through his system, he had a hard time managing.

Frozen in the spot, he stared in their direction, his red-hot vision not allowing him to see clearly. Before he stepped out of the vehicle, he had to get under control.

His cell buzzed.

Without checking caller ID, he hit the talk button, putting it on speaker. "Newman."

"From your tone," Jake said, "you're at the residence."

Impossible thoughts arose. Had his buddy set him up? "Affirmative."

"Old friends, agent. They're old friends. Going through a tough time. I don't know what you're seeing or what you're thinking, but remember they're friends."

"Say friends one more time, so I can reach through the phone and punch ya."

Jake chuckled. "If I was a betting man, I'd think Millstone has info. That's why you're there. Not to spy on Charlene."

"That's your cover story, isn't it? She told you where she was going and you sent me."

"I sent the best man for the job," Jake teased, as if he had the authority to tell Larry what to do.

Millstone eased away and Charlene crossed her arms over her chest.

"Gotta go."

Larry hit the off button. Shoved his phone in his pocket, stuck his gun in his hip holster, and slipped on a blazer.

Opening the door, the fishy odor gagged him. He covered his mouth and stepped onto the salt and pepper paved road and gently closed the door. Heart thundering in his chest, the effects of the green monster flying through his veins, all he could think about was Charlene reconnecting with an old flame. He light footed it toward them, wanting to overhear their conversation. Spying on friends wasn't in his gamut of past actions, yet he never thought about a woman non-stop, either.

"He's different," Millstone said. "Something's off."

"How?" Charlene asked.

All business, nothing intimate.

He worked his shoulders, easing the tension and preparing for the next onslaught of emotions. Thanks to Jake, he was about to piss Charlene off. No doubt, she'd jump to the conclusion that he followed her.

Larry cleared his throat. "Excuse me, Mr. Millstone? I'm Special Agent Newman." Larry handed him a business card from the small stack he carried in his shirt pocket.

Charlene inhaled a breath of air, a low shrill escaping her, and gaped.

For a brief moment, Millstone stared at the card before locking eyes with Larry, his features darkening. "What's this about?"

"Larry, why are you here? Jake told you, didn't he?"

"Not the place or time," Larry barked and regretted it.

She took the sharpness with a flinch of her head and pulled her lower lip inward, scraping her teeth on the soft tissue. The movement a kick to the gut, he wanted to kiss the pained expression from her face.

"You brought him to my home?" Millstone raised the card toward Larry and narrowed his eyebrows at Charlene.

Her gaze darted between him and Millstone, confusion etched in her brow and the downward curves of her mouth. "What? I didn't."

Angry red splotches appeared on Millstone's face, his hands curling into fists. "I can't believe this shit. Charlene, how could you set me up?"

Larry slid the edge of his blazer behind his holster and gripped the butt of his gun. Millstone getting jumpy he hadn't expected. "Sir, I need you to stay calm. I'm here to ask a few questions, nothing more."

"Uh, huh," Randy said, his head bobbing. He turned to Charlene. "This is how you repay me?"

A tear slid down Charlene's cheek. She shook her head. "I didn't."

Damnit! Larry caused her this grief. "I have a newspaper photo of you and Andrew Smith. Ms. Smith did not lead me to you."

She locked gazes with Larry and gave him a forced smile.

The effect chipped at his heart.

Millstone bolted.

Now what? Adrenaline crashed into Larry's veins and his muscles twitched with the potent thrill of a chance. He glanced at Charlene. "Don't move."

She diverted her gaze.

"Promise me," he said, eyeing Millstone. "I need to find you after I grab this guy."

She nodded.

Larry ran after him, his achy muscles reminding him of the fall yesterday.

Millstone cleared the fence into the neighboring yard, stumbled on the landing, and regained his balance.

The man was in shape. Larry cut the corner, bypassing shrubs and jumped the fence a yard over.

At this point, he needed to keep Millstone in his sights. The guy could take off in any direction and Larry could lose him.

A deep growl came from behind. Larry glanced over his shoulder in time to see a pit bull lunging toward him.

He jerked to the side, out of the line of its path, and sailed over the enclosure into another yard. The pit followed, his strong jaws snapping as he tried to bite Larry's legs and ankles.

Man, he hated to use force on an animal. No way could he outrun the beast. He unclipped the Taser from his belt and twisted.

The dog leapt, and his paws hit Larry square in the chest. He pressed the Taser to the dog's belly. He fell backwards. Air whooshed out of his lungs.

The dog yelped and ran in the opposite direction.

The sky and earth warped around him. He focused on the white, fluffy clouds against the light blue sky, shook off the dizziness, and regained his bearings. Climbing to his feet, he scanned the perimeter.

Millstone hopped over a neighbor's hedge and raced toward the beach along Potomac River.

Man, he hoped no one was there. Larry sprinted across the street and sank, the grainy particles bleeding around the edges of his hiking shoes.

Twenty-five yards ahead, Millstone ran toward the fishing pier, the heels of his bare feet kicking up sand behind him.

If Millstone reached one of the fishing boats floating at the end of the pier, chances of Larry finding information on Smith or figuring out why he fled were slim. Heart thundering in his chest and adrenaline darting through his veins, he forged ahead, shoving through the airy, yet heavy soil.

Millstone leapt onto the wooden pier.

Larry dug deeper, pushed harder, and closed in. He drew his weapon from his holster. "Freeze!"

Millstone's steps faltered.

The noise of an engine roaring blasted the air.

Larry tracked the sound to the end of the pier.

An average size man stood behind the wheel, a red baseball cap firmly on his head.

Mathews?

"Son of a bitch," Randy yelled. His back stiffened.

"Andrew," Charlene gasped from behind Larry.

Andrew? What the hell? And why had Charlene not listened? Her being here could make matters worse or…he could use her presence to his advantage. "Think of your friendship with Charlene. You don't want this situation to go south. Step off the pier and let's talk."

With his hands in the air, Millstone turned. His gaze darted between Larry, pointing the gun at his chest, to the water.

Describing the guy as edgy didn't depict the gleam in his eyes, nor his body twitching. All signs pointed to the situation ending badly. Millstone would take the bullet and not rat.

What did Smith have over him?

Millstone didn't budge. His eyes shot to Charlene.

Alarm pounded inside Larry's skull. "Come on, Randy. You don't want Charlene to see you get shot."

"I'm sorry, Charlene." Millstone jump.

Fuck! Larry squeezed the trigger.

A grunt shadowed by a splash of water followed.

"N-o-o!" Charlene screamed.

"Call 9-1-1."

Larry lowered his weapon and tossed Charlene his cell.

Eyes wide, mouth gaped, she nodded.

The strained expression on her face about undid him. Work had to come first. He shoved down his first instinct to hold her and hopped up on the wooden pier. His boots echoed on the slotted boards as he raced toward Millstone's body floating, face down, blood spotting the murky water.

Larry made quick work of removing his shoes and tugging his socks off, and stuck the gun in his hand and the one from his ankle holster inside the shoes before dropping into the water, clothed.

Larry rolled Millstone over and pressed two fingers to his neck. "He's okay," he yelled back to Charlene who stood at the edge of the water, a hand on each cheek.

Clutching Millstone by the shirt at the nape of his neck, Larry tugged him to the shore, then grasped him under his shoulders and laid him on the sand.

"Is he all right?" Charlene knelt beside them, concern etched into worry lines on her face. "Randy?"

Millstone coughed and sputtered, water oozed from his mouth for a few moments. He propped himself on an elbow then sat up and grasped his shoulder where the bullet had winged him. "I'm okay."

"Are you sure?" she asked, her hands and eyes inspecting the area near the wound.

"I said yes." Randy said around clearing his throat. "I'm fine. The wound stings, but I'm good."

"What the hell were you doing?" Frustration clearly welled inside her by the tone of her voice.

"What?"

She hit Randy on his good shoulder. "You left Larry with no choice but to shoot. Who does that?"

"Larry? You're on a first name basis with this guy?"

"That's not the point," Charlene bit back.

Larry chuckled. With Charlene occupying Millstone, he wasn't concerned if the guy would make a break for it and walked back to the pier to retrieve his guns before any spectators arrived. Gun fire in the area surely would bring onlookers. Still, he swiftly holstered his guns and made quick work of dressing his feet and returned.

"Leave it be, Charlene," Randy said, his manner like a scolded puppy.

"No." Charlene smacked his forehead and jabbed her hands on her hips.

Admiration filled him. Charlene took matters into her own hands. She didn't want someone else to fight her battles, she confronted them head on. At that moment, she earned his whole-hearted respect. He rubbed the area between his pecs, soothing the sudden tightness.

"You stupid son of a bitch. What has Andrew gotten you into?"

"Charlene." Larry joined her at her side. "You can't beat on my prisoner."

"Prisoner? The hell I am." Millstone straightened and reapplied pressure to the wound with his hand.

Larry snatched the gun off his belt and aimed. "Take another step, the next bullet will be more painful."

"I'd listen, you idiot," Charlene commanded, stepping to the side. "Don't let Andrew bring you down a road you can't recover from."

A cloud of darkness passed over Millstone's features before he nodded. "What do you need?"

Sirens approached.

Soon, the beach would be covered with police and rescue personnel. He lowered his gun to his side. "Why did you run?"

"You're FBI," Millstone huffed. "Of course, I ran."

"A citizen who's innocent doesn't run," Larry said, matter-of-factly.

"I haven't done anything wrong, so get that idea out of your mind." Millstone removed his hand and looked at the injury. Blood covered his palm, but the bleeding slowed.

"You warned Andrew! Why?" Charlene demanded.

"I owe him, Char. I would have helped you talk to him if you hadn't brought the Feds."

"This has been covered," Larry said choosing his words carefully and keeping his voice under control for Charlene's sake. "She didn't bring me."

Millstone forced a laugh. "I don't care what you say. I know you followed her."

Charlene observed Larry, the stink-eye showing. "Did you?"

Charlene questioning him in front of Millstone didn't set well. He gave the trail events that put him to this point, case closed. "We'll talk later." His voice came out more stern than he liked, but Millstone was really starting to grate on his nerves. Charlene siding with him for an instant sent a rush of disappointment through him.

She sucked in her bottom lip and surprisingly shook her head.

Suckerpunch in the gut. Again, he wanted to apologize for snapping. He winked. When her features softened, he focused on Millstone. "It'll go easier on you, if you tell me what's up with Andrew Smith before the uniforms and other agents reach us."

Millstone puffed out his cheeks. "A while back, he asked to stay with me while he straightened out his living situation."

"What living situation?"

Millstone lifted his good shoulder. "Beats me. He didn't tell and I didn't ask."

"Anything else?" Larry asked, suspicion he held back curling in his gut.

"That's all I know," Millstone said in a measured tone.

Larry wasn't buying the act. "Think. There's probably something he mentioned or you overheard."

A police car followed by an ambulance parked on the shoulder of the road near the beach.

"Your time is up," Larry said. "Right now, I have you on obstruction."

Millstone drew in a deep breath and stared out at the slight waves breaking on the beach.

"Please, Randy," Charlene pleaded.

He cut his eyes at her.

"For Henry. Don't make me tell him you went to jail." Charlene wiped a tear from her face. "I can't tell him another man he looked up to has let him down."

The moment Charlene's words registered with Millstone, he flinched and pressed his lips together. "He goes by Mathews."

The hair on Larry's neck rose. "Allen Mathews?"

"That's it. Phone calls came to my house for him. I hung up on a few, then one day I received a call and got pissed. I told them to stop calling. Andrew was nearby and snatched the phone from me. Shortly after, he disappeared. Today's the first day I've seen him for about six months."

"You didn't know he was on your boat?" Charlene asked.

"Nope."

"If you weren't heading toward him for help, why run toward the pier?" Larry asked.

"For my boat, the one Andrew took off in."

Smith, AKA Mathews, used Millstone for a pawn. The question still stood, why would this seemingly decent guy go to such lengths to help Mathews? "Want to tell me why you're so loyal to him?"

Millstone watched the advancing vehicles. "Nope."

****

Charlene sat on a bench under a group of trees, looking at the sudden crowd forming along the sandy beach. Minutes ago, the area was empty. Now, uniformed officers kept people at a distance as Larry talked with two men dressed in slacks and button down shirts. Now more than ever, she was glad she told Gloria to keep quiet about her involvement in the café.

Whatever Andrew was involved in, he pulled honest people into his web, preyed on them, and chewed them up, letting the remains fall in any direction without care. He'd proved that today when he raced away from the pier in his friend's boat, another thing to add to Andrew's long list of criminal activity. When would he ever stop? And at what cost?

She glanced over her shoulder at Randy, shirtless, sitting on a stretcher in the back of an ambulance. He still hadn't told her why he went to such extremes for Andrew. Not knowing drove her crazy.

Randy locked eyes with her as the EMT pressed white gauze to his shoulder injury. Unlike earlier when he wore a scolded childlike expression, anger vibrated off him.

The EMT patted Randy's good arm. "You're just winged. Keep the area clean and follow up with your doctor."

Randy slid his shirt on, jumped to the pavement and was met by an officer, holding cuffs.

Her heart went out to Randy. Still, no matter what Andrew did, Randy allowed it, always had.

Larry shifted, drawing her attention. She studied his profile. The tension from his jaw vanished and his eyes had softened. Every inch of him had been business while Randy tested him. Fierce, yet sexy…hard, yet soft. He possessed every quality she admired about a man.

Larry had looked out for her at the same time he worked the situation. She didn't blame him for shooting Randy. She did, however, kick herself for challenging Larry during a high stress period. First chance she got, she'd apologize. He wasn't anything like Andrew. Questioning his motives or what he said made no sense. If he said it then it was fact. She'd cause herself less stress if she remembered that.

Larry and the two agents approached. Larry stopped in front of her while one of the agents grasped Randy's elbow and the other opened the rear door to a sedan with darkened windows.

"What will happen to him now?" Charlene asked.

The ambulance, followed by the agents' car, and other marked police cars filed down the road and turned out of sight before Larry focused back on her and stretched out his hand. "Let's take a walk."

Hand in hand, they walked in the direction of the pier.

"Randy will be interviewed to see what else he might know." Larry squeezed her hand. "Your ex is up to his elbows in trouble. I'm asking that you stay away from him until loose ends are tied up."

She paused and gazed into his eyes. "He wants money from me. Why does that mean he's in trouble?"

"He broke into your house, Charlene. Hit a parked car. His behavior indicates irrational behavior. Other than saying that, I can't go into details until I have facts. If I say any more, it'd just be speculation."

Everyone shutting her out, not confiding in her, made her feel like she was alone in the dark, a little apprehensive, and a touch scared. "Do you always operate in such vague terms?"

"Not vague, cautious."

She gazed out to the water. "I hate being in the dark."

"Roger that." Releasing her hand, he reached around her shoulder, tucked her closer, and kissed the top of her head. "If I could tell you more, I would."

The subtle, tender touch sent her heart soaring. As they walked toward the pier, she relaxed her head onto his shoulder, enjoying the comfort of his warmth and not caring that his shirt wet her cheek and the side of her blouse. "I should have waited and questioned you in private instead of in front of Randy."

He shrugged. "No worries."

The impassive tone of his voice told her despite what he said, it had bothered him. "Anyway, I'm sorry."

"How you handle yourself today, minus not listening to me, was remarkable."

No compliment had ever made her glow inside. "Thank you."

He pecked her lips and motioned to sit on the pier. "Do you have any idea why Millstone is loyal to Smith?" They settled next to each other on the pier, their feet dangling inches above the water's surface.

A breeze tossed her hair into her eyes and the sun reflected off the water, all elements for a gorgeous, romantic day. "I don't."

"If Millstone cooperates, he will be released soon."

Larry's phone vibrated against her hip. She retrieved it and handed it to him. "What about the obstruction charge?"

Larry read the incoming message, shoved it into his pocket, and stretched his arm around her back. "It depends on if he cooperates. The information he gave identifying Smith as Mathews was a huge piece to the puzzle I need to solve."

"Mathews?"

Larry groaned and rested his chin against her. "He's someone of concern. I'm watching him now. Knowing he's actually your ex-husband puts a whole other spin on my concern."

She snuggled closer to his chest. Since this morning, her emotions underwent a one-eighty. The rush of wanting to get even with Andrew and the excitement of getting her restaurant back gave her hope and made her feel vibrant. Then the flipside, the man she wanted, craved actually, a relationship kept her in the dark

Needing to talk about something exciting and plunge out of the darkness that seemed consistently to enclose around her, she said, "I'm getting my restaurant back. Well, half of it."

He eased her away from him and locked gazes with her. "The one you and your husband owned?"

"Yes."

"Charlene, that's exciting news." He cupped her face and kissed her.

A rush of heat wove through her veins. His hand slid down her back to the small of her waist. He held her to him while his free palm tilted her head and caressed the curve of her chin.

A low thrill of excitement escaped her.

He eased away and his eyes squinted into small beacons of want as they slid over her face, taking in her every feature. "You get to me."

Her heart hitched, leaving a lump of emotion lodged in the back of her throat and tears stinging her eyes. The powerful passion passing through them locked her in place. She couldn't look away and couldn't identify what she felt. She could only stare and wait to see what he'd say.

He broke their gaze, kissed her forehead, and pulled her against him, wrapping his arms tightly around her. "You feel good, which brings us back to the issues we need to move beyond."

He was right. Neither of them had tossed their problems behind, at least she hadn't. She needed to tell him why she was here, what brought her to Colonial Beach to see Randy. "I came to Randy to find Andrew."

When he remained silent, she searched his eyes for signs he was upset, saw none, and added, "I wanted revenge."

"I figured."

She took the plunge and asked a question that had nagged her, one she consistently reconciled on her own when he was the only one who could answer it. "Will you always be honest with me?"

"Yes. At times I might not be able to tell you details of a case, just like earlier. When I can, I will."

The tenderness of his words…the intensity of his gaze, grasped her heart. The man was too good to be true. She pressed her lips to his.

A groan vibrated through his chest.

He cupped the sides of her face and slid his tongue over hers. The hunger in his kiss was so demanding it made her dizzy. "Larry," she said against his lips on a pant and grasped his wrists.

He eased back until their lips barely touched. "I have to leave to process the arrest."

She heard what he said, but the vigor she experienced in his presence dug its hooks into her, refusing to let her move. "I want you," she whispered.

"Ah, babe, you're killing me."

Larry's words held passion unlike the anger tone Andrew used when he said the exact words. She shut her eyes on the tears forming. "Thank you."

"For what?"

A watery gaze impeded her view. "For being you." Her lips trembled. The emotion came out of nowhere. Happy, yet a dam broke from deep within her she couldn't control. The excessive ill-treatment she'd endured from her life with Andrew escaped on a sob.

Larry hugged her, securing her tightly in his strong arms.

She pressed her face into his chest like she had earlier with Randy and cried. For a long moment, she basked in Larry's comfort, his powerful presence giving her what no man had ever given. He let her be herself and accepted her as she was. She wiped the moisture from her face. "I think I'm falling in love with you."

A low guttural sound vibrated from his chest and he squeezed her tighter.

When he remained silent, her nerves jumped with nervous energy that she'd spoken her feelings too soon. She had to see his face to know what to think and eased away.

Red eyes bored into hers, his mouth a firm line, and the pulse in his neck ticked.

She nibbled on her lower lip.

An array of expressions flitted across his handsome face before staying with tender eyes and an inviting mouth.

She believed Larry was falling for her, too. His reactions said so, but if his face and the whites of his eyes hadn't turned red, she wouldn't have known he'd even heard her.

Larry not acknowledging what she said released a shot of disappointment.

She wouldn't push. He'd let her know his feelings when he was ready. They both had issues that needed fixing before they moved their relationship farther. Her and her overwhelming feelings put them in an awkward position.

She rose and scanned the beach. The crowd from earlier had disbursed. With the exception of a few beach goers, only she and Larry remained.

Returning her focus to his, she held out her hand. "We better go."

He climbed to his feet, grasped and squeezed her hand. The return walk to her mother's car was quiet. When they reached it, he pinned her back against the door, braced his hands against the roof on either side of her. "Give me time."

Before she had a chance to digest his words and formulate a response, he took her mouth into a kiss that held as much fervor as it did possibilities, leaving her breathless and liquefying her muscles.

"See you in The Memory Café later?" he asked against her lips.

"Yes."

He opened the car door.

She slid inside and started the car.

Irritation, confusion, and with a heart full of warmth and hope, she drove away, eyeing his reflection in the rearview mirror.

He stared after her.

Chapter Fifteen

"Mother-fucker," Andrew fumed as he drove Randy's boat into a boat slip on the Rappahannock River.

He didn't give a fuck if the water gods towed the boat for illegally parking. Randy would have to deal with it. How in the hell could his trusted friend rat him out to big fuzz?

He swiped a hand through his hair, second-guessing his anger. Randy didn't know Andrew would come for a visit today. Hell, he hadn't been there for months. Besides that, Randy didn't know his alter-ego connection to the agent.

Holding onto the boat's rope, he climbed onto the wooden pier, secured the line around the cleats, and gazed at the flowing water. He recalled seeing Charlene at Randy's.

At first when he spotted Charlene standing in Randy's yard, he'd jumped to conclusions that she was two-timing him with his old buddy. But, he knew if Charlene and Randy were ever interested in each other, it would have happened before now. There was a time the three had been inseparable. Just the same, he'd decided to watch from a distance. He parked his car behind a neighbor's shed and walked on foot toward them. On neutral territory, Charlene might consider coughing up some money and give him a chance.

The idea went up in smoke when the red-headed fucker parked his Suburban on the road a little ways from where Andrew parked. At first, he thought the person was a stalker. Then he saw the binoculars and red hair. The black SUV had agent written all over it.

The only way out for him was by boat. If he drove his car, the agent would have a description and a license plate. In no time the pigs would track him down and make him pay for the damage he did to that Chevelle.

The image of Randy diving off the pier into the water filled his mind. The awkwardness in which he fell didn't look right. His body was disjointed as if his shoulder had twisted backwards. *Did big fuzz shoot him?*

The heat rose in Andrew's face and he curled his fists. "Someone will pay."

He tugged out his phone, hit Hulk on speed dial.

"Hulk, here."

"Hulk, Mouse. I need you to do me a favor. Come to the City Docks. Bring Monk's car."

"What?" The chicken shit's voice quaked. "He'll have my ass."

"Don't be a pansy. While Monk's gone for the week, I'm in charge. I need you to take a boat back to Colonial Beach and pick up my car."

After a few grumbles, Hulk agreed and disconnected.

Andrew stepped back into the boat, stashed the key back where he found it under the front seat, and went in search of a bar. He'd need some serious liquid encouragement to carry out what he had planned. *Payback.*

****

Parking in The Memory Café's rear lot, Charlene blew out a breath. The tense moment with Larry on the beach surprised and shocked her. She spoke her thoughts without thinking. The scandalous part? She was glad she had.

She used her key to let herself in the rear entrance. A scent of warm bread, cheeses, and an array of spices filled the air, making her stomach growl.

"Hi, Charlene," Marge said, looking into the hall from the kitchen, her arms, elbow deep in bread dough.

Charlene smiled and moved toward Pamela's stepmother. "Miss me?" They hadn't seen each other for the last couple of days.

"I sure do. No one makes crepes like you." Marge's sweet smile and bright, gentle eyes made her feel appreciated.

"You're too kind. I better head up front to collect Henry."

"He left, dear. Didn't your mother tell you? Henry had an upset tummy. I think he ate too many cookies. Pamela's father carried them home when he drove Grand Ann and Grand Ben back to their apartment."

"Oh." With all the commotion at Colonial Beach, Charlene hadn't heard any incoming alerts. She retrieved her cell from her purse and checked messages, two from Doris. The first, stating what Marge had said, and the second read: "Henry's better. Have a good time at Cocktail Hour. Is it okay if Henry stays the night with me?."

Charlene smiled. Her mother looked out for her and Henry well. So much so, she worried about her mom not having spare time to do her own socializing. "Yes, thank you," she said in the return text and gazed at Marge. "I'll treat myself to a margarita while I wait for the others."

Marge nodded toward the oven along the back wall. "Grab the two plates of food. Celine's already here, chewing Pamela's ear off about Steve. Those two have a rocky relationship." Marge shook her head. "If she doesn't eat, she'll get sick."

"Will do. Let me give Henry a quick call first."

"I turned the oven off a few minutes ago. They'll keep."

Charlene nodded as Henry answered the phone. "Hi, Mommy."

"Hi, sweetie. You doing okay?"

A long silence passed before Henry said, "Me and Grandma are watching *Spiderman*."

Now, she understood the long pause. "Does your belly hurt?"

Another silence.

"Sweetheart." Charlene couldn't keep her irritation from seeping into her voice.

"No, I'm good. Mommy, I should go Spiderman's about to..." his voice drifted off.

She smiled. "Go watch your movie. I love you."

"Love you. Bye."

The phone went dead. She sighed. If her mother needed to speak to her, she'd call.

"That boy of yours is adorable, so inquisitive and helpful. You've done an excellent job with him, dear. You're a good mother."

Swelling with pride, Charlene thought she'd bust. A sob worked up her throat. She cleared it. "Thank you. You're pretty awesome yourself." She picked up the oven mitts and retrieved a rectangle plate of quesadillas, her personal favorite, and a round plate of tortilla chips with melted cheese.

Her stomach grumbled in response.

Marge laughed.

"Like I said, you're awesome," Charlene sang, appreciating Marge's thoughtfulness and feeling eager to see her friends. She always enjoyed their weekly gathers, but tonight, she felt excited and lighter like the world didn't weigh down her shoulders. She pushed through the swinging doors, leading to the black and white tile dining room.

A man she didn't recognize worked behind the bar mixing a drink. By his buzz cut and fit body, she figured him for military and wondered if he was one of Pamela's step-brothers.

He winked.

The man oozed testosterone. Still, he didn't hold a candle to Larry. She nodded and rubbed her lips together. The taste of Larry lingered, filling her with excitement once more. She giggled. If she didn't control her giddiness, Pamela and Celine would know something was up and question her. Was she ready to share with them her feelings concerning Larry?

"Hi, ladies." She stepped onto the patio. Evening began to descend and the autumn scents of earth drifted over on the slight bit of wind, giving the outdoor dining area with several tables scattered around a cozy feel. She set the platters in the center of the table beside the stack of small plates then sat in a black iron chair next to Pamela and searched the street. Not much traffic stirred tonight. Talking over the engines made hearing each other a challenge. "How are you, ladies?"

Relief washed over Pamela's face. "I'm so glad you came early. I need reinforcements." She laughed.

"Wait a minute," Celine retorted, humor lacing her voice. "I listen to you girls whenever you have troubles. Look at it this way. You're lucky I only have one problem."

"Steve," Charlene and Pamela said in unison.

Celine's mouth fell open. "Jeez. Give a girl a break."

Charlene grabbed a decorative tumbler from a pile from the center of the table. "Are you expecting a crowd?"

"I hope so. It'd be nice to have everyone here." Pamela lifted one of the margarita pitchers from in front of Celine and filled Charlene's glass.

"How are you?" Celine covered her hand. "I'm sorry I couldn't come by yesterday. Fredericksburg Tourist was packed."

"No biggie." Charlene sipped the liquid and savored the taste of tequila, a refreshing drink after spending the day riding an emotional roller coaster. "That's good."

Pamela sipped some water. "I expected you'd want to talk about Andrew."

"I figured you'd be uptight and would need to blow off steam," Celine said around a mouthful of margarita.

"Nope. I'm declaring Cocktail Hour an Andrew-free zone."

Celine choked. "You had sex!"

"Shush!" Pamela's eyebrows slashed over her blue fierce eyes. "This is a PG establishment."

"Sorry," Celine said with a small, mortified smile.

Pamela gazed over her shoulder into the café.

No one watched them except for the bartender. He eyed Celine.

"No foul," Pamela said then faced Charlene. "Fess up, you have."

"How'd you two get the idea I had sex from me not wanting to talk about Andrew?"

Celine and Pamela exchanged a silent conspirator glance.

Oh, boy. So, much for wondering if she should talk about Larry, they'd do it for her.

"Larry?" Pamela's normally welcoming smile transformed into calm tone and she arched an eyebrow at Charlene.

If she hadn't known Pamela, she'd actually have been nervous and answered immediately. As it was, Charlene would use this time to collect her thoughts and work out what to say. Hanging out on the pier, her and Larry chatting with one another in a way that was so comfortable she felt like she'd done it forever. Well, until her mouth ran away from her and confided her feelings. After that, things between them had become awkward.

Her mind jumped to the kiss next to her mom's car…phew…she fanned herself and sipped more of her drink to camouflage the heat rising from her body to her face.

"That does it." Celine gulped her drink. "I want some of what Charlene's having."

"Oh, no. You can't. We're exclusive." Charlene looked at her half-empty drink. "This stuff is like truth serum."

"The bartender put a dash of serum in the pitcher to make people talk." Pamela laughed. "You have no choice."

"It'd do you good to tell us all the details." Celine braced her elbow on the table and rested her chin on her palm while sipping margarita through a straw. She gazed, dreamlike, at Charlene.

"I don't kiss and tell." Charlene grabbed a plate and slid a quesadilla onto it and ate. They could stare at her all they wanted, but she wouldn't spill, not when she really didn't know what to tell them. Was she in a relationship? Did Larry have feelings for her? Confessing her feelings for him when she didn't know his for sure, was that what girlfriends did with one another? She hadn't had close friends since high school. The problems with Andrew, she told Celine and Pamela everything, but this was Larry…their friend. She didn't want to say something that might make the relationship between any of them awkward.

Celine had told her and Pamela everything about her and Steve's relationship and he was Pamela's best friend, had been since high school. Pamela didn't think any differently of him.

Charlene swallowed the mouthful of food and blurted, "Yes, we had sex. It was the most incredible, delicious night I'd ever experienced. I think about him non-stop."

Celine sighed.

Pamela patted her hand. "I know the feeling."

Charlene locked gazes with Pamela. "I don't know his feelings for me. He acts like it, yet won't say."

Pamela snorted. "The life of an agent. They're reserved and cautious. The job and what's happened in their past dictates it. Give him time. Larry spending time with you tells me how much he thinks of you."

Charlene rested back in her chair. Larry said the exact same words, *give me time*. She planned to, but hearing a wife of a former agent drill the same thought home added that much more verity to his comment. "Thanks, Pamela."

"Anytime."

Charlene looked between her friends. The bond they'd formed over the last few months amazed her. They welcomed her and Henry so easily that emotion filled her heart and stung her eyes. "Love you, girls."

Chairs screeched and arms surrounded her.

"We love you, too," Celine and Pamela said, smashing her as if she was in the middle of a sandwich.

If they didn't back away, she'd be a puddle of water. She patted their arms and they settled back in their seats, drying their eyes with their fingers.

Charlene grabbed a tissue from her purse and blew her nose. She needed a safe subject to talk about and asked, "Where's Sue?" By this time of day, Sue worked the floor, joking and laughing with the customers as she took the orders.

"She's sick," Pamela said.

"Is that why there's a new bartender?"

"Jackson," Celine breathed, her dreamlike expression fixed on him behind the bar.

Pamela clicked her fingers together in front of Celine's face. "You're dating my best friend. You can't have eyes for my stepbrother."

"Correction." Celine lifted a finger. "Before your stepbrother was family, I had eyes for him. Besides, Steve and I are on a break."

Pamela slumped back in her chair. "There isn't gonna be a happy-ever-after with Steve and you, is there?"

Celine pressed her lips together and put food from each dish onto a small plate. "I hate to say. Besides, we're not talking about me. Charlene's in the spotlight." Celine stuffed a forkful of food into her mouth.

"Why is that?" Paul asked, his dimples deep on each cheek, as he stepped over the single linked chain separating the sidewalk from the patio.

"Where have you been?" Pamela stood and smacked his chest before giving her brother-in-law a hug.

Celine hugged him next.

He blinked his green eyes at Charlene, and spread his arms. "Come here."

She fell into his brotherly embrace. "Good to see you."

"You, too." He gave her a tight squeeze and sat next to her. "I hope you're not upset with me about Halloween."

"Why would I be upset? You needed someone to watch the place, so I did."

His groan and slight nod plunged what Larry had said into her mind. *I think we're victims of a matchmaking scheme.* She'd have to thank Paul later. For now, she winked.

His dimples grew deeper and his eyes brightened. "Time for a toast." He topped off Celine and Charlene's drinks and filled a glass for himself and eyed Pamela holding a water glass. "To the future."

They clicked their glasses and sipped.

All eyes turned on Pamela. For a long moment, no one said a word. Charlene knew what was on everyone's mind, the same thing that nagged at her since she saw the water glass sitting in front of Pamela. Either she was pregnant, or they were trying.

"How'd the competition go?" Pamela asked Paul, breaking the silence. "You've been in so many I can't remember which one you were just in."

He chuckled. "I can't either."

"Do you ever see the girl you used to love to race against?" Celine asked.

Paul's eyes widened before shaking his head.

"Niki," Pamela interjected. "That's been years ago. Whatever happened to her?"

"Subject change," Paul said, his voice suddenly withdrawn and expression impassive.

She, Celine, and Pamela exchanged glances with one another before focusing back on Paul staring at his empty glass.

Another subject she wouldn't inquire about. When he was ready to talk, he would.

"There they are," Jake said, stepping over the fence. A familiar guy with long hair pulled into a ponytail and piercing brown eyes trailed him.

"Hey, everyone, this is Quigley Collins. You know my wife, Pamela." Jake pointed to each of them as he spoke. "And you met Charlene earlier today." He patted Paul on the back. "My brother, Paul England…and this is Celine Marx."

"Nice to meet everyone."

"Quigley joined the Old Town Detective Agency a few days ago." Jake kissed Pamela's cheek and positioned a chair between her and Charlene.

Quigley sat on Charlene's other side, nudging Paul toward Celine.

"How are you feeling?" Jake asked his wife.

Pamela sent him the cold glare she'd given Charlene earlier and she could have sworn Pamela hushed him under her breath. "I'm good."

"Tell them," Jake urged.

"But not everyone's here."

The extra glasses on the table made sense now, but who was Pamela expecting?

Jake waved a hand. "Doesn't matter. Go for it."

She smiled and her face lit up like the morning star. "Jake and I have an announcement."

Charlene's eyes widened, excitement rushing through her that her friend would confide why she was drinking water.

"I'm pregnant," Pamela's words escaped on a shrill squeak.

Celine screeched, jumped up, and hugged Pamela. As soon as Celine walked away, Charlene hugged her. Paul was next.

"I see you told everyone," Steve said, joining them.

Larry followed, his gaze landing on Charlene. A small, knowing smile creased the corners of his mouth. Like earlier, he wore dress khakis. Instead of a button-down shirt, he donned a polo. The combination of the deep, rich burgundy color making his eyes pop and the cotton fabric pulling at the seams across his broad shoulders sent Charlene's heart into sudden palpitations. Her mouth watered to have his eyes on her, naked, and her hand itched to touch every muscle concealed from view.

Her expression must have given away her thoughts, for he tilted his head. The tender, sweet way he gazed at her with longing, appreciation, caring, hitched up her libido and sent a surge of want through her veins that pooled in her nether regions.

Not long ago, she debated if Larry looked at other women the way he had her that day he saved her and Henry on the mountain. Knowing Larry the way she did now, she knew he wasn't the type of guy to have wanderlust on his mind.

After the greetings to the new arrivals died down, Charlene was barely able to retain her giddiness toward Larry. "Hi."

"Hey, there." Larry pulled up a chair.

Wishing they could be somewhere private, she settled for scooting her chair over to make room for him between her and Quigley.

"Steve knew before me?" Celine's agitation broke through Charlene's sexual fog.

Paul chuckled. "Hell, he knew before me and I'm the uncle."

"Who's never home," Jake said.

"Touché." Paul accepted another pitcher of margaritas from a waitress Charlene didn't recognize.

"He's my best friend," Pamela said as soon as the young girl left, then smiled at Jake, "After you, of course."

He winked.

"Ever heard of girl code?" Celine pressed her lips together, but a smile tugged at the corners of her mouth. "I can't be mad. I'm too happy for you."

"We're all uncles and aunts," Steve said. "Again."
He grinned at Charlene. "Henry's the first nephew."

Her heart warmed that they included Henry into
the mix.

"When's the due date?" Paul asked, filling the
glasses for the newcomers.

"July tenth." Jake grinned and rubbed Pamela's
stomach.

"Here ya go," Jackson said, stepping onto the
patio. His dark eyes perused the group as he grasped the
handles of two margaritas pitchers in one hand, and two
pitchers of beer in the other. "I figured the guys might
want a cold one." He sat them in the center of the
rectangle table.

The position bunched his biceps and they were
some tremendous muscles. Charlene glanced over at
Celine, sitting at the opposite end of the table, to see her
take on Jackson. She all but drooled. Charlene flicked her
gaze to Steve.

He eyed Celine and stuck out his hand to Jackson.
"Hey, Jacks, are you home long?" Steve asked in a cool,
controlled tone, as if he hadn't noticed his girlfriend in
awe over another man. Pamela was right. There wouldn't
be a happily ever after for Steve and Celine. For some
odd reason, the thought saddened her.

Larry rested his hand on Charlene's thigh and
squeezed.

She smiled, covered his hand with hers. Curiosity
over how the conversation would play out had her
returning her attention to the end of the table.

"No, I'm heading out in a few days," Jackson was
saying.

Jake pointed. "Jacks, this is Quig—"

"We've met," Jackson interrupted, his words curt,
and his scowl clipped. "Later."

All eyes focused on Quigley as Jackson disappeared inside the cafe.

Quigley shrugged. "The guy's an ass."

Jake's eyebrow arched and he leveled an eye on Quigley. "You do know this is Pamela's café?"

Quigley lifted his hand, palm forward. "I meant no disrespect. Jackson and I have a history. Enough said."

Sitting between Larry and Jake, her thighs touching one of theirs, she physically felt Larry and Jake's tension. What shocked her was the tension radiating through the air from the other end of the table. Paul and Steve bristled and glared at the younger guy.

Charlene didn't know what was happening, and given the shocked faces on Celine and Pamela, they didn't either.

Jackson reappeared, stopped between the dining room and patio, arms crossed, shoulders squared. A Marine to the core, his presence gave her a chill. "Collins, a word." His tone didn't give any room for discussion.

Quigley rose without question, followed Jackson to the sidewalk, and stepped out of sight around the corner.

"Bad juju," Steve said. "Probably unresolved shit from the war."

Larry cleared his throat. "Jackson was the pilot when Quigley had the drop that went bad."

"Oh, no," Pamela gasped. "How do you know?"

"I saw the brief right after it happened," Larry said. "No one's fault."

"That's terrible." Celine placed a hand covered her mouth.

Before Charlene could digest what was said, tires squealed on the street, just in front of the outdoor patio, followed by a loud pop.

Her heart slammed into her chest and lodged in her throat. Her breathing quickened. Sweat pebbled on her forehead as awareness struck.

Someone shot at them.

Mouth wide and frozen in place, Charlene scanned the sidewalks and street. Pedestrians raced away. A few cars parked on the other side of the street. The road itself was empty. Why would someone shoot at them?

"What the hell!" Jake yelled, jerking her attention to her friends.

"Is everyone okay?" Charlene asked, seeking out the faces of the BOFs.

No one answered. All eyes stared, wide eyed, in the direction of approaching vehicles, and everything went into slow motion as if each act was freeze-framed. Two motorcycles passed, the drivers wearing brown leather jackets. The shadows the streetlights caused prevented Charlene from seeing what was stitched on their backs.

"No!" Pamela's raised voice sounded like she was petrified, her body vibrating from jerking her head back and forth.

A fury of activity simultaneously unleashed.

"Son of a bitch!" Steve yelled, taking off, his gun in his hand. Paul ran after him.

"Go to the left, I'll cover the next street," Jackson instructed Quigley.

"On it, Major," Quigley responded, jogging after Jackson.

"Everyone in the back," Larry ordered, his voice calm and controlled.

Heart booming in her ears, Charlene bolted out of her chair and followed Pamela and Celine inside.

Another shot reverberated through the air. Tires squealed.

Nausea landed in the pit of Charlene's stomach as the long tentacles of fear played down her spine. She glanced over her shoulder.

The dark colored car that parked across the street sped away.

"Man down!" Jake's voice boomed, dragging Charlene's gaze to him kneeling at the spot they just vacated.

Larry stretched out on the floor, eyes closed. Fear mixed with adrenaline shot through Charlene's veins. "L-a-r-r-y!" Ignoring people telling her stay inside The Memory Café, she rushed over to him lying on the patio floor. "Sweetheart, wake up!"

"I'm okay," Larry said.

"Larry," she cried, tears blinding her vision and her ears ringing. They'd just found each other. This wasn't fair.

Chapter Sixteen

"Psst, Charlene, really I'm okay," Larry said, his voice muffled.

Charlene's pinched face relaxed. She cradled his head in her lap, leaned over him and ran her hands over his stomach and chest, her breasts pressed against his forehead and head. A great position to stay in all night and day, but the customers inside The Memory Café may not appreciate his and Charlene's intimacy.

"Really?" She stretched further, her hands nearing the edge of his pants and dangerously close to triggering his hardening erection to spring into action. "I'm bruised where the bullet hit my vest."

"Are you sure? You're not just saying that?"

"As much as I like this position?" he chuckled. "Trust me, I love it, but I need to sit up."

"Oh, um...sorry." She removed her breasts from his forehead.

The evening air drifted across his face. He rose to a sitting position and twisted. The grief in her eyes gripped his heart. "I'm not just saying that," he said, stroking her hair out of her face and wiping an escaped tear with the pad of his thumb from her cheek. "And never apologize for putting any part of you in the vicinity of my face." He cupped her jaw and grinned.

She grasped his wrist, holding him to her. "When you didn't move," she sucked in a breath, "you scared me."

"The impacted of the bullet knocked me out momentarily."

"Don't do it again."

Emotions coursed through him. They were so overwhelming, so intense, words couldn't describe what he felt. He closed his mouth over hers and released every bit of the passions racing through his veins into their joining until their panting grew into groans. He greedily swallowed her sounds of ecstasy and dove for more.

Someone cleared their throat from behind and a hand patted his back. "Glad you're okay." Mischief colored Jackson's voice, cracking the dreamlike layer Larry had wrapped around him and Charlene and making him realize they weren't alone.

He eased back from Charlene's flushed face and looked at Jackson and Quigley, both with hands on their hips, composed as if they hadn't just sprinted a few blocks. "I didn't hear you approach."

Jackson chuckled. "No, I don't imagine you did."

Larry focused back on Charlene. She was pretty and sweet. He longed to hold her in his arms—so much so, he ached. Thoughts pinged around in his skull as he figured out a way to relay his feelings without the others reading between the lines more than they already had by him devouring her with his lips.. Then one line, which he said to her when he first let her know what he wanted, came to mind. He kissed the tip of her nose and whispered their inside joke, "Kick-off later?"

Charlene smiled, the dark gloom on her face moments ago disappearing, and the corners of her mouth twitched. "You bet."

He waggled his eyebrows and winked before turning his attention to Jackson. "Give me a hand."

Jackson grabbed his hand, and underneath his elbow, and tugged. The bruise on the outside of Larry's chest smarted. Another inch, the bullet would have hit the muscle in his shoulder and landed him in the ER. He was lucky, or had the shooter known he wore a vest?

"Here you go," Marge sung, approaching with her arms full of towels and bandages. Celine followed with a stack of plastic drinking glasses and a pitcher of water.

"Thanks, Marge, but Larry's okay," Charlene said. "He's not bleeding and won't need the bandages, but I will take a towel." Marge handed one to her and Charlene wiped the sweat from her brow.

Larry groaned. He hoped her overheated body came from their connection and not from him getting shot. The idea of him causing her any kind of pain, his fault or not, ate at him.

"Did you see the driver?" Larry asked Jackson and stretched out a hand to Charlene and helped her to her feet. She stood and shifted to move out of the way, and he tightened his grip, keeping her beside him.

"I didn't."

"If I can be of any help, dear, let me know," Marge interrupted and walked inside the café.

"Thank you," Charlene called after Marge and then accepted two glasses of water from Celine. "Thanks."

Celine touched Charlene's shoulder. "I'm going to help Pamela take care of the customers."

Charlene nodded and gave a glass to Larry.

"Let's move." Quigley waved his hands, herding them inside the café like a flock of geese before closing the French doors and locking them.

They went to the far right corner and pulled out a couple of chairs. Thanks to Pamela, the patrons were paying their bills and clearing out of the restaurant. The group chose a table in the far right corner, free of dirty dishes. Larry pulled out a chair for Charlene.

"I should help Pamela," Charlene said.

"Nonsense," Pamela said from a few tables over and picked up a rectangle tub full of dishes. "Take care of Larry. There's not much left for us to do."

Charlene slid into the chair next to Larry as Pamela and Celine disappeared into the kitchen.

"Did you get eyes on the license plate?" Larry asked, motioning to a chair for Jackson to sit down and one for Quigley.

Jackson refused the chair Larry motioned to and remained standing, arms folded, feet a shoulder width apart. The man had the military bug bad. Quigley stood beside him.

"By the time I reached the corner," Jackson said, "the car turned again. I glimpsed the rear tail lights, possible muscle car."

"A Challenger, early seventies," Quigley added, joining Jackson.

Whatever hard feelings existed between Jackson and Quigley earlier, they shoved it aside and worked together.

Paul pushed through the main entrance of the café, held the door open for Steve, and then locked it.

"Anything?" Larry asked.

"I got nothing." Steve dragged a chair along the tile floor, flopped down, and sucked in air. "Give me a sec."

"The driver wore a cap," Paul said, barely winded, propping his back against the wall.

Elbows on knees, Steve pinned Paul with a scowl. "I get how these two guys aren't tired." Steve tilted his head toward Quigley and Jackson standing off to the side. "They do vigorous KPs every day, but you? You exercise to prepare for competitions, but I've never once heard you speak of running in a race. How are you not out of breath?"

"I'm a natural."

"Bullshit. I train my ass off and still suck air when I sprint," Steve voiced, the undertone bitter.

"You need to train for triathlons," Paul said, his posture easygoing.

A rattle sounded at the front door, followed by Jake grumbling as he passed through the foyer to the main area of the café. "I'm too old for this shit." He wheezed, pocked his keys, and slumped into a chair next to Larry. "I need to jog on a daily basis."

"Tell me about it. Ever since I started collecting intel, I don't have as much physical activity."

"There's one way to keep your body fit." Quigley smirked.

Jackson nailed him with a glare. "Hey, a lady's present."

"No worries." Charlene smiled and pulled out her cell.

"Everything okay?" Larry asked, bumping shoulders with her.

"Yes. I'm texting Mom and Henry to let them know everyone is okay, just in case they hear about it. The rumor mill runs rampant."

"Good idea." Charlene's loyalty to her son and mom was admirable, one of his favorite traits.

"Where'd you end up?" Jackson asked Jake.

"Celine's place…Fredericksburg Tourist…left to the lights."

"See anything, boss?" Quigley asked, handing Jake a glass of water.

All eyes stayed on Jake until the glass emptied. He dropped the glass on the table with a thud and refilled it. "I called the shooting in, to the office. I also had an agent call the surrounding businesses so I can check their videos." He finished the water, breathed a sigh of relief, and dragged his arm over his mouth. "Okay. The shooter drove a 1972 dark green Challenger. License plate… Oh, get this…INPALE4. I'm waiting for a call from Missy with the DMV record."

"By now, the office should have feedback," Steve said tugging his cell off his belt loop. "I also called in the shooting and the suspicious motorcycles to the local authorities and the FBI office.

"When they arrive, Quigley will you take care of the questions? We'll give a statement when we're done."

"On it." Quigley scooted out the door after unlocking it.

Larry rubbed the spot the bullet hit his vest, feeling the sting from the blow. By tomorrow, a black and blue bruise would form.

"The hit is better than falling down that well at Greenwood Manor," Steve said, his voice colored with sarcasm.

"You fell in a hole? You didn't tell me." Charlene eyebrow's flew into her hairline and disappeared.

Until now, he hadn't noticed her disheveled hair or the black smudges under her eyes. Larry caressed her cheek with his knuckles. "Yesterday—"

Marge barged into the dining room from the kitchen. Pamela and Celine followed. Their presence saved his hide from having to respond, giving him a few minutes of reprieve to think of a way to explain since he hadn't told her last night. Pamela stood behind Jake, a hand on his shoulder. "Marge insisted on fixing everyone a plate."

"You need to eat." Marge's gaze lit on Pamela then to the group. "Everyone needs to eat before chasing any bad guys. It'll be ready shortly," Marge said and headed toward the kitchen.

Thanks came from around the table.

"I want to hear what happened at the well." Celine dropped into a chair near Steve and rested her elbows on the table, and arched a brow.

The issue hung in the air for a moment before he decided making light of the situation would bring less tension to him and Charlene. "Funny, really."

"Barrel of laughs," Steve said, staring at his phone. "You 'bout gave me and Jake a heart attack."

"The rattler hyped up the tension," Jake added, rubbing a hand over his jaw. "High pucker factor."

"What?" A storm bowled over Charlene's pretty, fawn eyes. "A snake in the well? With you?"

Guilt he hadn't said something before his former friends had slithered through his gut. "Thanks, Jake," Larry said, his voice tight. "Could have led into that bit of information slowly."

Jake shook his head, chuckling. "Nah, might as well rip off the scab, and get it over with."

"Is that what you do?" Larry asked, only half teasing. "Rip off the scab to see how much it hurts?"

Jake gave a nod.

"Let's see if your theory works. Pamela, did your husband tell you about how he was supposed to protect—" Larry paused, waiting for a signal for him to stop.

Jake shifted and his movements turned squirrelly, yet he remained quiet, arms folded across his chest and his gaze aimed at the table's surface.

"—a child of the American Ambassador?"

"Wait—" Jake raised his hand, "—point taken."

Hating when one of them forgot their pact, Larry fixed his best friend with a stare.

"No, I'd like to hear." Pamela leaned closer. "Go on."

Jake narrowed his eyes on Larry and jutted his chin. The silent agreement made. Neither would say a word.

Larry knocked his knuckles on the table. "I can't. It's classified."

"Classified my ass," Pamela said, sending a sharp glare at Larry, then Jake.

"Pamela!" Marge shouted from the kitchen.

Pamela's sigh was echoed through the dining room. "Jeez, I can't get away with anything."

"Welcome to my world." Jackson laughed. "Since when do you swear?"

"Since, I'm pregnant."

"You don't say." Jackson straddled a chair. "I'm going to be an uncle."

Pamela beamed, like a white-lighted Christmas tree. "Looks that way."

"Well, I'll be." Jackson smiled, but his gaze became detached.

Larry understood Jackson's distant expression. Having your close friend go down the path of parenthood put a different twist on life as he knew it.

Charlene touched his arm. "Back to the well and snake." Her voice dripped with honey, spear heading straight to his cock. She blinked. When she opened them, her eyes were wide as saucers. "What happened?" She pulled out the entire arsenal to get him to talk.

He'd rather tell her in the comforts of one of their beds, naked, so he could show her each of the places that hurt. Maybe he could convince her to kiss the bruises away.

The playful smack on his arm from Charlene alerted him that his thoughts showed on his face. "A bed of fake grass covered a hole. I didn't see it, fell to the bottom, to a pissed off rattlesnake."

Charlene covered her mouth and said around her spread fingers, "What did you do?"

He lifted his hands in the 'what could I do' gesture. "I did the only thing I could. I shot it."

By the fire in her eyes, he expected her to hit him. She leaned closer. "Last night," she whispered beside his ear, "did it—"

He chuckled. She didn't want to hit him, didn't question why he hadn't told her. "Was wonderful," he said, his mouth a fraction away from hers. The concern she showed him was unexpected and sweet. He kissed her lips.

"Hey! Earth to Larry." Jake snapped his fingers. "We have business."

"Either the gunman knew you wore a bulletproof vest or he wanted you dead," Steve said, a serious look on his face.

"Whoa!" Pamela raised her hand. "Charlene, Celine, let's go in the other room. I've learned from past experience there are some things I don't need to know."

Charlene hesitated, her gaze darting between Pamela and Larry.

"It's your call," Larry said, when he really hoped she would go with Pamela. At times, Steve's direct approach was rough for anyone to take.

"I trust you'll tell me what I need to know." She kissed his cheek and followed Pamela and Celine into the kitchen.

At least, she trusted him. He didn't know if he trusted himself to discern when to inform her of certain details. When emotions came into play, it strained his rationale.

"You were the intended target," Steve said. "Why?"

Larry shrugged. "Could be one of a number of things."

"Start listing them," Steve said. "Jackson, is there a pad and pen behind the bar?"

Jackson rose, reached over the counter and retrieved a napkin and pen. "Here you go."

"Thanks." Steve eyed Larry. "Shoot."

"Start with what you told me earlier," Jake said. "Andrew, A.K.A. Mathews."

"You're shitting me." Steve looked under his brow at Larry. "That yellow belly is involved with Greenwood Manor?"

"Works on the manor, yes," Larry supplied. "Connection to the lights, anyone's guess. Today, I went to Randy Millstone's residence. He's a lifelong friend of Andrew Smith. I hope to find a lead on Smith. Millstone ran. I ended up winging him in the shoulder, just a scrape, nothing major, but I got his attention. He told me that Andrew Smith was indeed Allen Mathews. Millstone didn't know why Smith used an alias. Two agents brought Millstone in for questioning while I talked to Charlene."

"Wait, Charlene was at Colonial Beach, too?" Jackson asked.

"Yes, she went to Millstone for the same reason I did, to locate Smith." Larry grimaced. "I wish she hadn't. After he forced his way into her home … and what with him taking a bat to Jake's car, I don't trust him. Who knows what he's capable of? But she's a strong-minded woman who wants to take care of herself."

"Do you think she'll continue not asking for assistance?" Quigley asked, returning from talking to the local police. "You two seem pretty chummy."

Larry gazed at the table. Figuring out what Charlene would do next was anyone's guess. Her independence was one of the numerous things he loved about her. "I don't know. While at Colonial Beach, Smith spotted me, Charlene, and Millstone talking from Millstone's boat. Up to now, Smith has not been apprehended."

"Did the agents get any more information out of Millstone?" Steve asked.

"Nope." Larry sighed. "Smith has something hanging over Millstone. He won't crack. I'm shocked he told me Smith's alias."

"So," Steve lifted the napkin. "We have three scenarios, which could have been responsible for the bullet you took. One, Smith wants you dead because you're with his woman."

Larry hadn't thought of the situation in those terms, but he supposed seeing his ex-wife with someone else could be a kick in the gut.

"Two, us visiting Greenwood Manor yesterday, finding the traps and reflective metal we believe is used for signaling potential buyers, pissed someone off. Since you fell in the hole I'm assuming you've been marked."

"Or three," Jake broke in and knocked his knuckles against the table. "The two leather jackets on the motorcycles were Black Scorpions and Larry wasn't the target, but I was."

"Hell, Jake, the Scorpions could be after you, Larry, or me." Steve slumped against the back of his chair. "If they were the Black Scorpions, they would have shot to kill and you would have been on the top of their kill list. Remember the last time they came through here? They opened fire."

"Keep your voice down," Jake whispered harshly. "I don't want Pamela reliving it."

"They used machine guns, sent bullets flying," Steve said, keeping his voice controlled, yet red hot fire rolled over his tan skin. "Not two single shots."

"I remember. All too clear." Jake's body vibrated with anger.

"How could anyone forget?" Anger laced Jackson's words. "Sent my mom to the Emergency Room and I couldn't get leave." Jackson wiped at his eyes. "Damn, move on."

A moment of silence passed before Quigley spoke. "Don't discount the random guy who shoots into businesses for shits and giggles."

"I'll add that to my list." Steve jotted on the napkin. "Shits and giggles. That's plausible."

Quigley angled his head and glared at him, his jaw ticking.

"Don't go Marine on me," Steve said. "I'm agreeing with you. There're lots of crazies out there."

Simultaneously, Jake's and Steve's phones rang.

Steve listened for a long moment and hung up. "Damn, they got away. No one could confirm the identity of the drivers of the motorcycles. Neither bike had a license plate."

"Missy texted," Jake said. "The Challenger belongs to a Kevin Steele, known connections to the Impalers. His position in the organization is unknown."

Larry laced his fingers together and rested them on the back of his head, and leaned his head into them, using his linked fingers as a pillow. "The Impalers are small time, a group of kids who want to make a small dent in the crime world in order to feel important. They don't want to involve the heavy dogs like the Black Scorpions."

"True, as a whole they don't," Jackson said. "But one bad apple can screw up their whole operation."

"Rona Thomas came by the office today looking for help," Larry said. "She said, something was going down on Greenwood Manor, but she didn't have the details. Tomorrow, she and a man named Hulk will be isolated from the others while they check the fences. She believes Hulk knows the information and wants me to arrest both of them on trespassing to question them."

"She's an Impaler?" Jackson asked.

"Yes."

"That's a start," Jake said. "I'm in."

"I'm waiting for confirmation. I may have to head out in the morning." Steve scoffed.

"Before, Pamela gets back in here," Jackson said. "Jake, what are the chances of the Black Scorpions coming back and retaliating on you and Pamela for killing their leader?"

"No matter where we go, we will have to look over our shoulders. We assumed staying in the area would be the last place they'd look for us."

"Whoever the bad apple is must want something from them," Quigley said.

"There's no proof the Scorpions are in town," Steve refuted. "We can't go on just what ifs."

"Steve," Pamela's voice squeaked. "What are you saying about the Black Scorpions?"

Steve swallowed and eyed Jake, an 'oh shit' look in his eyes. "Sorry, man."

"Jake? Sanjar's men can't be after you, can they?" Pamela's voice was low, nervousness laced in it. "I mean, I know he's dead, but could a follower come after you? After me?"

Jake tugged Pamela toward him until she stood between his legs. "I don't think so. A Black Scorpion is not brave enough to challenge Rambo."

Larry smiled at Jake using the nickname he labeled on Pamela after the ordeal in the mountains.

She laughed and hit his chest. "If The Memory Café gets shot up again, I'll lose my business."

"Not hardly," Jake said. "The food's delicious and everyone loves you. They won't stop eating here because of a couple of bullets."

Charlene slid into the seat beside Larry. "What are they talking about? Are the Black Scorpions back?"

He didn't want to scare her. If the members ever chose to come back and retaliate, Charlene could be in danger, too. Her first-hand dealings with the notorious gang also made her a possible target. Until the FBI could put together enough information and take down the key players of the gang in Louisiana, the risk would remain. Larry scanned the faces of everyone sitting around them. He, Charlene, Pamela, Jake, and Steve all had contact with the gang in one form or another, and would have to continue to look over their shoulders.

Without eyes on the identifying scorpion insignia on the back of their jackets, he couldn't say for certain. In his gut, he believed they were here. "No one has ID'ed a member, no."

"The motorcycles," her voice quivered, "the brown jackets. It looked like them."

"Yes, but looking like them isn't verification."

"Okay." She pulled her lips inward and her gaze went distant. "What about Andrew? How does he tie into all of this? And please don't tell me he's not involved...You told me Andrew used a fictitious name."

Here's where his job got hard—telling people what they least expected. From what he could tell, Charlene didn't have any empathy for Andrew Smith. Still didn't change the fact he was the father of her child. "As I said, I met him on Greenwood Manor the night I ran into you. I didn't know he was your ex-husband at the time."

"

"Has he done something wrong?" Charlene's manner was more of a mother concerned over the father of her son than affection.

"I'm not aware of him doing anything criminal using his alias. As Smith, he's done plenty to warrant an arrest."

Charlene sucked in a gasp.

They hadn't talked about Smith to any length for him to know how she wanted to proceed, if she wanted to charge him or not.

"I don't." She pressed two of her fingers and thumbs against her forehead and rubbed. "Henry... I don't know how his father getting arrested would affect him."

Larry nodded toward Jake. "Either you or Jake could press charges for what he did to the Chevelle. It's Jake's car, but it was on your property when Andrew vandalized it."

"I haven't decided." Jake groaned, his jaw tightening, his frustration clear. "I want to take the bat to him the way he did my car."

Pamela slid her arm under his and squeezed.

Jake gazed at his wife and looked between Larry and Charlene. "I won't. I haven't made a decision about prosecution. My window of opportunity for obtaining a warrant hasn't closed. I'll let you know soon."

Larry nudged his knee against Charlene. "What do you want?"

"Take care of it myself."

"I'm not the only Rambo at this table." Pamela snickered.

Steve grasped the back of the chair behind Celine and twirled her hair between his fingers. "No, you're not."

Celine smiled and leaned into him.

Larry shook his head and focused away from the turbulent couple to Charlene. "I understand, but confronting Smith right now is tricky. Not knowing what he's into, what he might be capable of."

"Do you think he shot at you?" Charlene asked, her eyes going wide.

"Possibly. He could have shot me back as payback for me shooting Millstone."

Charlene whispered. "No. He wouldn't."

Larry groaned. "Are you positive that you can speak so confidently on his behalf? The Challenger that drove by here is registered to a Kevin Steele, a known gang member of the Impalers. Without seeing his features, we don't know for sure if it was Steele or someone else. Smith, acting as Mathews, could have driven it."

"I don't understand," Charlene said, "he's never been violent."

"Money, greed, brings out the worse in people."

Charlene stared at the table and fiddled with her fingers. "He's a stranger, a complete spook to me and Henry."

"Yet he's Henry's father," Pamela said, her voice tender as she touched her stomach.

"You guys are more family to Henry than Andrew ever was," Charlene said, her words tight.

Larry pulled her into him. "We'll work this out."

She nodded and rested her head against his chest. Damn, he hated to admit how it felt to have her lean on him, emotionally and physically.

He scanned the room. The best investigative minds surrounded him. Each in their own right excelled in one area or another. Paul sat toward the end of the table quiet and listening to every word. He was an anomaly.

Between them all, they could resolve this situation quickly. The lights, Smith, and the Impalers were all linked together somehow.

"Consider this," Larry said. "Someone's trying to make a name, become a big dog. They want Steele out of the picture, so they call in tips. If we find enough evidence, we'll arrest him, opening up the head spot. The Impalers are small time crooks. They don't have the loyalty or the hierarchy established yet."

"Sounds logical." Jackson straddled a chair. "Think it's Smith?"

"I do."

Charlene released another gasp, but remained silent.

"Here we are," Marge sang, coming into the room. Her arms were layered with plates.

"Amazes me how you can carry so much at once without dropping them," Jackson said, nodding at his mother's arm.

"Oh, hush before every one of these fall." She smiled.

"Let me help you, Ma." Jackson hopped up and reached for a plate she balanced on her arm.

"No! Don't take that one. They would for sure hit the floor. Here, take this." She handed him one and he grabbed another. He set them on the table in front of Steve and Celine, reached for two more, and placed them in front of Larry and Charlene.

"Hmm, smells heavenly," Charlene said, waving her hand above the plate to bring the steam toward her, breathing in the aroma.

"It should," Marge giggled. "It's your recipe. I'll be right back with the rest."

A moment later, she returned, her arm lined with plates again.

Jackson grabbed two of the plates and set them in front of Jake and Pamela. "Here, mommy-to-be."

"I'm going to be a grandma," Marge said, her voice excited. She brought her hands toward her chest, forgetting she had two plates stacked on her arm.

"Whoa, ma!" Jackson saved one, but not the other.

"Fiddlesticks."

Chicken Parmesan covered her apron and shirt. The plate shattered on the tile floor.

"I'll get the mess for you, ma'am." Quigley knelt and gathered the broken pieces.

"Oh, phooey," Marge sighed. "I'll fix another one."

"No need. I ate before coming tonight." The swinging kitchen doors said Marge didn't hear Quigley or she ignored what he said.

Quigley straightened and tossed the pieces behind the bar in the trashcan. "Where's the mop?"

"It's in the supply closet at the end of the hall," Pamela said. "Thanks."

"It's none of my business, but what's up with you two?" Paul asked between swallows of water. "One minute, you and Quigley are sending each other glares, the next he's puppy-dogging behind you."

"An Afghanistan issue. Water under the bridge." Jackson forked a piece of chicken and stuffed it in his mouth, ending the conversation.

Charlene twisted and kissed Larry's cheek. "I'm glad you didn't get hurt tonight or in the well."

He wrapped a hand around her back. "I still could use R&R."

She giggled. "I can help with that."

"I'm counting on it."

"All better," Marge said, returning with two plates. "Quigley, I won't take no for an answer. Sit and eat."

"Yes, ma'am." Quigley sat next to Jackson's mom.

"Larry, I think you should go to the hospital. You might need a shot." Evidently, Marge hadn't mothered anyone for a while.

Larry held back a smile. "I'm up-to-date on my shots, ma'am."

"You sound like a dog," Quigley laughed and forked a piece of chicken.

Quigley disrespecting what Marge said didn't settle well with Larry and he bristled.

"Q," Jackson ground out.

"Maj, that was too good to pass up. Admit it, it was funny."

Larry shook his head, realizing he was being too serious, and chuckled. "He's right."

"Why does everyone call me ma'am? It's Marge."

"Yes, ma'am," Larry and Quigley said in unison.

Steve clipped his cell back on his belt. "I'm officially on standby. So much for the Director giving me some slack."

Celine's face fell. "I'm done," she said, and disappeared into the kitchen, carrying her plate.

"Storm's a brewing," Paul said, not making eye contact with anyone.

Steve groaned.

The doors busted open. Celine stormed in carrying a tray. Evidently, everyone was done eating.

Larry and Charlene ate faster.

"Figures, you're leaving," Celine screeched. "You probably have a second family."

The storm hit and rolled right over Steve. His face turned beet red and his hands fisted. "Why would I?" He scooted his chair back and straightened. "I can't take any more nagging than what you give me. I'm out of here. Larry, I'll check the cameras in the area after I stop by the police station. Touch base later."

Celine slumped into her chair.

"Why do you give him so much shit?" Paul asked her.

Celine stared at her hands, her expression switching from pissed to confounded. "I don't know."

"Better figure out what you want or you might as well say adios." Paul ate the last bite of the food on his plate and straightened. "Gotta go." He kissed the top of Celine's head. "Ease off. Steve has a tough job." He pecked Pamela on the cheek, ditto Charlene, and then stopped in front of Marge. "As always, your cooking is out of this world. Thank you." He lifted her hand and kissed the back of it. "Night, everyone," he waved. "Congratulations, Pamela and Jake."

"Thanks," Jake said.

Pamela smiled.

Charlene turned toward Larry as he read an incoming text message. "Promise me, we never behaved that way."

Maintaining a relationship took time and energy. The continuous arguing made no sense. For the life of him, Larry couldn't understand why Steve dated Celine when she stayed pissed. Larry twisted, so his knees straddled Charlene's chair, and he grabbed her hands. "I promise, but I need you to swear that you won't get mad at me when I have to go to work at a moment's notice."

Celine made an odd sounding noise.

Charlene gazed between his eyes. He could see the wheels working as she considered their possible dilemma. She didn't want their relationship to end up like Steve's and Celine's any more than he did. "I swear."

"I have something I need to take care of," Larry said, and kissed Charlene on the lips. "I won't be long."

"Okay."

The quicker he took care of this little detail, the faster he could get home to Charlene. Larry untangled himself and eyed Jake. "You coming?"

Jake arched a brow. "You bet."

Chapter Seventeen

Knowing her mother's concern about the shooting at The Memory Café and wanting to cuddle with Henry, Charlene drove to her mother's house.

"Hey, sweetie," Charlene said, walking into the kitchen. Off to the right, the light from the TV shined on her sleepy-eyed son.

"Mommy!" He rushed over, eager and excited as if he hadn't been almost asleep, and grabbed her hand. "We popped popcorn."

Charlene closed her eyes, cherished hearing her son's excited voice, and shoved back the emotions that wanted to erupt. This evening had been much harder on her than she'd realized. And when Jackson insisted he'd follow her home, she dug her feet in. If the Black Scorpions were in town, they wouldn't use their man-power to go after her. She'd done everything they wanted. Her concern stayed with Pamela. In the end, Jackson and Quigley escorted an uptight Pamela home.

Henry squeezed her hand, snapping her out of her musings, and dragged her into the family room.

Doris rose from the armchair, closed the distance between them, and held Charlene so tight she didn't think her mom would ever let go. "I'm so thankful you're okay," Doris whispered, a sob choking her words.

Exchanging kisses on each other's cheek, Charlene said, "I love you, too, Mom," and sat beside Henry on the couch.

He grabbed a bowl of popcorn, put it in between them, and started munching. His eyes were glued to the animated figures flashing on the screen.

Charlene draped an arm around his shoulder and dug into the popcorn. They watched the movie, which ended way past Henry's bedtime, and she glanced down at him sleeping next to her on the couch. His head rested against the crook of her arm and he held the stuffed bear Andrew had given him against his chest.

At the moment, she wished a miracle could bring back the man she'd married, and get rid of the maniac he'd become. Not because she wanted anything to do with him, but because Henry deserved to have his father, to know the man he once was.

A loud snore, comparable to a chain saw, jarred Charlene to look at her mother. Her mother's head rested against the back of the cushioned chair and her mouth hung open, snoring.

Some things would never change. Thank goodness.

Charlene eased away from Henry, scooped him up in her arms, and carried him to the room her mother designated as his. Spiderman didn't cover the walls and bedspread here—Batman did. Last year's obsession.

She pulled the cover up to his neck and gave him a kiss. "I love you, sweetie."

"Love you, Mommy. See you tomorrow." Henry rolled over to his side, his even breathing hardly interrupted.

Charlene made her way back to the family room and kissed her mother's head. "Bye, Mom."

Doris opened an eye and grinned. "I'll bring Henry home in the morning. Have fun, dear."

****

An hour later, Charlene sat at her kitchen table, sipped some wine, and gazed down at the black, silk teddy she wore. The last time she and Larry were together, she hadn't gotten a chance to wear the sexy lingerie. She hoped they'd make good use of it tonight, if he ever showed up.

Celine's dating reservations became clear. Seeing an FBI agent was difficult, their schedule unpredictable. But the way Charlene saw a relationship was simple: if you loved someone, then you'd do whatever was necessary to keep the relationship going.

She smiled. Had she fallen for him? Earlier, she told him she thought she was falling in love with him. Now, she realize there was no thinking, she had. Ever since she met him, her body hummed with need. The last few days, the sensation had deepened, a fact she didn't know how to manage.

A motor sounded in her driveway. She rushed to the door, opened it, and ran into the crisp, cool, night air, not giving any consideration to neighbors seeing her, or if by chance someone else stopped by.

The chuckle that greeted her warmed her heart.

"You are a sight, babe." Larry moved closer until the motion detector light affixed to the corner of her house shined on him. A grin brightened his face.

She ran and jumped into his arms.

He gripped her butt, held her against him, and planted a kiss on her lips. A low masculine moan followed, vibrating his chest and tickling her breasts.

"I'm assuming we're alone," he asked, against her lips.

"Yes."

"I'm sorry it took me so long. I had to follow up on the camera images. Steve had hoped one store in particular had the images we needed to confirm the identity of the drivers."

"Is he the one who texted you?"

Larry nodded. "The quality of the film wasn't good enough to enhance the pictures."

"So—"

He swallowed her next words in a hot, needy kiss, mimicking the act they craved.

Heat rushed through her body, sending a buzz to her core, a need that demanded attention.

"Let's get inside before someone sees us and gets jealous."

Giggling, she rested her head against the hard plains of his chest and thrilled in the stacked muscles in his biceps and shoulders bunching to hold her against him.

He crossed the threshold and kicked the door shut with his foot. "Where to?"

"Bedroom," she breathed and trailed kisses over his neck.

He climbed a few steps and stopped. "I need to get something from the GTO first."

She hadn't noticed the car. "You have a GTO?"

"I do. Does it turn you on?" He waggled his eyebrows.

"Eh…The owner does."

"I'll be right back." He kissed her lips and lowered her.

She intertwined her fingers behind his neck, not letting him release her. "No need. I have a condom."

Lines formed on his forehead. "Just one?"

"A box."

"You're my type of woman." He moved up a couple more steps and groaned, his expression turning serious. "Do you mind if we talk first? I should tell you a few things."

His words pinged around in her mind for a moment. "Okay, but just say no to sprinkling bad mojo on what we have between us."

Lines etched his face and the corners of his mouth and his honeyed eyes filled with worry.

She slid down his delicious body until her feet touched the step. A numbing-tingling awareness ran rampant through her body, even stinging the tips of her fingers. "Okay," she said, trying to control her shaky voice. Just a moment ago she couldn't wait to see him, but now his visit worried her. "Do you want a glass of wine?"

"Does it taste like the peach on your lips?"

She placed a couple fingers on her mouth. "Yeah."

"Okay, but later, I want to sample the wine from other parts of your body."

Goose bumps pricked her skin and she flushed. "I have a case of wine."

He chuckled, tucked her to him, and caressed her arm. "Like I said, you're my type of woman."

His light-heartedness gave her hope whatever he had to say wouldn't be a deal breaker.

They walked into the kitchen. Charlene moved away from his embrace to reach for a sweater, hanging on the hook by the door.

"Are you cold?"

She sensed his appreciative gaze and peeked behind her. "No."

"Then, do you have to wear the sweater?"

She thought it'd be awkward wearing a barely-there nightie while he talked. "No." She dropped her hand. "I don't."

"Good." He closed the distance between them and grasped her waist. The silk glided over her skin, caressing her. "I'll hurry, but first…" He bent, put his mouth on the base of her throat, and nibbled.

She closed her eyes and leaned her head back in response to the pleasure. Her nipples went tight and liquid heat shot to her core. "Larry," she breathed, grasping his shoulders and locking her knees to prevent from falling. "We won't have a conversation if you keep this up."

He eased back and blew out a breath, heat blazing in his eyes. "You're right."

Standing practically naked in front of him, while erotic and thrilling, put her on an uneven playing field. "I have one condition, though."

His mouth curved. "Let's have it."

"I'm at an unfair disadvantage." She slid a finger down his cheek, tapped his chin, and moved lower to his chest. "You can see most of me, but I can hardly see any of you."

His low chuckle sent another shot of liquid heat low in her belly.

"You want me to strip?"

"I do." She grinned.

He slid one shoulder out of his shirt at a time, and tossed his shirt onto a chair. His movements, the heat in his eyes, made it one of the most erotic acts she'd ever seen.

Her eyes traced over every dip and ridge in his abdomen, his chest, before landing on the bruise from where the bullet hit his bulletproof vest. An ache pinched her heart. If he hadn't been wearing the vest…she shook her head, dismissing the thought. She couldn't go there. "I can't believe what went down in the café."

"I know." He sat down in the chair next to hers and shifted until he held the outside of her thighs and his knees straddled hers. "This shooting wasn't as bad as the last. Jackson phoned that none of the bullets hit the building. Last time, the McDowell Brothers had to repair the damage."

He gripped the wine bottle. "Want a glass?"

On her nod, he filled a goblet and handed it to her, then poured his. "To us," he said, lifting his glass.

"To us," she repeated, wondering for the hundredth time what he was about to say.

The intensity in his eyes lessened. The heat in them turned down to a lower simmer, as his expression turned serious. She wasn't ready to stop their fun banter. "You're not done disrobing."

A mischievous sparkle gleamed in his eyes. "I'm not?"

"No. You see, I'm wearing a see-through thong under this nightie. This again puts me at an unfair advantage."

His honey-colored eyes crinkled at the corner as his gaze slid over her body, devouring every inch of her, and his face reddened. "I noticed. And as you'll see, I appreciate the outfit."

She flushed. "Then you better hurry, so we can get to it."

He choked on a sip of wine. "Damn, woman. You're killing me. You're full of surprises." He untied his boots, toed them off, and removed his socks before standing. Undoing his belt, he stopped. "Should I dance to?"

"Okay." She giggled.

"Ha. If only I had some rhythm. You should know I can't dance." He dropped his jeans. Black material puffed up as if a pole lifted it. Her mouth watered and the nerves between her legs jumped with joy.

"Should I remove my briefs?"

Yes, please. "If you do, we won't talk."

His eyes went wide and excited. "No?"

"No. I would be in your lap in a flash."

"I'm game," he said, then cupped a breast and tweaked her nipple.

She grasped his hand, holding him to her, and swallowed harshly. Stimulation made it hard to breathe, to think, but he had something to tell her. "I want, but later."

"Deal." She sat.

He rested in the chair beside her and straddled her knees. The tip of his penis broke free of its confines. "This will be hard."

She giggled, "Already is," and scratched his shaft with the tip of her finger as if it was a cat's chin.

"Whoa." He gripped her wrist. "Not yet."

The electricity in the air snapped around them. She had no idea hanging out with a man could be so fun, exhilarating. "I'm sorry. I can't resist. Go."

The laugh lines around his eyes disappeared. He stared at his glass. "I want to tell you the rest of what happened between my father and me."

By the seriousness of his voice, she sensed how much he needed to be able to talk without interruption. She draped an elbow over the chair's back to prevent temptation.

His eyes drifted to her chest, desire shining before focusing on her face. "I told you I killed my father."

"Yes," she said, a lump parked in her throat and her mouth went dry.

"That's only half true. My father held my hand on the gun. My finger was on the trigger when he applied pressure to discharge it."

Charlene gaped. *What type of man does that to his son?*

No words were spoken for several minutes. She thought maybe he wanted to say more. When he remained silent, she tried to figure out why he withheld the details earlier. "I don't understand. Why didn't you tell me?"

"I didn't want you to think I was weak."

She closed an eye and tried to comprehend his thoughts. "Come again?"

His stern expression softened into a smile. "I plan to, shortly."

She swatted his bare knee at his irony. "Did you think the way the shooting happened makes a difference?"

"The thought crossed my mind. My father held my hand on the gun." Larry rested his elbows on his thighs, his hands hung between his knees. He looked beaten. "How does a man not move his hand?"

"He didn't let you!" Larry's insistence that he was the bad guy in what happened to his father tore at her heart and infuriated her. Larry didn't deserve any of the responsibility. "Why do you blame yourself for what he did?"

"It's as if I shot and killed him."

"Whoa! Back up, big guy." She dropped to her knees in front of him and covered his hands with hers. "You did nothing wrong. He was sick. Any person in their right mind would see what a prize you are. You continually help your mother when she faults you, disowns you. Wait a sec." She kissed his lips and uncurled.

This situation demanded the harder stuff. She reached into the cabinet above the refrigerator and pulled out a bottle and two shot glasses. Tequila would remove Larry's funk. She filled the glasses and set one on the table. "Drink."

He eyed her for a second and downed the liquid.

She handed him the other. "This one, too."

"You're not having any?"

"I'm not the one who needs to shake off a twisted father. Drink."

His throat moved. The glass hit the table with a clink. The wrinkled skin between his eyes smoothed out.

"Better?"

He pulled his lips inward. She craved to touch them, but not until he said his fill.

"That day," Larry's voice was sullen, "when Ben gripped my hand, just before he made me squeeze the trigger, Dad said, "I don't deserve to live. Be a better man than me.""

"What an awful person." Charlene filled the glasses again and placed them on the table, one for him, the other for her, and sat. "Is he the reason you don't like the name Ben?"

Larry nodded. "Which reminds me, did you ever figure out why you called me Ben?"

She had, but admitting it was embarrassing "I vaguely remember. I thought you were the teen who had died at Greenwood Manor."

His eyebrows scrunched. "How'd you know about him?" He waved a hand. "Doesn't matter, but why did you think that?"

"I have no clue. Like everything that night, weird objects, strange occurrences materializing…" She shook her head. "Did you know a witch flew over the moon?"

He smirked.

"Yep. And the rabbit from Alice in Wonderland visited." She giggled. "I'm surprised I remembered. Actually, I didn't until now."

"That wine was potent."

"That it was. Since we're airing stuff out, I have a question."

"Okay." His voice sounded tight.

"Did you put a tracker on my cell or my car?" She didn't remember what source Celine said the guys used, just that they did.

"Huh?" After a short pause, he said, "No. I haven't."

She narrowed her eye and gave him her world-class stink-eye. "Are you sure?"

A low chuckle erupted. "Yes. You should have given Randy the eye. We would have extracted more information sooner."

Laughing, she said, "It works every time." Gratitude for Larry's honesty washed over her at the same time disappointment struck. "I wish I knew why Randy is loyal to Andrew. I doubt he'll ever be forthcoming."

"One day, maybe he will tell you."

Since Randy hadn't yet, she seriously doubted he would. "Has he said any more since his arrest?"

"No. He's been released with the understanding if he made contact with Smith without informing the authorities, charges will be brought against him for aiding and abetting, and obstruction."

This conversation needed to end. She was done talking about anything related to Andrew. She rose.

"Are you going somewhere?" There was an upward lilt in the end of the last word that told her he knew what she was up to.

"I am." Tucking a hand inside the band of her panties, she pulled out a foil packet, and grinned.

"Wow. My dream girl." He straightened, reaching for her.

She pressed a hand to his right shoulder, staying him.

His intake of ragged breath sent a shiver down her spine and jostled the daring minx, craving to be set free. She ripped the packet open.

A hiss of satisfaction escaped him, encouraging her to continue. She pulled his shaft out of his briefs and rolled the condom over him and shifted to remove her panties.

He slid his hands around her waist, stopping her, and wrapped her in his warm comfort. Holding onto her butt, he stood.

"I want you in me," she whispered.

"Always in such a hurry?" He kissed her earlobe.

"With you, yes. Maybe one day the sizzle will die."

"Doubtful." His voice was strained.

A hand towel hung on a cabinet door. He snatched it and covered the chair's seat.

This guy was too much. Everything he did made her heart sway.

Shifting her in his arms, the briefs discarded, he plopped his bare butt onto the towel and set her on his knees. His fluid, skilled actions gave no clue his shoulder was bruised or he had fallen down a hole.

Slowly, he leaned in and claimed her mouth. A gentle glide across her lips, his tongue tickled the gateway to her heart. She opened, welcoming him into her space. Sharing herself with him came so easily.

His tongue swooped into her mouth, bringing warmth, the flavor of tequila, and the mind-blowing taste of Larry. It danced with hers in such a way his earlier allegations that he had no rhythm went out the window. The man had everything she wanted in a guy.

Feathery swirling motions touched the inside of her thigh and moved toward her core. His hands were hot as his fingers teased their way under her panties. Her body throbbed, and she grew wet, needy. She wiggled, trying to entice him into moving faster.

"Always in a hurry," he whispered, repeating his earlier claims, and deepened the kiss even more.

"Only with you," she hissed.

The pressure built, tight as a spring. Ever since he pulled into the driveway, she'd craved him.

His fingers traveled down her seam.

She whimpered. The touch was so exhilarating, she wanted to jump him hard and fast.

He held her hips, held the edge of her panties aside, and guided her down on him. The awareness of him filling her shot through her body, stole her breath, and chased away all thought. She stilled, watching his eyes glaze over.

"You feel so good." He latched onto a nipple, sucking and caressing with his tongue. An uncontrollable yearning flooded her body and threatened to explode if he didn't stroke her straightaway. She dug her fingers into his scalp, tossed her head back, and gave her body over to him.

He sucked her through the silky, thin fabric. Every stroke, kiss, and nibble heightened the excitement in her already overheated body.

She melted. The ecstasy overwhelmed her. "How can any person feel so good?" The comment escaped on a whisper, barely loud enough to hear. But he did, for his chest came forward, flattening her breasts against him. The intimacy of him wanting to be so close increased the mountain of pressure.

"I love you," the words flew out of her mouth before she considered what she said.

He eased back, studied her for a long moment. "I love you, too." Sincerity burned from his gaze as the words had escaped his lips, reaching into her chest and gripping her heart, but apprehension snuck its way into her mind. When she said she thought she was falling in love with him previously, he'd remained quiet. What had changed in the short time?

She diverted her gaze to their joined bodies, trying to grasp reality. Could the throes of passion convince him to say the words of endearment?

"Babe, look at me." Larry cupped her cheeks until her eyes locked on his. "I'm not blowing smoke. I'm in love with you. Earlier, I couldn't wrap my mind around what I was feeling. I don't say the words lightly, never have. Actually, I've never spoken them to another person."

Whoa. Charlene's heart boomeranged against her chest. Her eyes watered and her body tightened around his shaft.

"Hello!" Larry's eyes lit on their connection. "What was that? Miracle fingers?"

She smiled. "My acceptance of what you said."

"Ah, babe."

He gripped her waist, rocked his hips, thrust harder, faster, in and out of her core until his eyes rolled back in his head. She met him thrust for thrust and exploded with him.

She rested her head on his shoulder and caught her breath. "Wow."

"Yeah," he said between pants.

They didn't move…in the chair…in her kitchen. She'd never be able to look at the room or furniture again without getting a warm flush. Tonight, she realized something phenomenal. For the first time, she truly fell in love.

He stroked her hair out of her face and kissed her lips. "I need to discard the condom."

Barely able to move or see through the sexual haze they had created, she eased off his chest.

He guided her up and off him until she stood.

"The bathroom is to the left of the door."

"Be right back."

Muscles loose, body sedate, she could curl up and go to sleep, but the tingle residing between her legs wasn't ready to give up the ghost yet.

She uncorked another bottle of wine and headed toward the hall as Larry reappeared.

"Where are you going?" he asked, stepping out of the bathroom.

"We have a date." She held up a blue bottle. "You game?"

"Hell, yeah." He swiped the tequila and followed.

Chapter Eighteen

Larry barged into the cinderblock FBI office, holding a scruffy teenager's handcuffs. The boy known as Hulk stood a good three inches taller than Larry. His hair hung around his neck in dreadlocks.

Jake followed, escorting Rona, the pint-sized girl who came into Larry's office, requesting this meet and greet.

Larry pushed open the door to the interrogation room and moved forward. Hulk dug his feet in and leaned his weight into Larry. "No, man."

Hulk hadn't resisted when he arrested him on the trespassing charge. He'd almost gone voluntarily. So what gives? "Get in there!" Larry forced him inside, showed him a chair, and closed the door behind him as he headed toward coffee on the far end of the room, near Missy's desk.

This part of his job, he hated…being tired, grumpy, and having to interview a man when he just wasn't feeling like it. Larry unclipped his cell from his belt, hoping Charlene had tried to contact him and shine a little brightness on his gloomy day. *No messages.*

Jake snatched a Styrofoam mug from the corner of the break table and filled it. "Are you ready to quit from the FBI and work for Old Towne Detectives?" Jake asked Missy.

A growl escaped Larry.

Her eyes bugged out. "Not if he's gonna be a bear."

Jake smacked Larry on the back. "Don't let Mr. Personality scare you away. I'll protect you."

Larry studied Jake over the brim of his mug. "How can you be so chipper?"

Jake shrugged.

The coffee slipped down Larry's throat and warmed his insides. The caffeine stoked his adrenaline. "Nice and strong. Thanks, Missy."

"You're welcome."

Jake jutted his chin upward. "So, what did you decide?"

Larry didn't want to deal with this bullshit right now. As much as he hated to admit it, if Missy preferred to switch to the private sector, he wouldn't stand in her way. "If you want to work for this lug, go ahead. I'll support you, but know you'll be missed."

"Won't you be joining the agency, too?" she asked.

She'd already made up her mind. *Damn.* The thought had occurred once or twice, but at this point he didn't have a reason to switch jobs. "I have no plans."

"Don't worry, he'll be working with me again soon." Jake winked at Missy and turned to Larry. "Pow wow in your office?"

"In a sec." Larry grabbed his phone messages off Missy's desk and scanned the department. "Thanks for covering. I wished the higher ups would hire us an assistant. Where is everyone?"

"An issue, up north, a car bombing in Crystal City."

"Why didn't I receive word?"

"I don't know. Check your phone, make sure you have service."

He pulled out the phone again. The 'no service' symbol showed. "Damn, phone."

"Turn it off for a while. In the meantime, I'll write up an order for a new one."

Missy was a gem. "Thanks."

Inside Larry's office, Jake reclined in Larry's chair, his ankles propped on the corner of the desk. His head slumped back mouth open. The coffee cup balanced in his lap.

The jackass had fallen asleep.

"Wake up!" Larry slapped the top of Jake's shoe.

Jake jerked and darted his coffee cup off to the side, as the hot liquid splashed over his hand. "Crap." He grabbed a couple tissues from the box on the corner of the desk and dabbed his skin. "Did Hulk give any useful information?"

"Not yet. He's a scared teen. I'm hoping after he stews in the room alone for a few minutes, he'll spill like Rona said."

"Well, let's get this over. My bed is calling my name. A nap is in order."

The sixth sense Larry experienced at Greenwood Manor thundered into his mind. "Something's off."

Jake's gaze snapped to Larry's. "I've got the same feeling."

Larry snatched a soda and a pack of donuts from the snack area and headed into the interrogation room holding Hulk. He tossed them on the table and sat next to Jake, facing Hulk. "Hungry?"

Hulk eyed the treats next to his cuffed wrists then shot his gaze to him. "What do you want?"

"Answers. Why have you been lurking around Greenwood Manor?"

"Don't got to tell you anything!"

Larry rested back in his chair and sipped more coffee. "You're right, you don't. I don't have time to sit in here if you're not talking. That means no deals will be made. Make no mistake. We will discover what's going on at Greenwood Manor. When we do, you'll be charged."

Hulk's jaw tightened.

Larry knocked his knuckles on the table and stood. "Keeping quiet won't save your ass from what's about to go down on the manor. Think about it. If Rona tells me everything I need to know, she'll get the deal, not you. I hope you enjoy your time in prison."

"Sweat and vomit don't do it for her." Jake added. "She'll talk."

"Just like the girl. She complains about everything," Hulk said, wringing his hands together and diverting his eyes to the floor.

"At least she'll have a deal." Larry eyed him and waited for him to unload. When he didn't, he patted Jake's back and moved toward the door.

"Wait." Desperation laced Hulk's voice. "I'll talk."

Jake removed the cuffs from Hulk's wrists, scooted the soda and donuts closer to him, and settled back in his seat. "Okay, talk."

Nervous energy bounded off of Hulk. He removed his Impalers cap and threw it on the table. "I don't want any part of it."

The guy talked in riddles. "Part of what?" Larry asked.

"Monk's boss. That's all I know."

"Explain." Jake's gaze narrowed to slits.

Hulk shoved a miniature donut into his mouth. Powder covered his lips and chin. "Mouse wants to take over."

Man, Larry hoped they'd didn't have to get rough with this guy. "Come on. Stop talking in riddles." He glared. "What's there to take over?"

"Monk was easy to work for, but with Mouse trying to take over…" Hulk shook his head and popped the top on his soda, "it's got hard."

Impalers had a boss. News to Larry. "Explain."

Hulk swallowed. "They're fighting. Mouse says, just wait, I have back up that will take care of that asshole."

"Monk's the asshole?" Jake asked.

"Yeah." Hulk nodded. "And Monk says that fuckwad doesn't know who he's dealing with."

"Does Mouse have a name?" Larry scooted out a chair and sat.

Hulk's dark beady eyes darted between them. "You don't know jack shit that's goin' down over there, do ya?"

When they remained quiet and glaring, he gawped. It was almost comical the expressions that crossed his face, from *you've-got-to-be-kidding* to *I'm-screwed*, ending with his mouth turned down and his shoulders slumping. "Mathews, Allen Mathews."

For Charlene and Henry's sake, Larry hated that his hunch about Andrew was right.

"It's Rona you should be talking to," Hulk muttered, spit flying out of his mouth. "She's screwing the old fart."

"What about the marijuana? Where is it grown?" Larry drilled.

"I don't know."

"Don't know?" Jake straightened and braced his hands on the table in front of him "Or won't tell?"

Hulk's face turned ashen. Sweat beaded on his forehead.

"Better spill," Larry advised.

"I don't know where it is now. They had it in an underground room, but they made me load it onto the back of a truck. That's all I know."

"Who are they?" Larry asked in a calm tone when he felt everything but. Getting the information out of the guy was like his mother listening to reason. It just didn't happen.

"The two cock-fighters we've been talking about and some others."

Jake cleared his throat, obviously trying to keep his composure, too. "Who's Kevin Steele?"

Hulk groaned. "Man, I can't give up my crib."

"You better or you'll be finding a whole new bed to sleep in," Larry said.

Several minutes went by. Tears watered the guy's eyes. "Monk."

Larry and Jake eyed each other.

One mystery down, several to go, Larry released a breath. "Why the small metal sheets nailed to the trees in the field closest to the road?"

"I don't know. I'm not aware of the reasons. I'm just told what to do."

"Uh-huh," Jake said, "Did you dig the holes, too?"

"And cage snakes in them?" Larry asked.

Tears slid down Hulk's face. "What? No, man. I didn't touch no snake. I dug the holes with the tractor and post-hole digger. Others helped dig the rest by hand. Man, I didn't do anything wrong!"

"We'll be back," Jake said, rising. "The cuffs will stay off but the door is locked, so don't try anything."

They left the room. Jake swiped another packet of donuts and a soda from the snack area and opened the door to speak to Rona.

Her hands were cuffed in front of her. Tears mixed with mascara streaked her face. The hood that had covered her purple and pink hair rested on her back. The Impalers hat lay on the table. She eyed them through long eyelashes and thick makeup. "Why am I handcuffed?"

Jake unlocked her cuffs and gave her the food and drink. "Tell us about your boyfriend, Allen Mathews."

Her eyes shifted from one to the other. "He's not my boyfriend."

"Figured he was since you're banging him," Jake said, sitting down beside her.

For several minutes she stared at the donuts in her hand, then finally, she peeled off the wrapper and ate one. "We've been seeing each other."

"It's like this," Larry sat in a chair across the table, "either you're honest with us or you'll go down with Mathews."

"He's not involved in anything illegal."

"That's not what you told me yesterday."

"Well, yesterday, he scared me. He was talking all crazy and shit. We're not doing anything criminal."

Larry arched a brow. "Come again? You're growing marijuana illegally."

She stared at her clutched hands. "He's not like the others."

"How's that?" Jake asked. "He's competing with Monk to be boss."

She played with the wrapper. "I want a lawyer."

"Do you think you need one?" Jake asked. "We're not pressing charges...not at the moment."

"I haven't done anything wrong." She turned to Larry. "I thought we were working together."

"Not telling me everything is lying by omission," Larry said. "You wanted my help. I did what I said I would, then I find out that you and Mouse are an item. Care to explain why you didn't tell me?"

"I couldn't do the ratting."

Larry studied her for a few moments. What she said made sense. She didn't look the type to be mixed up with criminal activity, neither did Hulk. "I believe you,"

Larry said. "But the people you consider friends will pull you farther down the hole to hell. If you want out, level with us, we'll help."

She studied them, the same way Hulk did before he started talking. These kids were amateurs. Probably came from dysfunctional families and ended up at the wrong place at the wrong time. The same thing could have happened to him so easily.

"Allen has a plan to remove Monk as leader. What he said scared me."

"Which is?" Jake leaned closer, his eyes narrowed to slits.

"Mathews is waiting for the big deal to go down and hopes the FBI will show up."

"What's the big deal?" Jake asked.

"I don't know." Her head moved so fast, it vibrated.

"You're holding back," Larry demanded. "Coughing up what you know can only help you."

She searched their faces for a few seconds. "Some guys, bad ones, are coming in today." Her voice trembled. "Allen said The Impalers needed to beef up their game. Some rough guys, mean ones, are arriving from Louisiana."

Larry's sixth sense intensified a couple of notches, creating an unusual hollowness in the pit of his stomach.

"What guys?" Jake's shoulders went rigid, his jaw ticked, and the pulse in his neck jumped with the sudden strain in his voice.

"The Black Scorpions."

"Mother-fucker!" Jake bolted upright, fists clenched as he darted out of the room.

Adrenaline raced through Larry's system as he charged out the door after Jake. The Black Scorpions had played havoc with Jake's family. Afraid his friend would go off halfcocked, Larry motioned to Missy to stay alert and headed into his office where Jake paced.

"Settle down." Larry said, closing the door. "You won't be able to think rationally if you don't."

Jake whipped around, his eyes red. "Don't you think I know that?"

"Get Pamela out of town," Larry said, his voice deadly calm. "Stay focused."

"You're right." Jake sucked in a deep breath, released it, and nodded.

Larry stood by as Jake called his father-in-law then Pamela. The strain in his friend's voice when he told Pamela he had confirmation that the Black Scorpions would arrive in town if they hadn't already, nailed Larry in the gut and reminded him he'd best call Charlene. The odds were doubtful that the Scorpions would mess with her, but figuring out what they'd do was playing the slot machines. You never knew what you'd get.

****

Last night, the things they did…What Larry did… Charlene sighed. The wine…his tongue…she melted and couldn't put a complete thought together. Her body tingled. She curled her arms around her pillow, pulling it under her naked breasts and touched something soft and velvety.

Her heart skipped a beat. Not one rose, but a handful lay in a bundle on the pillow Larry had used last night.

In no time, he managed to melt her resolve to keep her distance. Surprisingly, she was okay with that.

She lifted the roses, breathed in the fragrant scent, and wished Larry hadn't been called out in the wee hours concerning a case. After he received a phone call, he'd given her one hell of a kiss that would have knocked her socks off if she had been wearing any, and left.

Her cell rang, interrupting her blissful musings. She pushed the talk button. "Hello."

"Charlene!"

Hearing the gruff voice, she flipped and sat straight up. Her muscles went rigid. How'd Andrew get her number? "What do you want?"

"The money."

"This is bullshit," Charlene raged back. "I don't have any."

"Char, you know your face twists when you lie. It's not a becoming look for you."

Footsteps sounded in the hall.

Oh, shit!

Panic tripped her heart into a sprint, pumping an excessive amount of energy to her feet. She jumped out of bed, raced to the door, hitting it with a thump and managing to slam it closed on Andrew.

"Give up, Charlene. I don't want to hurt you, but I will come through this door one way or another." His heavy breathing sounded through the wood.

She braced the heels of her feet against the bench at the end of her bed and pressed her hands against the closed door. "Get out!"

Cool air drifted over her body. She glanced down at her naked form.

Double Shit!

Her nightie from last night dangled off the corner of her bed. Her phone was who knows where.

The door edged inward.

She pushed harder against it.

"I'm coming in."

She locked her arms.

The breathing on the other side disappeared.

Where'd he go? She eased her ear to the door. What he planned lit into her mind—he was ramming the door. She couldn't stop him from busting in and raced for the nightgown.

The door flew open and Andrew fell into the bench. "Son of a bitch!"

She eased backwards. "Get out!"

He righted himself and his gaze slid down her body. "Nice jammies."

Crap! She grabbed the see-through nightie she'd worn last night, not the cotton one. Where the hell was her brain? She yanked her robe off the chair and covered her body. "How'd you get in?"

Darkness covered his face and his nostrils flared. "I want the money."

"Get out of my house!" she shot back.

"The money," he demanded, his fists clenching. "There's money due me for the sale of our restaurant."

The man was dense. "You dropped the ball. The bank foreclosed. I didn't get any."

"You're lying. That Jameson fellow bailed you out."

Who told Andrew about the stupidest mistake she'd ever made? Randy didn't even know everything she did where the restaurant was concerned. "He didn't bail me out!"

"And you have the award money."

"I bought the house for your son and me. I have no money left."

His eyebrows dived into angry slashes. "I'd believe you, if I thought you were honest."

"I'm not the liar," she panted.

"Really?" He shifted toward her bathroom. "You're sleeping with an agent, the agent that shot Randy."

She didn't want to chat about her personal life.

"Your silence is confirmation."

"It's none of your business!"

He stepped inside the bathroom and held up the trashcan.

Her throat stung and her mouth went dry.

"You've turned into a whore!"

The situation turned from bad to worse. "Get out!" She scanned the room for a weapon.

He threw the can on the floor, the contents spilled over. Several condoms fell out, the ammunition that would send Andrew over the edge.

"You're fucking him! You slut!" His pupils grew wide and his face turned red.

She'd never seen him this angry, but she couldn't back down. If she did, he'd think he could control her like he had when they were married. She pressed her lips together and returned his glare.

"I ought to kick your ass. If you weren't the mother of my son, I would."

He stormed toward her so fast she backed up without thinking.

He gripped her shoulders and shook her. His face an inch away, he stormed, "You're crazy. The agent is using you to get to me." His last word came out on a sullen note.

"Why would anyone use me to reach you? We're not married, not living together. I don't even like you."

His expression pinched.

Andrew's questionable behavior turned desperate. Why? "Why would an agent be searching for you?"

He stiffened. A flash of tenderness crossed his hard features. "I've done some stuff I'm not proud of. Put you and Henry in a bad situation. I'll get us out of it soon, but I need the money."

What the hell was he talking about? "There is no us!"

The jumping pulse in his neck clued her in that he was about to do something really irrational. Telling her feet to move, get the hell out of the way, and have them listen was a maneuver her brain and body couldn't finagle.

Anger raged in his expression. A vein popped up on his forehead. He grabbed her throat and squeezed.

She grasped his wrist, hit at him. "St-o-p," she huffed out.

"Tomorrow. I want the money tomorrow."

"Fu-ck yo-u!" She spit in his face and jerked her knee upward.

His grip lessened.

Heart beating double time, she darted out the door, banging the door closed behind her, and ran down the steps for the bats.

They were gone.

Ugh!

She raced to the kitchen for her mother's car keys.

Gone.

"Charlene!" Andrew yelled. His footsteps pounded down the stairs. "I promise I won't hurt you."

His voice was tender and sweet, but she wasn't staying around to see if he meant it.

She raced for the kitchen door. The doorknob was gone.

Her heart fell to her stomach. Fear crashed into her gut. For the first time, she was truly scared of her ex-husband.

Andrew grabbed her arm. "Please, Char." He spun around until she faced him. "I shouldn't have touched you. I'm in a bad situation. If I don't get the money, I'm a dead man."

Her chest heaved, sucking in air and coming down from the adrenaline rush. Her nerves stayed on edge, but the fear that had vibrated through her body had died down. "I don't believe you."

He spread out his fingers in front of him. "Please trust me."

"Like you told me to trust you the day I said 'I Do'." She forced a laugh. "That's rich. For you to think I'll believe you again, you're kidding yourself."

"Consider it...please. I'm at your mercy." He marched toward the front door. "Tomorrow morning," he said over his shoulder.

She followed.

"Oh, yeah," he smirked. "Tell lover boy, payback's a bitch."

Rage ignited her blood. She charged after him. "Tomorrow."

The door closed in her face. She locked it and looked out the window to Andrew driving away in an Impala. *The car used in the shooting?*

What to do darted around in her brain before alarm settled in. *Henry!*

She raced up the steps and searched for her phone. A glow from underneath the curtain grasped her attention before the theme music to *Spider-Man* played.

She snatched the phone. "Mom." Her breath rushed out in pants.

"Dear, is everything okay?" Doris asked.

If her mom had to ask that question, then she and Henry were fine. Charlene sucked in a deep breath and released it. "It is now." She gripped the edge of the curtain and peeked out the window.

All four of her mother's car tires had been slashed.

Her phone beeped. "Mom, I'll call you back in a second. Don't go anywhere."

She clicked the phone. "Larry?"

"Tomorrow at 9. Charlene," Andrew said and the line went dead.

Heart thundering in her chest, she hit the button and called Larry, her fingers shaking.

Voice mail came on.

She tried Jake. No answer.

"Damn it!"

The cell rang. "Larry?" she shouted into the phone.

"No, it's Celine. I'll be there in a few."

Celine was coming there. Why?

"You sound upset," Celine said. "Did Larry not show last night?

"Uh." Charlene's mind was scrambled. She tried to figure out what to say in the midst of her confusion. Telling Celine Andrew was here would only make her friend act hastily and possibly put her in danger. "He did. I'm trying to reach him this morning."

"Well, do you need a ride to Greenwood Manor to pick up your car?"

She'd forgotten about the arrangements she and Celine made last night before she left the cafe. She didn't know what she was in for today with Andrew, but not having a car wasn't good. "Yeah, yeah, I do. Thanks, Celine."

They disconnected and she called her mom back. Doris answered on the first ring. "Hi, honey, what's going on?"

"Andrew was here again," Charlene said, fighting back tears.

A gasp came across the line. "No."

"He still wants money."

"Have you called Larry?"

"I tried, but his phone went to voice mail," Charlene said. "I'm sure Larry will call as soon as he can."

"Maybe you should phone the police."

"I don't know." Charlene swiped her forehead and her robe gaped. She better get dressed before Celine showed up. "Celine's taking me to get my car. If Larry hasn't called me by the time I get back, I'll call the police."

"Okay."

"Is Henry awake?"

"He was. Right after he ate breakfast, he fell asleep watching *Spider-Man*."

Charlene sighed. "I kept him up too late last night. Give him a kiss for me. I'll be over after I get back."

"Be careful," Doris said, concern reflected in her voice.

"I will."

The doorbell sounded.

"Gotta go, Mom, love you."

"Love you, too."

Charlene disconnected, dressed in blue jeans, a shirt and tennis shoes before grabbing her spare car key off her dresser. She rushed downstairs and peeked through the window. Seeing it was Celine, she opened the door. "Hi, Celine. Thanks so much."

"No problem. Driving to the country will relax me as long as I don't have any more flats."

Charlene settled into the passenger seat of the Camaro and rested her head against the headrest. For a long moment, she stayed that way as her breathing evened out and the adrenaline fueling her blood into hyper alert slowed.

Before she knew it, Celine turned past the Greenwood Manor's stone posts.

Charlene's stomach twisted. The strobe lights and odd noises from the other night flashed in her mind, haunting her. From what Larry had said, the drug in the wine played tricks on her brain. She believed that, but still the images were so vivid it was hard to put the incident into perspective.

Celine parked beside Charlene's Hyundai.

"Do you mind if we look around a bit?" Charlene asked, climbing out of the car. Larry had said Andrew worked at the farm under an alias. If so, maybe she could figure out what he was into.

"Sure, I could use some fresh air, but I'm stuck wearing flip-flops."

Celine joined her on the sidewalk and a shoulder bumped her. "How was staying here the other night?"

"Can I tell you something without you believing I'm crazy?"

Celine gave a single nod.

"The other night, I saw strange things."

Celine raised a sculpted eyebrow. "Yeah? Like what?"

Charlene figured she'd start with one incident and judge Celine's reaction before telling her the more peculiar things. "I saw the lights the guys talked about." They followed the sidewalk passed the back door and stopped. Charlene pointed to the front field. "Out there."

Celine scanned the area. "Honestly, the place gives me the creeps. At the same time, it's fascinating. Want to take a walk? We'll stay clear of the fence row where Larry and Jake said the traps were."

How wise was it for them to trounce around the place when gang members, snakes, and traps had been seen? Yet, she really wanted to put an end to the mystery that surrounded Andrew. "I need to figure out what Andrew is up to."

Celine nodded. "I can understand that. He is, after all, the father of your child." She nodded toward the field. "Do you think the answer is out there?"

"I don't know."

A low rumble came from somewhere in the distance.

"What's that noise?"

"I—" Celine's words broke off and the color drained from her face.

Adrenaline spiked through Charlene's blood stream. Men with guns sped toward them riding four-wheelers. "Oh, shit!"

"No...don't say oh, shit," Celine snapped. "Oh, shit means something really...really bad is about to happen"

Two more four-wheelers came from the sides of the house.

Charlene raised her hands and pressed her back against Celine's. "They think we're trespassing."

"We are." Celine's voice rose. "I told you when Larry appears, something big is going down."

"Oh, shit."

****

Rage bolted through Andrew's veins and he fisted his hands. His eyes narrowed on the man he'd fought against for the leadership of the Impalers for the last month. The battle turned personal as soon as Monk sent his goons after Charlene. "She's my wife, you imbecile. Let her go."

"Mouse...mouse...mouse." The beady eyed man shook his head, making a tsking noise. "You're out of your league now. Imposing your authority on my crib won't work."

Andrew thought about the Black Scorpions arriving today, how the gang members would have his back. "I have backup coming. You'll regret ever tangling with me."

"I already do." Monk shifted his hat on his head and rubbed a fresh scar above his right eye. "Thanks to you, I've had dealings with a group I never wanted to come in contact with. The Black Scorpions are ruthless, vile, and don't give a shit about anyone. And look what you did."

Andrew swallowed around the lump lodged in his throat. No one was supposed to know about them.

"You call the sons-o'-bitches to come here and try to take over my small-time operation. You fucking tell them that if they take the reins from me that you'll hand them over an FBI agent." Monk slid another hand over his face and tugged a gun out of the back waistband of his pants and aimed it at Andrew. "How the fuck could you? I gave you a job. I knew you were power hungry, but to call them? Try to deal with them? You just signed the entire group's death certificates."

'Oh-fucks' pinged around in Andrew's skull.

"Now, I have to try and deal with them. Our gang will have to disperse and hope to hell the Black Scorpions won't track us down. I'm already missing two people. Rona and Hulk didn't return from checking the fences."

Andrew looked around the underground room Monk forced him into, the scent of dirt and weed making his head spin. The plants that filled the room had disappeared, leaving a table and a chair. If Monk decided to leave Andrew in there, no one would ever find him.

His mind flicked on his sweet Charlene wearing the see-through nightie this morning. Why had he ever threatened her? When she arrived at the Manor, Monk had gotten all weirded out and forced Andrew into this pit of a hole. "Let me go. I'll straighten this out."

Monk's brown eyes lit into Andrew. "You've got that right. You will iron this out, but on my terms. Push the button on the wall behind you."

Andrew twisted. A small brown knob, almost the color of the ply board, was an inch from the ceiling.

"Push it!" Monk ordered, and thrust the gun at him.

Andrew did. The door opened into a smaller room, he'd never seen.

"Get in there!"

Monk might as well kill him then let him rot in the hole. "No."

"If you want to see your wife again, you'll do as I say. Between you and her, somehow, someway I hope to get the gang out of this fucking mess." Monk's gaze went distant before shooting back on Andrew. "Now, move!"

Andrew stepped into the room and stared at the empty cell, his gut plummeting. He fucked up. "Come on, Monk. I'm sorry."

"Are you sorry you stole my car? Used it to shoot a federal agent? You set my ass up. I won't only be dealing with the Scorpions but the fucking FBI. Because of you, I have to do things I promised my mom I wouldn't ever do. I'm not made for this type of shit."

Andrew twisted toward the guy that he became close to in order to use. "Really man. I am sorry."

"You know, you're not dumb, but in all your scheming there's one thing you didn't count on."

Andrew arched a brow.

"My brother is a Black Scorpion, you stupid fuck."

Andrew saw the club swinging at him a second before sharp pain pierced his skull. Darkness invaded his vision and his body went limp.

Chapter Nineteen

Charlene swallowed, trying to shove down the golf ball-sized lump in her throat. It didn't work. Four-wheelers surrounded her and Celine on all sides. Fear barreled through her system while adrenaline shot through her veins, leaving her antsy and shaky.

The drivers, wearing Impalers hats, flannel shirts, and blue jeans parked the butt of their guns on their thighs glared at them.

"Roach, get them!"

Charlene followed the direction of the woman's voice to a four-wheeler off to the right. A petite woman with purple hair, cascading around her shoulders, eyed her.

"I'll help." A shaggy, brown-haired man with a porker-sized belly rolled off his seat and stormed toward them, a rifle in his hand.

Nerves wracked through Charlene's body. "Support me," she whispered over her shoulder to Celine and intertwined their arms.

The closer Roach came, the more foreboding he looked. A wad of something stuck under his bottom lip. His face was caked in dirt as if he hadn't washed in ages. "Let's go!" he shouted, motioning with his gun.

Charlene and Celine didn't move.

Roach gripped the gun in one hand and reached for Charlene with the other.

She leaned back against Celine, kicked out her foot, hitting his stomach, and flung out her other leg. Charlene's foot connected with his wrist.

He grunted, dropped his gun, and slumped to the ground.

"Run, Celine!" Charlene yelled and darted into the open field at the back of the house toward a rock pile, just behind a fence.

Lungs burning and muscles screaming, she dug the soles of her shoes into the spongy ground, pushed harder, and raced through the knee-high grass.

Reaching the pile, she grabbed a hand-sized rock, and pivoted.

A hand covered her mouth and an arm pinned her stomach to a fat one, stopping her movement. "Don't." Foul-smelling breath hit the back of her neck and drifted over her face. Fear shot through her. She hauled her arms backwards and plunged the rock into Roach's head.

He grunted, but held onto her left arm.

She smashed the heel of her hand into his nose. Bones cracked.

The grip loosened.

She shoved off him and darted for the wooden fence.

"Bitch, don't run or I'll shoot." Roach's voice was a little more than breath, but the tone was deadly.

Charlene stopped half way up the boarded fence. Guilt and regret gnarled its way up her spine, as she couldn't leave Henry motherless. She jumped to the ground and faced the man, sitting on a pile of rocks and pointing a gun at her, blood dripping from his nose and the dark circles forming under his eyes.

"You boys can't do anything right." With her eyes fixed on Charlene, the purple-haired woman approached, tugging a thin piece of plastic from her pocket and spun Charlene by the shoulder. "You, missy, will behave yourself." The woman looped the plastic around Charlene's wrists. "You run. You get hurt."

The binding tightened. The plastic dug into her skin.

"Understand?"

Charlene nodded.

"That's my girl." The woman patted Charlene on the arm and looked down at the man Charlene bloodied. "For fuck's sake. Roach, go help." The woman pointed to the field off to the right.

Charlene glimpsed a barefoot Celine ducking into the woods. She must have run right out of her flip-flops. A thin man, with hair pulled back in a ponytail, chased her on his four-wheeler.

"Damn, Lavender, my head hurts" Roach whined, pressing a palm to his head.

"I don't give a God damn what ails you. Go."

Roach braced the butt of the gun on the ground to right himself then motioned for Charlene to go to the four-wheeler. "Move," he hissed, his eyes narrowing into angry slits.

The sound of engines roared. In the next field over, three four-wheelers sped toward the wood line, stopped, and the drivers rushed into the woods.

Tears stung Charlene's eyes. *Please be okay.*

"Now," Roach screamed from the seat of the four-wheeler.

"I'd do what he said, honey," Lavender said, patting a gun she cradled to her chest.

Reluctantly, Charlene moved toward the four-wheeler. The balancing act of steading herself on one foot without the use of her hands made swinging her leg over the seat behind him that much harder. Tobacco scent, dirt, and old sweat hit her nose. She gagged.

"I smell like petunias," Roach laughed, started the motor, and drove through an opening in the fence to the edge of the woods to the other four-wheelers.

They reached the tree line. Roach didn't move, just sat there letting the motor idle. In the distance, voices erupted. A moment later, Celine's beautiful face came into view. Charlene's heart plummeted. Celine had a bruised eye, fat lip, and blood dripped out of her nose.

Tears threatened to escape, as Charlene pulled her lips inward. This whole situation was her fault. If she and Celine had just gotten Charlene's car and left, instead of nosing around to find out more about Andrew, none of this would have happened.

Two men clutched each of Celine's elbows and a third trailed them. Scratches and scrapes marred their faces. A third man with two cuts on his forehead and a bleeding nose trailed them.

"What the hell happened to you fellas?" Roach asked. "Did you run into a tree?"

The one with the cuts on his forehead jutted his chin. "Probably the same thing that happened to your head."

Charlene's mouth gaped and she gazed at Celine. A darkness etched into Celine's face, her jaw tightening. The sweet, carefree person Charlene grew to love had disappeared. In its place was a person with dark eyes and hard features. Celine looked ruthless and ready to kill. Judging by the scars on the three guys, she'd tried.

"You putz!" Lavender yelled, stopping her four-wheeler beside them. "Why'd you mark her up?"

"She fought us! Look at my face," Albert yelled, binding Celine's wrist. He grasped her shoulders and shoved her onto the seat of a four-wheeler.

"Don't be a pansy, Albert," Lavender snapped, gunning the engine and taking off.

The rest of the ATVs trailed.

Charlene grabbed the bar in the back of the four-wheeler and hung on. The bumps and dips in the rough terrain made the idea of her falling not only possible but probable.

The scent of pine, hay, and the smell of musky animals intensified, upsetting her stomach.

They rode through three fields and passed numerous buildings. Roach made a sharp turn, almost tossing her off, and stopped near a two-story rustic building in the midst of a thick grove of pine trees.

"You know what to do," Lavender said. "Meet back at the shop."

She and two other ATVs drove away.

Roach climbed down, grasped Charlene's arm, and jerked her off the truck. Albert did the same to Celine.

Through tall grass, the foursome made their way to the opening of the building. Cow manure turned dirt covered the ground. Charlene's tennis shoes sank in, and flakes of dirt seeped over the edges of her shoes.

If Celine didn't like the feel of the composite against her bare feet or was grossed out by what they walked in, she didn't make it known. Her expression was stoic, yet distant.

"Up there." Albert yanked Celine to a ladder, leading to a small hole in the ceiling. "Go!"

Celine looked up at the ladder. "I can't climb with my hands tied."

The men glanced at each other before Albert tugged a knife from his pocket. He cut Celine's tie, then Charlene's.

Celine climbed the few rungs, braced her hands on the floor above and hauled her body out of sight. Albert went next.

"Your turn," Roach snarled. He touched Charlene's back and nudged her forward. "Move!"

She grasped a rung, made her way to the next floor, and scanned the interior. While the slats in the floor butted up to one another, the wallboards did not. Gaps of various sizes separated them. No windows, just a four-foot closed door.

Charlene's gaze locked on the hooks hanging from the ceiling. She shuttered, her mind conjuring different scenarios from horror movies.

"Albert, throw me one of those nylons," Roach said. "We'll hang them by their wrists,"

Albert's face twisted as he tugged out a plastic tie from his pocket. "How long will they stay here?" His voice was shockingly sympathetic.

"Until Monk arrives," Albert said, working on tying Celine's hands together.

Roach grasped Charlene's wrists..

Monk? Who was he? She closed her eyes and tried to remember if Larry mentioned him and came up empty.

Albert grunted.

Charlene snapped her eyes open.

Albert bent over, holding his stomach. Celine rushed toward the opening in the floor.

Roach banded an arm around Charlene's chest and brandished a knife against her throat. "You do it, she'll pay."

Fright shot through her and butterflies somersaulted in her stomach.

Celine paused, her shoulders stiffened, and slowly she turned toward them, her wrists still bound in front of her

Albert coughed, held a hand to his stomach, and straightened. "Get over here. Now!" he ordered Celine.

Celine sent Charlene a *we-better-do-something-now* look and slithered back toward them.

"Good girl." Roach removed the knife from Charlene's throat, closed the blade, and tucked the knife into his pocket. He clutched Charlene's waist and lifted.

Albert stepped close, his vile breath assaulting her senses, as he maneuvered her wrists to slip over a hook.

The plastic ties cut into her skin as she hung from the ceiling. Her feet dangled inches above the floor.

"Let's take care of that bitch," Roach nodded at Celine. "Time for you to know who is boss."

Like a shot of adrenaline pumping into her veins, Charlene used the hook for support, swung her legs upward, wrapping her legs around Roach's neck, and squeezed.

Gasping, Roach hit at her legs and dug his fingers into her thighs.

Celine charged forward, head first into Albert's stomach. He lost his balance and fell backwards into the wall.

"What the fuck?" Albert wheezed, curling into a ball and rolling onto his side, moaning.

Celine popped back to her feet.

Charlene squeezed her thighs tighter, pulling Roach closer to the hook. The strain on the binding loosened. She lifted her hands up and off the hook, clasped them together and leaned far enough back not to fall off but to slam her intertwined fists into the back of his neck.

He gasped and sunk to his knees.

Charlene fell backwards, hitting the wall and floor with a thud. Pain pierced her back and hip. The boards popped and creaked before giving way. She plummeted through the floor onto the ground below. A cloud of dirt sprayed her face and hair.

Celine dropped beside her, her hands free at her side. "Can you move?"

Thanks to the pile of crap, offering a cushion, she could move. "Yes." Charlene eased up into a sitting position. "How did you undo the strap?"

"Knife." Celine cut the binding on Charlene's wrists. "Let's go."

Charlene jumped to her feet, swiped at the dirt clinging to her face, and ran after Celine toward the two four-wheelers.

"No keys," Celine shouted, through heavy breaths.

Charlene hit her hand against the other seat. "Damn, none here either."

"Get away from them." Roach peered at them from the open door on the second floor. "Get the bitches," he ordered Albert.

"Oh, shit," Charlene gasped. "Come on."

She and Celine rushed through thick brush and briars to the right of the shed. Thorns dragged across Charlene's skin and snagged her clothes, but she didn't care about the scratches stinging her hands, or that her lungs burned with each labored breath she sucked in. Determination lodged in her gut. She would see her son, her mother, and the one man who rocked her world…Larry, again.

"Stop just before the clearing," Celine panted, pointing to a patch of grass a little ways ahead of them.

Charlene slowed, dragged her hand on a tree, and stopped. Panting breaths escaped her on a wheeze.

"Jeez," Celine stepped onto the patch of grass and rested her palms on her knees, dragging in air. "I don't know which hurts more, my feet or lungs."

Celine sat on the ground and examined her blackened feet. "I bet I have shit all over me."

"At least it's not covering half of your face and body."

Celine snorted. "There is that."

"Easy for you to say."

Sounds of motors, nearing, pounded adrenaline through her system again. Charlene yelled, "Go!"

They rushed from the clearing into the thicket of woods, leaves and sticks crunching under their feet. Charlene glanced over her shoulder, caught a glimpse of the field, and changed directions to go deeper into the woods.

"Ouch!" Celine hopped on one foot in the mixture of dead leaves and pine needles before bracing a hand against a tree and examining the bottom of her foot. "I have a freaking thorn."

"Get it out!"

"I'm trying," Celine snapped, pinching the skin on her foot together. "I can't. Grab it!"

Charlene scanned Celine's black feet and zoomed in on the spot between her fingers. A small briar stuck out.

The engines quieted.

"Hurry!" Celine ordered.

Charlene pinched the intrusive object between her fingernails and yanked.

"There they are. Behind the trees." Roach's voice boomed.

Blood rushed through her ears, matching the pace of her heart, and the speed of her feet. She forged ahead, listening to Celine crunching leaves behind her.

She rushed by a tree, hit a barbed wire fence, and flew backwards into Celine, knocking them both to the ground.

"Enough," a deep, raspy voice ordered, his tone frosty as his face.

A toothless man, eyes black as tar glared at them. A bandana hung around his neck, and the all-telling Impalers cap on his head. "On your feet!" With the barrel of his gun, he motioned for them to move.

"Monk." Albert approached, gasping and holding his stomach, eyes wide. "You got them."

Roach appeared, panting. Sweat tripped off his ashen forehead.

"Take them to the pits!" Monk barked, his eyes narrowing into angry slashes.

"Oh, shit," Celine said.

The day on the mountains slammed into Charlene. Fear like no other raced through her, stopping her heart. She gasped for air and came up empty. The ground and trees warped. Everything went black.

****

"Damn." Larry tossed his cell onto the console of his Suburban next to the two jewelry boxes he planned to give Charlene tonight. He hoped she was ready to move forward as much as he was.

Jake sat in the passenger seat, calling Quigley.

"Charlene's still not answering" Larry said.

Jake glanced at his watch. "She's probably spending the day with Henry."

Larry propped his elbow on the driver's door and rubbed his jaw. Jake had a point. Charlene didn't spend much time with Henry yesterday and probably wanted to make it up to him today. Still, a niggling feeling stayed in the back of his mind that something was wrong.

"Thanks, Quigley," Jake said, capturing Larry's attention. He'd missed their conversation.

"Can they make it?"

"Yep. Quigley's calling Jackson. By the time we get to Greenwood Manor, we'll have eyes in the sky and boots on the ground." Jake raked a hand through his hair, tension and anger radiating off him. "Wish Steve was here. We could use the backup."

"Me, too." Missing the third man in their team, a team that could predict each other's next move and thoughts, was tough on cases that hit so close to home.

Larry snatched his ringing phone. "Charlene!"

"Benny, it's me, Mom."

He ignored the worry of regret that Charlene wasn't on the other end of the line and focused on Doris. "I'm kind of in the middle of something. What's up?" he asked, waiting to hear her say, "I need help."

"I won't keep you."

Larry's eyebrows shot up and his hand tightened on the wheel. Something was seriously wrong. "Mom, what is it?" He couldn't stop his worry from invading the tone of his words.

"Let's just say, I'm taking you up on your offer. I found your hide-a-key and settled in to your guest bedroom. This is temporary. I will find a job and my own place. I'll start looking tomorrow."

His mother's overzealous tone of voice was icing on the cake. She'd stepped over the imaginary line from accepting abuse to saying no more and healing. Overwhelmed with joy and pride, Larry's head tipped back and he chuckled. "You can stay with me as long as you want."

"Thanks, son."

"Welcome home, Mom." Larry disconnected and gazed at the country road. "Mom finally left."

"Good to hear," Jake said, sounding relieved. "I worry about her."

Larry knew the feeling. Many nights, he stayed awake, trying to figure out what to do to help. One problem solved, yet he stared in the face of another, one he was afraid that was more menacing.

From that moment until they reached the abandoned road, not far from Greenwood Manor, Larry's mind jumped. When he didn't focus on Charlene and why she didn't answer, he fixated on Mathews and the Black Scorpions. They were loose cannons. It was anyone's guess what they'd do next.

A half hour later, Larry parked on the side of a dirt road, leading to a pond, and climbed out of the car. Squinting against the afternoon sun, he opened the back doors and grabbed two fishing poles. He propped them against the side of the car for a decoy, masking the real reason they were there, and reached for the artillery.

Jackson approached, parking his Camaro on the opposite side of the road, near the intersection. He and Quigley popped out of the car, wearing all black like him and Jake, and lifted the hood, making out that they had car trouble.

"Team two going in," Quigley said over the radio, transmitting to Larry, Jake's, and Jackson's earpieces.

"Roger that," Jake said, snatching his equipment from the backseat.

Larry shoved his backup weapon into his ankle holster and caught movement slithering up behind him. "Take cover," he ordered, picking up a fishing rod to pretend he was checking the line.

Quigley and Jackson bent over the engine and looked under the hood.

Jake stood on the side of the Suburban, his body between the road and the trees, his gun drawn. A moment later, he exhaled. "Stand down. Jogger."

Larry returned the fishing rod to the side of his Suburban and glanced over his shoulder. A woman disappeared around the corner in the opposite direction from the manor.

"It's a go." Larry slipped his night vision goggles onto his forehead, closed and locked the Suburban.

Quigley and Jackson climbed the gate and rushed toward the front corner of the field.

Larry and Jake sneaked across the road, slid between the strands of barbed wire, and made their way through the woods, leaves crunched under their booted feet.

Not seeing anyone near the location Hulk gave for the underground bunker, Larry said, "Team one heading toward the target."

"Copy that. Meet at rendezvous," Jackson replied.

Jake and Larry moved farther into the woods, jumped a gully, and moved toward the field.

"Found it," Jackson said in the earpiece.

Through the woods, Larry could see Jackson and Quigley in the open field flat on their stomachs this side of the tree line from the traps and snakes.

"On the way," Larry replied. He and Jake jumped the three-foot wide creek, maneuvered through rough terrain, and jogged toward Quigley and Jackson, staying low to the ground.

When they approached, Jackson moved to a crouching position, gripped the handle to the bunker door flushed to the ground, and held up three fingers.

Larry lowered his night goggles, drew his gun, and gave a single nod.

Quigley and Jake followed suit.

Jackson lowered one finger at a time and lifted the door backwards on its hinges.

On high alert, Larry examined the entrance and climbed down a ladder into an underground room. Marijuana mixed with an earthy scent accosted his senses.

Jake descended next.

Larry swept his gaze and gun over the room. Dirt covered the floor, and boards shored up the walls and ceiling. An empty six by six table sat in the center of a twenty by thirty room; grow lights suspended from the ceiling, water hoses stuck out of the walls.

"Empty." Jake stuck his gun in the back of his jeans' waistband.

"All clear," Larry said in his earpiece. Not surprised, but still, he expected to find a clue.

Quigley slinked down the ladder and scan the room. "Someone's here. I smell him."

Larry narrowed his eyes and shot Jake an inquisitive glance.

"I have my own personal hound dog," Jake said. "Watch him work."

"There's another room." Quigley ran his hands over a wall. "Search the wall for some sort of lever."

Larry slid his fingers over the board next to him, grazed a raised object, and pushed it.

The wall scraped open. Larry shined the light into the dark room and motioned he'd take the lead.

Quigley and Jake stood on either side of the entrance, guns drawn.

With his weapon out in front of him, he entered the six by six room and fixed his gaze on a man sitting in the corner, his back to Larry. Hands and ankles bound.

Larry did a quick swipe of the rest of the room, then holstered his gun, and walked around to face the gagged captive.

Jake and Quigley joined him. A momentary shock silenced the room.

Smith, A.K.A. Mathews, was the last person Larry expected to see as a prisoner.

"I have a warrant for your arrest," Jake said, tugging down the gag.

Smith's flat brown eyes landed on Larry and widened. "You're the agent Charlene's screwing…"

A wild feeling engulfed Larry, forcing reckless anger to boil his blood. He drew his fist back and punched Smith in the jaw. The force knocked him and the chair to the dirt floor, and a cloud of dust rose.

Quigley and Jake righted Smith's chair.

"Want to make another stupid comment?" Jake asked.

"F-u-ck! I had enough," Smith mumbled.

Larry studied Andrew. Besides the bloody lip he gave him, he was black and blue. "Did you run your face into someone's fist?"

"They have Charlene."

Larry stiffened. He despised this asshole saying her name. "They have who?"

"They have her and some blonde chick."

Larry's heart jackhammered against his chest.

"What did he say?" Jackson's deep voice boomed from above."

"I planned to fight them," Smith said.

"I don't want to know about you, asswipe," Jackson snarled, coming into the room. "Who do they have?"

"Whatever, man. Like I said, they have Charlene and some Barbie-looking dame. Can you untie me?"

"No," they said in unison.

"I told him my wife was here to see me, nothing more, but he wouldn't listen. He called me a traitor and stuck me in here," Smith rambled.

Larry swallowed hard, trying to gain moisture to his sudden dry throat. "Charlene's here?"

"Yes, you fuckwit. Haven't you been listening?"

Larry drew his fist backwards.

"Don't! We need him awake to talk," Jake's gaze warned Larry not to get emotional.

Larry sent him a silent okay and turned to Smith. "Where are Charlene and Celine?"

"I don't know. Lavender's crew picked the women up on Monk's orders. I don't know where they went."

Quigley crossed his arms over his chest and jutted his chin toward Smith. "Who clobbered you?"

"Monk." Andrew squirmed. "He said I set him up."

Larry paced, feeling like a caged lion. Logically, he knew questions needed asking but his skin crawled from not searching.

"Did you?" Jake asked. "Did you set up Monk?"

Andrew nailed Jake with a glare. "Money talks. I needed some. The Black Scorpions could give me what I wanted and I have what…"

"You have what?" Larry asked, his gut instinct sending out warning flares.

With a snarl, Smith met Larry's stern gaze. "You stole Charlene from me."

"You lost her on your own." Larry braced his hands on the arms of the chair. "What do you have?"

Smith sneered. "It's too late. The plan is in motion. You know what's even funnier and I couldn't have orchestrated it better if I wanted to? Monk, the timid guy who never wanted to hurt a flea, is the brother of a Black Scorpion." Andrew laughed, unfeeling. "I would hand over the FBI agent who killed the leader—"

Jake growled and lunged forward.

Larry flung his arm out, hitting Jake across the chest.

At the same time, Quigley clutched Jake's shoulders from behind. "He's not worth it."

Jake shook Quigley off and walked over to the far wall and propped his shoulder against it, anger vibrating off him.

Smith chuckled.

"Don't toy with me," Larry said, seeing red. "You're in no position for smugness."

"Let me take a whack at this," Quigley said, patting Larry's shoulder, and pivoted toward Smith. "Did you shoot at The Memory Café?"

"Yep," Smith said, eyeing Larry. "An eye for an eye. You shot Randy, a guy who never harmed anyone."

"I'm the one asking the questions," Quigley said, a hard edge to his tone. "Eyes on me. Who were the guys on the motorcycles?"

Smith lifted a shoulder. "What guys?"

"The ones that followed you," Larry snapped.

"Were they Black Scorpions?" Jake growled.

"I haven't a clue."

Jackson stepped forward. "If Millstone's so decent, why is he a friend of yours?"

For a beat of time, Smith didn't say a word, just studied Jackson.

The amount of information Smith had willingly given them thus far surprised Larry. He expected some fist action to get the man to talk. With Smith staying quiet, maybe he was at his limit for playing nice. Larry would wait a few more minutes before relieving the stress that ran rampant through his system. In the same room with Smith, Larry's nerves wanted to fight each other.

Smith cleared his throat. "I saved his ass when he rolled a car he was too young to drive. If I hadn't pulled him out, he would have caught on fire with the car he wrecked."

Larry had to admit, it was civilized of Smith, if what he said was the truth. "Back to my question, what was your deal?"

"I get the manor's operation, clout, and the Black Scorpions' acceptance, and most importantly," he squared his shoulders as best as someone could while sitting in a chair with their hands tied behind their back, "I'd get Charlene back. She and I had one last roll for old time's sake this morning. I appreciated you keeping the bed nice and warm. I didn't have to do any work."

Anger that had been holding at a boil bubbled into a full out fire. Larry saw red. He struck Andrew in the jaw. The hell Andrew put Charlene through tumbled through his mind. Larry's fist connected with Andrew's eye.

Andrew and the chair fell to the ground, blood spewed from his mouth.

"Whoa!" Jackson gripped the back of Larry's shirt. "Stop, man!"

Ready to nail the son of bitch in the nose, Larry shrugged Jackson off and drew his arm back.

Jake caught the blow in his open palm. "Larry!"

He snapped from blind fury and gazed at his friend.

"Get out." Jackson pointed to the stairs.

Larry bolted up the ladder to fresh air. Way too much emotion battled around in his mind. If he had any hope of saving Charlene, he had to get a grip.

Jake approached. "Are you all right?"

Larry's temper had him blowing out steam. He walked a few feet, placed his hands on his hips, and gazed at the mountains, releasing another breath. He prayed Smith was full of shit. That he hadn't touched Charlene.

Larry ground his teeth, the only way Smith could have—his face flushed and the pulse in his neck thumped.

"Man, don't let your thoughts go there. Nothing happened. He's trying to rile you up," Jake warned.

—was to force Charlene. Rage spurred Larry into action. He raced to the bunker.

Jackson came up the ladder, shoved a hand into Larry's chest. "Don't!"

Larry drew back.

Jackson held his ground. "I'm not your enemy. Cool your jets before this situation turns from bad to dire."

Damn, Larry wanted to cold cock someone. He'd rather hit Smith, but with the uncontrolled anger flowing through him, he didn't care who was the target as long as he could unleash it. That in itself wasn't a good idea. He forced himself to take a calming breath and uncurled his hands. "I'm all right."

Quigley slammed the door shut.

Larry backed away from Jackson. "That fucking piece of shit could rot in the hole as far as I'm concerned."

Jake smacked Larry on the arm "I think he's already made his death bed."

"Abort mission, abort!"

A male voice blasted Larry's eardrums. He pressed a hand against his earpiece. "What the hell?"

"Scorpions, twelve o'clock."

Jake's eyes shot toward the sky. A helicopter hovered above. "Paul?"

"Get the fuck out of there!" Paul yelled back. "You're sitting ducks."

Larry drew his gun and pointed it toward the house. On the other side of the tree line and the snake pits, a fence presented barrier for the motorcycles maneuvering around before they could reach them. Still, it'd only take a second for the bikes to blast through the metal gate.

"Fuck a duck!" Quigley yelled.

"Take cover!" Jackson shouted.

Chapter Twenty

Larry's heart beat double-time, pounding in his ears so loudly other noises were wiped out as he ran for cover toward a small run down garage along the road. Ten Black Scorpions rode motorcycles heading toward his way. Four against ten, no way would he, Jake, Quigley, and Jackson outrun motorcycles once they broke through the gate.

"Coming in," Paul shouted in their earpieces.

Larry ducked behind a tree next to the garage, a few feet from the fence bordering the road, his gun at the ready.

Jake, Quigley, and Jackson fell in around him, guns drawn. Their bodies were shielded by either a tree or the garage.

Paul maneuvered the helicopter, darting it back and forth as if he was *it* chasing the advancing motorcyclist in a game of tag.

From their location, they had no choice but to keep cover and wait for the outcome of Paul's one-man team.

The nose of the helicopter aimed toward the ground and lowered.

"No, man, no!" Jake yelled, his hands raking through his hair.

The weight of the anxiety Jake felt vibrated off him at the difficult maneuver Paul undertook. If the nose of the helicopter didn't pull up in time, Paul would crash. Larry held his breath, along with the rest of the wide-eyed men.

"Shut up, bro." Paul replied, his voice deadly calm. "You're messing with my concentration." The helicopter leveled out and flew at the Scorpion leading the pack.

The bike swerved, lost control and flipped, front end over rear. The driver flew off the seat, landing on the ground in front of another motorcycle. The wheels rolled over the down Black Scorpion and the bike toppled over.

"There's more than one way to skin a cat." Paul chuckled. "Eye patch and his side kick are down."

"Two down," Quigley said, crossing his arms and chuckling. "I love this guy."

The helicopter lifted.

"What the hell is this?" Jake cut his eyes at Jackson. "The owner of a sports store is your eyes in the sky?" Skepticism laced his voice.

"You're not the only one who keeps secrets." Jackson remained stoic, not giving any indication if his high-school friend's five year disappearance had irked him or not. "I'm not at liberty to say any more."

Jake's jaw stiffened and he gave a slight nod. The silent agreement to discuss it no further was made.

The helicopter banked right, lowered, and rocked back and forth, inching toward the bikes as if the massive machine was a border collie herding sheep.

"Damn, he's good." Admiration for Paul's ability reflected in Quigley's eyes. "Guns!"

Gunfire erupted in a storm of pings against the aluminum sides of the helicopter.

"Shit." Larry tapped Jake's shoulder on the run past and took off. "Team one heading to trees," he transmitted.

"Team two covering," Jackson said, snapping a rifle together and flattening to the ground. Several yards away, Quigley mimicked the act.

Bypassing the tree line where they'd found the snake pits, Larry climbed the stock fence and headed toward a grove of trees midway down the field.

"Damn, they have all the toys," Jake said between breaths, his pace even with Larry's.

Larry took cover behind one of the five trees in the dip of the field and hoped Quigley and Jackson were as good as their fine tune actions said they were. "Paul's got a good cat and mouse game going on." He aimed his gun at a driver, firing at the helicopter, and squeezed the trigger.

The guy fell to the ground. The bike spun out.

"You boys and your secrets," he said.

Jake rested against another tree and let off two rounds. "Yeah, go figure."

A shot missed and the other hit a Scorpion in the shoulder, but didn't deter him from driving toward them.

"You just pissed him off." Larry swung around the trunk of the tree to get in a better position.

"That or he recognized me." Jake moved away from the tree. Feet shoulder-width apart, , he fired his gun until the gun's magazine emptied.

Larry covered, firing at the remaining moving targets.

Jake's target jolted and collapsed to the ground, the bike went with him.

Five more Scorpions tumbled over. Either Larry hit them, or Quigley and Jackson had.

"Paul had all the signs. No show." Larry pushed the lever on his gun, discharged the magazine, and snapped a spare from his belt. "Take off at the last minute."

"I can hear you," Paul said. "Open mike, remember?"

Except for the whirl of the helicopter, the rest of the motors quieted. Larry moved out from behind the tree, scanned the area.

"Six o'clock!" Paul said, his words firm, but tone urgent.

On full alert, Larry whirled.

Bullets whizzed by.

Two men dressed in Black Scorpion jackets stormed toward them, guns blasting, and crumbled to the ground.

"Hoorah!" Paul shouted. "Snipers Jackson and Quigley are on fire."

Another well-kept secret. Larry eyed Jake, his mouth pulled down cartoonlike in disbelief.

"Snipers?" Jake asked. "Where the fuck have I been?"

"Playing dead," Paul responded in a patronizing tone and made another pass with the helicopter over the now quiet field. "All clear."

Larry motioned toward the woods on the other side of the field. "Let's roll!"

Confirmation in his earpiece from each of the guys told him they followed his lead. He jogged across the expanse of land at a steady gait, surveying the motionless bodies and watching for sudden movement. Ten brown jacket-wearing Black Scorpions lay on the ground, their bodies disjointed and blood seeping out of bullet holes. Larry couldn't help but wonder what retaliation would be in store for them over this battle.

A gunshot pierced the air.

Larry hit the ground, a sickening sensation smacking his gut. A quick look over his shoulder confirmed his raw feeling. The leader of the group, identified by an eye patch, swayed over Jake's motionless body. "You fucking pig!" he gruffed, anger blazing in his eyes.

No. Fucking. Way. Larry squeezed and held the trigger. The automatic unloaded the magazine, pumping ammo into the man's upper torso. The Black Scorpion jerked and flinched until he hit the ground.

Pain pounded in Larry's ears in a deafening roar. He raced over to his friend, knelt, and pressed two fingers to the pulse in his neck. "Jake!"

****

"Charlene!"

In the distance, Charlene heard her name called, but her eyes wouldn't open.

"Wake up! Charlene!" She recognized the familiar female voice. By the high pitch, the person was excited, yet the shaky edged tone gave away she was scared. The evil men took her to the pits. She held her breath, scared she'd hear a rattle like Larry had, and would have to fight off a snake with nothing more than her hands and feet.

Pressure wrapped around her wrists, comparable to what she figured a calf underwent at a rodeo.

"They're going to drag you behind them," Celine sobbed.

Celine. Had she been moved? Were Celine and her in the pit?

Charlene came slamming back into her body and opened her eyes. Her vision blurred then sharpened on the dark green horizon and the outline of the mountains way off in the distance. Earthy, hay scents drifted over her.

She hadn't been moved to the pits.

A headache flared behind her eyes. She went to rub them, but couldn't. Her arms stretched over her head and her wrists were bound.

Sunlight hit her face from all directions. Squinting, she eyed three figures standing nearby then twisted to see what held her against her will.

Sheer fright radiated through her body. A piece of rope connected her to the backend of a four-wheeler.

"Take them off!" Celine yelled. Desperation mixed with tears laced her words.

Angry faces popped into her line of vision.

"Untie her, Albert," Roach ordered, grasping Celine's shoulder and shoving her backwards.

Albert smelled of sweat, dirt, and cow manure. He removed the rope and grasped the elbow to the hand she used to cover her nose and mouth. "Get up."

Charlene rose, almost crashing into the woman called Lavender, her face pinched with worry and her eyes wide. "Monk, there's a problem," she said, touching his arm and guiding him a few steps to the side.

Charlene glanced at Celine, standing behind Roach and focusing on Lavender and Monk.

"The Black Scorpions arrived, found the agent Mathews used to bait them here, and..."

A wave of fear mixed with excitement slugged Charlene's stomach. Larry was there! He came looking for her, for them. Still, his name was used simultaneously with the Black Scorpions. She held her breath and waited for Lavender's next words.

"And what?" Monk barked. He nailed Lavender with a glare, yet a touch of tenderness edged the corners of his eyes.

Her gaze dropped to her hands, clutching together. "Um, none of them made it."

White-hot terror blanketed Charlene's skin, intensifying the pain behind her eyes and leaving her strangely detached from her body.

Monk stiffened and his hands fisted. "Who didn't make it? The agents?"

The withering expression washing over Lavender's face gave Charlene an inkling of hope that Larry was okay. "The Scorpions. No one is alive."

Charlene heaved a sigh of relief and heard Celine's exhale. She had to be as worried as Charlene. If Larry was here that meant he brought backup. Steve could have been in danger, too.

"What!" Monk's eyebrows narrowed. His voice sounded as if he swallowed a wad of paper. He tugged off his cap and ran a hand over his face. "You're mistaken. My brother is the best fighter in the gang."

Lavender nodded, tears leaking down her face. "I know."

Rage boiled over Monk's expression; his face turned beet red and his nostrils flared. "That fucker!" He stormed over to the fence, gripped the top row of barbed wire, and stared out into the dense woods.

After a few minutes, he faced them. "Roach, go to the bunker and bring Mathews to me." The emotion that had overwhelmed Monk's features disappeared. He was composed, yet his eyes held a toughness that told Charlene he flipped a switch from a mild mannered Impaler to a callous criminal, *a Black Scorpion*.

Lavender's intake of breath confirmed her hunch and sent goose bumps over Charlene's skin.

"Get them out of here," Lavender whispered over her shoulder to Albert.

Monk's hard eyes landed on Lavender then on Albert shooing Charlene and Celine to the four-wheeler. "Stop!"

The three of them didn't move. Albert's body stiffened as if he was more a squeamish teenager than a gang member.

Monk walked over to Charlene, leaned in until his nose was a mere fraction from hers. "Mrs. Gibson?" He arched a brow.

Charlene shook her head so fast she thought it'd go into convulsions. "No, I'm not."

He narrowed an eye on Celine. "You?"

She pressed her lips together and shook her head.

He studied them for a long moment, looking between Celine and Charlene, before his chin jutted outward. "Get them out of here."

****

Quigley and Jackson made quick work of removing Jake's shirt and undid the Velcro on his vest.

A hole lodged into the right-hand side of Jake's shirt, stopping in his bulletproof vest.

"Damn, you all keep manhandling me, I'm gonna wonder about ya," Jake said, his voice weak.

Releasing a sigh of relief, Larry ran a hand down his face. No matter how many times he was faced with this scenario, each one cut him to the quick. "Hey, buddy."

"Hey, back." Jake rose to a sitting position. "Damn, that stung."

"You guys got to stop with this shit!" Quigley said, stepping aside and puffing out air.

Larry took in the fit, stealthy soldier. Quigley's hands rested on his hips and he stared at the sky. Something bad must have gone down for him to be this shaken up.

"Package found. At your one o'clock," Paul said in their ears, "near an old abandoned shed. No access by air. Guns alive."

A deluge of adrenaline slug through Larry's system and he shot across the field over bumpy terrain into the woods. Darkness invaded, and the branches blocked the last remaining light. He lowered his night goggles and perused the expanse.

The rusty trailer and goats were set off to the right. The goats kicked up their hooves and butted each other with their horns.

"They're active for this time of day," Jackson said, catching up to him when Larry slowed. "They high?"

"Looks it. They've been known to nibble on plants in the past." Larry hopped over a dip in the terrain and advancing toward a field bordered with trees. He had two choices: either to stay undercover amongst the trees and take twice as long to reach Charlene and Celine, or sprint across the field and get to them before trouble worsened.

"Found their crop," Paul said into their earpiece. "Going in."

"Wait for backup." Jake's voice was much stronger and he panted.

"The man is on the move," Jackson chuckled. "Glad you're amongst the living."

"Thanks." Gun fire blasted over Jake's words.

"Fuck!" Jake yelled. "He didn't wait."

No need for Jake to say who *he* was. The shots came from the direction Paul landed the helicopter.

Sirens sounded in the distance.

"Locals are here," Jackson said and went for the tree line.

"This way," Larry said and proceeded. At the top, he and Jackson dropped to the ground.

A stream divided them and what looked like a makeshift camp. To the left, there was an old two story building. The bottom floor opened on one side. Off to the right, a bonfire and a strange looking contraption behind it.

"Damn. That's a crop." Paul whistled in the earpiece.

"Another perky voice," Quigley said. "Take any hits?"

"That's a negative," Paul said. "Rendezvous at the shed. Coming in on foot."

"Roger that," Larry said, focusing back on the camp. A burly man with a gun crossed between his arms walked in front of the structure and paused. Larry's heartbeat thundered in his throat. "The girls are in that structure."

The sound of a motor approaching had them pressing their bodies to the ground. Out of a gap in the woods, a four-wheeler advanced toward the camp. Two riders, one unknown gang member and Smith, his hands tied behind his back.

Larry lowered the googles. Through them he could see the scowl on Monk's face. "This isn't looking good for Smith."

"Nope." Jackson pulled out a laser listening device and aimed it toward the camp. "You guys will hear everything they say."

"Damn, you have some toys." Jake dropped to the field beside them.

"He's my hero," Quigley said, peering through night goggles.

The four-wheeler stopped near the fire. Smith and the Impaler stepped off.

"That's Ellis Goldberg, A.K.A. Roach. Done time for small stuff, nothing major," Larry informed.

Jackson did something to the listening device. "Listen."

"You dumb fuck!"

With the listening device, Monk yelling sounded like it was right beside them.

And through the night vision googles, his body language said *pissed*. "You led the agents here."

Roach moved backwards toward the fire.

"I didn't lead them here," Smith's voice rose. "You captured one of their women."

"Aw, fuck!" Larry mumbled on a growl. The asswipe just put Charlene's life in more danger.

Monk spit on the ground next to Smith's boots. "You killed my brother."

Smith's eyes widened. Nervousness flowed off him in waves. "What? No, man!"

"Incoming," Quigley said.

Larry ignored the twitching in his eye. "What's the count?"

"A scared tweet, two guard, two Scorpions, one purple-headed person, two sitting near the fire," Jackson said, "Monk, and a partridge in a pear tree."

"For those who can't count, that's nine," Quigley said.

"Can anyone get a visual inside that structure?" Jake asked.

"Two men inside," Paul said, "watching the packages."

"Your location?" Bewilderment laced Jake's voice.

"In the trees. The vines aren't covering the top. I have clear shots," Paul whispered.

"You think he can take them both before they fire?" Quigley asked.

"Yeah, I do," Larry said. "Let's roll. On three. One…"

"You thought you could make a deal with the Black Scorpions to take over my operation," Monk fumed. "Instead, you set a trap and get my blood killed."

"No, no, that's not what I did," Smith went from nervous to withering. "I just wanted my wife back."

"Two…" Larry said, his adrenaline kicking in full gear, making it unbearable to wait.

Monk scuffed. "I want my brother back. He's paid the ultimate price for your actions. Now, your dear wife will pay for what you have done."

Larry's heart clenched. The pain seeped through every inch of his body. He bolted upright, raced through the tall grass toward the camp.

"Damn it!" Jake shouted in his ear.

Larry ignored his friend, but knew the men would have his back.

A barrage of activity happened at once.

Two shots discharged. "Go…go…go," Paul commanded in the earpiece.

Monk pressed his gun against Smith's head and pulled the trigger. Smith's lifeless body collapsed to the ground.

Larry felt Charlene and Henry's loss like a serrated knife to his gut and tore after Monk heading toward the vine structure.

Screams sounded.

Larry lifted his gun, aimed at Monk's head, and…

Monk crumpled to the ground.

"You're welcome," Quigley said in the earpiece.

Larry groaned. He appreciated Quigley acting fast, but he wanted to take the guy out for threatening Charlene.

Chaos broke loose. The men sitting around the fire scrambled for their guns.

Jake and Larry made quick work to incapacitate the remaining men, and Larry targeted the guard heading inside the structure. The burly man slumped. The other guard ducked behind the structure out of sight.

A gun discharged.

Dread plummeted like a lead balloon into the pit of his stomach. The gun's report came from inside the vines where Charlene and Celine were held.

"Scorpions!" Jake hopped onto an ATV.

"Your woman's a good shot," Paul said into the earpiece and dropped from a tree limb onto the four-wheeler beside his brother and drove off after him

The ball of fear taking up residence in his stomach broke apart. Still, he needed eyes on her. He slipped to the entrance, peeked inside, and froze.

With her back pressed against Charlene's, Celine cradled the barrel of AK-15 in her lap and scowled at the purple-haired woman.

Charlene looked over her shoulder and Celine's, glaring at the woman. She clutched the grip of the gun, her finger resting on the trigger. "Untie us, Lavender!"

Wide-eyed, Lavender shook her head and dropped her gaze to the dirt. "I'm sorry, girls. This was never in the plan," she sobbed. "Monk was decent. He didn't want the life his brother had."

Quigley pushed past Larry, standing at the entrance. "Let's go. Tell your story in court." He grabbed Lavender by the nape of the neck and they disappeared.

Charlene met Larry's gaze and her eyes softened.

Excitement that she was alright did a number on him, almost taking him to his knees. "You're okay," he said more to himself than asking a question, giving his worst fears a voice.

She smiled and gave a single nod.

Hair mussed, dirt covered her face, and yet, she was so unbelievably gorgeous he ached.

****

Emotions rushed up Charlene's raw throat and stung the backs of her eyes. The last hours had been treacherous, scary, and sent her heart into rapid palpitations more than once. Seeing Larry, looking so gorgeously handsome, so lovable, her heart's wild beat returned. He was alive!

"Is it over?" Charlene asked, gazing into his eyes too afraid to blink for fear he'd vanished.

The affection and relief in his honey-colored eyes warmed her insides and clenched her heart. She choked on a sob.

"Yes, babe." His voice was strained. He slid the AK-15 out of Celine's and Charlene's grasp, handed it to someone dressed like Larry that she didn't recognize.

The ties binding her hands and Celine's broke apart easily with one swipe of Larry's knife. He helped Charlene to her feet and engulfed her in a bear hug. She wrapped her arms around him, pressed her cheek against his chest, and listened to his heartbeat. For a long moment, she stayed that way, savoring the deliciousness of him. She rubbed her eyes and forehead against him, feeling his heartbeat and warmth, and closed her eyes. She never wanted to leave this position.

A moan leaked from him. He squeezed her closer to his body, his body vibrated. "I've never been so scared," he said, his voice raspy. His mouth caught hers in a kiss so demanding and hot, her heart flipped.

"You gals are fighters!" Jackson's deep voice resounded, splitting Charlene and Larry apart.

Celine buried her face into Jackson's chest, tears streaming down her face.

"We need to talk," Larry said to Charlene and grabbed her hand, leading her out of the vine shelter she'd been held captive in.

The bonfire Lavender started earlier had died down. Still, the flicker of the flames illuminated bodies on the ground. The man Charlene had shot slumped against the vine structure. Her insides were a roaring ocean of reactions. Anger. Fear. Guilt. She swallowed hard at taking another's life and shuddered, remembering the act of pulling the trigger. The man's grunt had told her the bullet made its way through the thick grape vines to her target. She hadn't wanted to kill him, just stop him from coming after her and Celine. She dragged in a ragged breath. If the situation had been different, he would have shot and killed her without second-guessing his actions.

"You okay?" Larry asked, stroking her arm.

She nodded. "As well as to be expected, I am."

"I hate being the bearer of bad news," he said on a long sigh.

Andrew's last words rushed toward her. *You captured one of their women.* She felt numb toward the loss. How sad was it that the father of her baby was murdered, yet she felt nothing. Maybe in time, it'd hit her and she'd feel remorse. Still, her ex served her up to a killer. If Larry hadn't arrived when he had, her son would be an orphan. Her gaze landed on Larry. "Thank you."

He gazed at her and looked into her soul. "I love you." His voice was calm, firm, and confident. Together they had removed the demons that resided within each other to be able to fall in love again.

Goosebumps raised on her arms. At that moment, there was no second-guessing his motive, or her feelings. She loved Larry with all her heart. She placed a hand over her mouth and her eyes filled her eyes. "I'm in love for the first time in my life."

Tears welled in his eyes.

In the background, she sensed people milling around. Friends yelling to one another, but their gazes stayed locked on each other.

He stepped closer, slid a hand through her hair, stroking her cheek as if she was a precious gem. "I want to marry you. Have more Henrys or Harriets."

She snickered. "Um, maybe we should call our daughter by another name."

"Will you marry me, Charlene Webber?"

A sob escaped. The sweetness of him using her maiden name touched her. Never in a million years did she think she would feel this much joy. Her mom's princess wish for her came true. She whole-heartedly felt like a princess in Larry's presence. "Yes."

"Thank goodness for haunted houses." Larry captured her lips in a soft, sweet passionate kiss filled with promise and love.

The End

www.caitjarrod.com

Evernight Publishing

www.evernightpublishing.com

www.ingramcontent.com/pod-product-compliance
Lightning Source LLC
Chambersburg PA
CBHW031545240626
47153CB00002B/393